TRACKERS 2:
THE HUNTED

NEW YORK TIMES BESTSELLING AUTHOR
NICHOLAS SANSBURY SMITH

GREAT WAVE INK
PUBLISHING

Books by New York Times Bestselling Author
Nicholas Sansbury Smith

The Sons of War Series
(Offered by Blackstone Publishing)

Sons of War
Sons of War 2: Saints (Coming Fall 2020)
Sons of War 3: Sinners (Coming early 2021)

The Hell Divers Series
(Offered by Blackstone Publishing)

Hell Divers
Hell Divers II: Ghosts
Hell Divers III: Deliverance
Hell Divers IV: Wolves
Hell Divers V: Captives
Hell Divers VI: Allegiance
Hell Divers VII: Warriors

The Extinction Cycle (Season One)
(Offered by Orbit Books)

Extinction Horizon
Extinction Edge
Extinction Age
Extinction Evolution
Extinction End
Extinction Aftermath
Extinction Lost (A Team Ghost short story)
Extinction War

The Extinction Cycle: Dark Age
(Season Two)

Extinction Shadow
Extinction Inferno
Extinction Ashes
Extinction Darkness

The Trackers Series

Trackers
Trackers 2: The Hunted
Trackers 3: The Storm
Trackers 4: The Damned

The Orbs Series

Solar Storms (An Orbs Prequel)
White Sands (An Orbs Prequel)
Red Sands (An Orbs Prequel)
Orbs
Orbs II: Stranded
Orbs III: Redemption
Orbs IV: Exodus

NicholasSansburySmith.com

For my Dad, relentless in his pursuit and fight for a better world.

"Humankind has not woven the web of life. We are but one thread within it. Whatever we do to the web, we do to ourselves. All things are bound together. All things connect."

—Chief Seattle, 1854

Note from the Author

Dear Reader,

In Spring of 2020 I updated this section to reflect the current international medical crisis. As you all know, we are in the middle of a pandemic with extreme damage being done to the global economy. Trade has come to almost a standstill and the major gears of the supply chain have ground to a halt. We have an overwhelmed medical industry focused on COVID-19 and a shortage of personal protective equipment (PPE). The meat and poultry industry has been hit hard, slowing production, and resulting in shortages. Over thirty million people have filed for unemployment in the United States.

And that isn't even the full picture of just how much has changed in the past five months. An EMP attack now could cripple the United States to the point of no return.

If this attack were to occur, I believe North Korea is the country that would be the most likely to carry it out. Despite international efforts to stop them, they are still advancing their nuclear weapons and ballistic missile programs in defiance of the United Nations Security Council resolutions and sanctions.

At the end of April 2020, there was another twist to this explosive situation, with reports coming out of the Korean peninsula and Japan that North Korean leader Kim Jung Un was either dead or in a vegetative state. If this is true, it adds a new element to the fragile international conflict.

Whoever replaces Kim Jung Un could be worse, furthering the risk of war. On the contrary, they could help bring unification to the peninsula. I've updated this note again in May to reflect reports of Kim Jung Un being spotted in public. Some analysts are saying it's a body double, others say it is indeed the leader. Only time will tell if he is still alive, but either way, the situation remains a powder keg.

And that is exactly what this story is about.

Before you dive in, I've included some background on how this story came to be. In 2016 I was finishing up book five of the Extinction Cycle, and at that time, I thought Extinction End would be the "end" of the series. I decided to write a new type of story—a story without monsters, zombies, or aliens—about a different type of threat.

Rewind ten years. I'm a planner with the State of Iowa sitting in a meeting with other agencies and utility companies talking about solar flares and a weapon called an electromagnetic pulse (EMP). It was there that I realized just how devastating an EMP could be to the United States if it were strategically detonated in the atmosphere. The longer I heard about the effects, the more I started to wonder—why would our enemies poison our soil and destroy our cities with nuclear weapons or waste their troops in a battle they probably couldn't win, when all they had to do is turn off our power and sit back and watch the chaos and death that would ensue?

During this meeting with other agencies, I was shocked to learn there wasn't much being done to harden our utilities and critical facilities to protect against such a threat.

A few years later, I started working for Iowa Homeland Security and Emergency Management. I had several duties as a disaster mitigation project officer, but my primary focus was on protecting infrastructure and working on the state hazard mitigation plan. Near the end of my time at HSEMD, I was also assigned the duty of overseeing the hardening of power lines in rural communities.

After several years of working in the disaster mitigation field, I learned of countless threats from natural disasters to manmade weapons, but the EMP, in my opinion, was still the greatest of them all.

That brings us to today. We're living in tumultuous times, and our enemies are constantly looking for ways to harm us, both domestically and abroad. We already know that cyber security is a major concern for the United States. North Korea, China, and Russia have all been caught tampering with our elections and our systems. We also know other countries are experimenting with cyber technology that can shut down portions of our grid. But imagine a weapon that could shut down our entire grid. The perfectly strategized EMP attack gives our enemies an opportunity to do just that. And that is the premise of the Trackers series.

Before you start reading, I would like to take time to thank everyone who helped make this book a reality. Many people had a hand in the creation of this story. I'm grateful for all their help, criticism, and time. I'd like to start with the people that I wrote this book for—the readers. You are the reason I always try to write something fresh, and the reason I strive to always make each story better than—and different from—its predecessors.

Secondly, I'd like to thank the Estes Park Police Department.

In the spring of 2016, my wife and I spent a few weeks in Estes Park, Colorado, a place I had visited many times growing up. I wanted to show her this gorgeous tourist town that borders Rocky Mountain National Park, and I decided it would also make a good setting for some of the scenes in Trackers.

The police department very graciously allowed me to tour their facilities and ride along with Officer Corey Richards. Department officers and staff explained police procedure for tracking lost people, and their operations and response to natural disasters. Captain Eric Rose, who is in charge of the Emergency Operations Center, described what they went through in the flood of 2013, when Estes Park was quite literally cut off from surrounding communities.

I've spent time with many law enforcement departments over my career in government, and I can tell you Estes Park has one of the finest and most professional staffs I've ever had the pleasure of meeting. Thank you to every officer for serving Estes Park and assisting with Trackers. I hope you find I did your community justice.

I'd also like to thank my literary agent, David Fugate, who has provided valuable feedback on each of my novels. The version you are reading today is much different than the manuscript I submitted, partly because of David's excellent feedback.

I also had a great group of beta readers that helped bring this story to life. You all know who you are. Thanks again for your assistance.

Trackers is more than just a post-apocalyptic thriller about the aftermath of an attack on American soil. It's meant to be a mystery as much as it is a thriller. There are a lot of EMP stories out there, but I wanted to write one that included new themes and incorporated elements of Cherokee and Sioux folk stories. I spent years researching and reading Native American history at the University of Iowa where I received a certificate in American Indian studies.

This story, like many works of fiction, will require some suspension of belief, but hopefully not as much as my other science fiction stories. Any errors in this book rest solely with me, as the author is always the gatekeeper of the work.

In an interview several years ago, I was asked why I write. My response was that while my stories are meant to entertain, they are also meant to be a warning. Trackers could be a true story, and I hope our government continues to prepare and protect us from such a threat.

Captain Eric Rose of the Estes Park Police Department told me that he wasn't sure he was ready for a post-apocalyptic Estes Park. I'm not either. Let's all hope this story remains fiction.

With that said, I hope you enjoy the read, and as always, feel free to reach out to me on social media if you have questions or comments.

Best wishes,
Nicholas Sansbury Smith

Foreword

Dr. Arthur Bradley

Author of

Disaster Preparedness for EMP Attacks and Solar Storms
and The Survivalist.

When used conventionally, a nuclear warhead could destroy a city and cover the surrounding region in deadly radiation. Horrible to be sure, but at least it would be localized. When detonated in the atmosphere at the right altitude, however, that same warhead could generate an electromagnetic pulse (EMP) that would cause almost unimaginable harm to our nation.

The most significant effect of such an attack would be damage to the nation's electrical grid. Due to the interdependency of systems, the loss of electricity would result in a cascade of failures promulgating through every major infrastructure, including telecommunications, financial, petroleum and natural gas, transportation, food, water, emergency services, space operations, and government. Businesses, including banks, grocery stores, restaurants, and gas stations, would all close. Critical services such as the distribution of water, fuel, and food would fail. Emergency services, including hospitals, police, and fire departments, would perhaps remain operable a little longer using generators and backup systems, but they too would collapse due to limited fuel distribution, as well as the loss of key personnel abandoning their posts.

In addition to the collapse of national infrastructures, an EMP could cause widespread damage to transportation systems, such as aircraft, automobiles, trucks, and boats, as well as supervisory control and data acquisition hardware used in telecommunications, fuel processing, and water purification systems. Such an attack could also damage in-space satellites and significantly hamper the government's ability to provide a unified emergency response or even maintain civil order. Finally, many personal electronics could also be damaged, including our beloved computers and cell phones, as well as important health monitoring devices.

With the collapse of infrastructures, loss of commerce, and widespread damage to property, an EMP attack would introduce terrible financial ruin on the nation. Consider that it is estimated that even a modest 1-2 megaton warhead detonated over the Eastern Seaboard could cause in excess of a trillion ($1,000,000,000,000) dollars in damage.

Testing done in the 1960s, such as Starfish Prime and the Soviet's Test 184, provided some idea of the potential damage, but weapons have become even more powerful and our world more technologically susceptible. No one really knows with certainty the extent of the damage that would be felt, but expert predictions range from catastrophic to apocalyptic. What is universally agreed upon is that the EMP attack allows for an almost unimaginable amount of damage to be done with nothing more than a single nuclear warhead and a missile capable of deploying it to the right altitude. Given that there are more than 128,000 such warheads and 10,000 such missiles in existence, it seems prudent to better understand and prepare for this very real and present danger.

What many do not know is that the U.S. has been

openly threatened with an EMP strike by Russia, Iran, and North Korea. Leaderships of these countries have come to appreciate the truly asymmetric nature of such an attack. Consider that an EMP strike would be largely independent of weather, result in long-lasting infrastructure damage, and inflict a damage-to-cost ratio far greater than any conventional weapon, including a nuclear "dirty bomb." Worse yet is that our enemies would not limit themselves to a single EMP strike. Rather, they would detonate several warheads, carefully timed and positioned across the nation to achieve maximum damage.

Author Nicholas Sansbury Smith understands how an attack could cripple the United States. I first spoke with him when he was working for Iowa Homeland Security and Emergency Management in the disaster preparedness field. He reached out when he was writing a science fiction story about solar storms with some questions about my book, Disaster Preparedness for EMP Attacks and Solar Storms. Since then, Nicholas has also spent a great deal of time researching EMPs.

Trackers is a work of fiction, but many of the places in the story are real. Utilizing his background in emergency management and disaster mitigation, Nicholas has done an excellent job of describing a realistic geopolitical crisis that sets the stage for an EMP attack. The following story is a terrifying scenario in which brave men and women must adapt to a challenging new world—a world that we could see ourselves being thrust into. Part of me wishes Nicholas had continued writing purely science fiction stories about aliens and government designed bio-weapons because Trackers is a novel that could become non-fiction.

— Prologue —

Dr. Martha Kohler staggered down Highway 7, somewhere south of Rocky Mountain National Park, in a radiation suit she had constructed out of garbage bags. A pair of ski goggles and a scarf shielded her face, but she was all too aware that they wouldn't be enough to block the radiation drizzling from the skies.

A nuclear blast had almost blinded her three nights ago, and the fireball had set fire to the surrounding forests. All around her were views of the apocalypse. Blackened evergreen trees swayed in the wind to the northeast, carrying the scent of burning pine needles. Flames engulfed an entire forest to the southwest, filling the sky with a wall of black smoke that choked out the sun.

When her car stalled out on the road, she'd been stranded. The National Guard soldiers had told her to stay put and wait for help. After two days, she decided to take action. Waiting meant dying. Running at least gave her a chance to reach help before it was too late.

Martha's heart had been firing out of control since she had left her car. As a doctor, she knew what irradiation did to a human body. She had done everything she could to keep the radioactive material off her skin, but there was little she could do to stop breathing it into her lungs. A flimsy cotton scarf was no replacement for a CBRN suit.

The deep rattle of a cough rose in her throat. The sound seemed to echo in the quiet afternoon. She licked her cracked lips, desperate for a drink of water. A stream snaked along the left side of the road, but drinking the water would be a death sentence.

She slogged along, searching for supplies or someone to help her. She hadn't seen another living person for three hours. Before that, a man had run from her, screaming nonsense about an alien invasion. Delirium was another sign of radiation sickness. For now, Martha's mind seemed whole—but if it wasn't, would she even know?

She'd seen plenty of bodies on the road over the past few days. Another victim lay ahead. The elderly man was on his back, hands twisted like a praying mantis. A second corpse, rigid from rigor mortis, lay a few feet from the man. The gray-haired woman was facing him, curled up in a fetal position. They had died within reach of one another.

At least they were together, Martha thought. She'd lost her husband to a heart attack ten years ago. Regrets surfaced in her mind. They always found a way of coming to a head when disaster struck, things she would have said or done differently during their marriage.

She sighed and pressed onward, even though stars were bursting before her vision. The journey was taking its toll, and she was only halfway to Denver. The soldiers had said to head that way to avoid radiation, but the bodies here told her she was still in the middle of the dead zone.

Reaching out, she steadied herself on the side of a mini-van. Over the howl of the wind came a faint, scratchy sound like someone was trying to clear their throat. Something moved inside the van. Martha peered inside the back window. Two small figures were huddled together in the back seat. A body was slumped against the steering wheel, and judging by the pale, blistered skin on its exposed arm, the kids were probably orphans.

She had been careful to avoid other people on the road. If anyone found out she possessed potassium iodide pills, which she carried in her medical bag, they would surely take them from her, maybe even hurt her to get them. But these kids weren't going to hurt anyone, and she couldn't just leave them here to die.

She scanned the road again. There was motion down the highway to the east, directly under a bridge. Several clusters of bodies rested beneath the overpass. Loose clothing rippled in the wind, but there was no sign of anything or anyone alive that way.

Satisfied, she opened the van door. The two kids reared back from her, their curly brown hair a disheveled mess.

"Don't hurt us," the boy sniffled.

Martha pulled down her scarf and pushed up her goggles so they could see her eyes. She could only imagine how terrifying she probably looked with the garbage bags covering most of her body. From a child's eyes, she probably looked like an alien.

She summoned the same calm voice she used with kids at the beginning of a pediatric visit. "I'm not going to hurt you. I'm here to help."

"Can you help our papa?" the girl asked.

"Your father is sleeping," Martha lied. She pulled a piece of duct tape away from her waist and reached to retrieve the bottle of pills from her pocket.

"I'm Doctor Martha Kohler, and I'm going to help

you both feel better, okay?"

They just stared back.

"What are your names?" Martha asked.

The girl started sobbing, tears streaking down her red skin. The boy scratched at a sore on his cheek.

Martha unscrewed the lid and placed two pills in the palm of her glove. She managed a smile with her cracked, dry lips. "I want you two to take these. Okay? It will make you feel better."

"Papa said to never take candy from a stranger," the boy said. He rubbed at his bloodshot eyes and then squinted at her like he was looking into the sun.

"I'm a doctor, and this isn't candy," Martha said. "Didn't your parents teach you to listen to doctors?"

The girl sniffled and dragged her sleeve across her nose while the boy slowly nodded.

"It's okay, I promise," Martha said, holding out the pills. "These will make you feel better."

"Do you have any water?" asked the girl. "I'm really thirsty."

Martha shook her head and held out her palm. She could see these kids had already been exposed to the radiation for a period of time. The pills helped block radioactive iodine from being absorbed by the thyroid gland, but they wouldn't reverse what had already been absorbed. They needed water, and they needed protection from the radiation. She might be able to cut the tarp down and tape it around them, but it wasn't an ideal solution.

First, though, she needed to get the children to trust her. She leaned in and mustered up a warm smile.

"How about we play a game?" she suggested. "Do you want to play a game?"

The boy tilted his head, his blue eyes brightening slightly.

"I do," the girl said.

"No, Emma. Papa said we have to stay here until help comes."

"I'm the help your father was talking about. Now, I know your name is Emma. What's your name?" Martha said, looking at the boy.

"Micah," he said shyly. His eyes flitted to the front seat. "Papa isn't sleeping, is he?"

"I need you to take these pills," she said, "and then we can play a game."

The boy and girl both reached out and plucked them from her glove. Doubtfully, they examined the pills and then swallowed them with difficulty.

"Can I see that tarp?" Martha asked. "I need it to make you suits like mine to protect your skin."

Micah hesitated but then pulled the plastic away. A fetid stench rolled out, confirming her fears. The kids were already sick. The initial symptoms of radiation poisoning were vomiting and diarrhea. Dehydration wouldn't help matters. She needed to get these children clean water and medical care immediately.

"Come here," she said, holding out her hand.

Emma and Micah scooted across the back seat, and Martha helped them both onto the road. It took her several minutes to carve up the tarp with her multi-tool, but when she was done she had enough pieces to wrap the children in makeshift suits.

"Hold up your arms," Martha said.

The kids did as ordered, and she taped the plastic around them. Emma shivered in the wind, gooseflesh prickling over her arms.

"You ready?" Martha asked the kids.

They both nodded. She grabbed them each by the hand and guided them toward the stalled vehicles.

"Bye, Papa," Emma said.

Micah was silent, but he looked over his shoulder several times as they walked away. Martha had to gently tug his hand to keep him moving.

"I'm sorry about your father, but he would want you to be safe," she said.

A sniffle sounded behind her. She wasn't sure if it was Micah or Emma.

If they started crying, they'd become even more dehydrated. Water wasn't the only thing on her mind. She still needed to find a way to cover the children's faces. She turned her attention to a Toyota Prius ahead, hurrying over with the kids in tow. A few of her friends drove Priuses, and all of them were the prepared type.

"Stay right here," she said.

Micah and Emma remained at the bumper while Martha checked the front of the car. She opened the door and did a quick sweep of the dash and glove compartment. An empty bottle of raspberry tea was stuffed in the cup holder on the door. She climbed into the backseat and moved a blanket aside to reveal a pair of tennis shoes and a sweatshirt. There was a gym bag on the floor. She rifled through the contents and pulled out a nearly full water bottle.

For a moment, she just stared at the bottle. Then a natural smile formed on her face for the first time in days. She opened the back door, anxious to show the children. Smoke drifted across the road to the west. She clutched the bottle against her chest. The forest fire was shifting, but it wasn't the flames she was worried about—it was the smoke. She couldn't see through the black cloud creeping up on them.

Emma and Micah reached up for the bottle.

"Don't drink it all at once," Martha said.

Emma greedily gulped down the water anyway, a trail bleeding down her chin.

"Not all at once," Martha repeated.

"Sorry," Emma said. She handed it to her brother. He took several gulps and then handed it to Martha. She took a slow slug, licked her lips, and sealed the container. Then she placed it inside her suit, tucking it into her waistband.

Martha guided them onward, clutching Emma and Micah's hands in the shifting winds. There were more bodies crumpled on the other side of the bridge ahead. There was no way to shield the children from the corpses, but nothing could be worse than watching their father die of radiation poisoning.

A faint whistling sounded over the gusting wind. It seemed to come and go as they walked. She listened for the sound again, catching it a moment later. Martha craned her neck to search for the source, but everything was shrouded in smoke. She turned back to the vehicles ahead. There were only two more before the bridge—a black sports car and a passenger van.

Halfway to the car, the rusty rattle of a motor vehicle rang out, stopping her mid-stride. The noise grew louder, clinking and clanking, and the cough of an engine joined the din. She pivoted back to the cloud of smoke. To the northeast, an army of skeletal trees jutted out of the hills like candles on a chocolate birthday cake. The frontage road twisting through the area was clear, with no sign of movement down the dirt path.

Was she hearing things? Was this the beginning of delirium?

She glanced down at the children and asked, "Do you hear that sound?"

They both nodded. "Sounds like a car," Micah said.

Martha turned around just as a pickup truck broke through the wall of smoke. Several men wearing green CBRN suits stood in the bed of the vehicle. They were the same type of suits the National Guard men had been wearing.

Her instincts told her something was off. These men weren't in a Humvee like those other soldiers.

Martha pulled the kids toward the black sports car and ducked behind the bumper. The pickup truck weaved around stalled cars, the tires screeching. Whoever these guys were, they were in a hurry.

"Are they going to help us?" Micah asked. He stood and looked around the car.

Martha pulled gently on his arm. "Be quiet," she whispered.

The truck slowed, and Martha strained to hear their conversation over the clatter of the engine.

"Where'd you see those people?" one of the men asked, his voice distorted by his mask.

"Over there."

Martha peeked around the bumper. The truck had slowed to a crawl. She glanced back over at the kids and said, "Get under the car and don't come out until I tell you. Okay?"

The children stared back at her.

"Come on," Martha said. "Doctor's orders."

She helped them crawl under the vehicle, and when they were safely hidden, she darted toward the van.

"There!" shouted a voice.

Martha halted and turned toward the pickup, praying her gut was wrong about these men. She held up her hands as the truck came to a stop. The passenger door opened and a soldier hopped out. The men in the bed angled assault rifles at Martha, forcing her throbbing heart into her throat. She squinted to see their features, but their faces were mostly obscured by their helmets.

"Stay where you are," one of the riflemen said.

The passenger checked the surrounding area as he strode toward her with a hand on the grip of a holstered pistol. She could see his eyes behind his visor. They were crystal blue and focused on her.

"You're the first person we've seen on the roads for a while," he said calmly. "That means you're either really stupid, or really smart for staying alive out here."

Martha kept her hands in the air and didn't reply.

"Not saying much, are you?" He took a few steps closer—so close she could see a snake-like scar on his forehead. It looked like someone had carved the squiggly design on purpose.

He glanced back at his men, motioning for them to lower their rifles. Coughing sounded from the back of the truck, and several small faces covered with gas masks peered around the side. The children were all wearing protective suits covered in ash.

Martha relaxed slightly, but she kept her hands up. The old pickup wasn't a military vehicle, but maybe these men weren't bad after all if they were trying to help those kids.

"Looks like you got a pretty fancy suit on," the man said with a chuckle. He gave her the elevator eyes treatment, up and down, to look at the garbage bags covering her body. "I'm willing to guess that you know a thing or two about fallout. Am I right?"

Martha decided to risk answering him. "I'm a doctor, and this isn't fallout per se. That only really happens when a nuclear warhead detonates on the ground. The radiation from an air detonation is actually more dangerous in the short term than fallout."

The man turned to look at the other soldiers. "Well damn, she does speak—and she's smart, too!"

"What unit are you with?" she asked.

The man cocked a bushy gray brow. "Unit?"

"I assumed you're a soldier. That CBRN suit is military issue, isn't it?"

"You are a *very* smart lady." He turned back to the truck and shouted, "Boys, what unit are we with?"

The men in the back of the truck all yelled, "Sons of Liberty!"

Martha had never heard of that one, but she didn't know much about the military. Maybe that was some sort of team call sign or something.

"You out here by yourself?" the man asked.

"Yes," she replied a bit too quickly.

"Carson, didn't you say you saw three people near the bridge?"

One of the men in the back of the truck nodded. "Her and what looked like a couple of kids."

The man in front of Martha stepped closer. That's when she noticed the holes patched with duct tape on the breast of his suit. The area was stained with something dark—something that looked a lot like blood. A chill spiked through her sweaty body.

"Now why would you want to lie to me? Do I strike you as someone that would hurt a kid?" he asked her.

Martha remained silent and took a step back. Were those bullet holes in the front of his suit?

His demeanor suddenly changed. "Now you're just making me mad," he growled. He closed the distance between them and stopped directly in front of her, hot breath hitting the inside of his visor.

"I was thinking about giving you a lift out of here, but you're testing my patience, and we already have a doctor back at our base."

"I'm sorry," Martha said, her mind racing. "I've seen some bad people on the road. Never know who you can trust, right?"

The man grinned again. "Damn right."

"So you'll give us a ride somewhere safe?" she asked.

"Sure, you and those kids. Just tell me where they are."

Martha moved to get a better look at the children in the back of the truck and the riflemen standing in the bed. She couldn't see their faces clearly because of their masks and visors, but she did notice other details on the truck from this angle; the number 88 stenciled on the passenger door, the double lightning bolt of the SS symbol made from strips of duct tape, an armband with a crudely painted eagle clutching a Swastika. These men weren't soldiers—they were some sort of white supremacist gang.

"Well? You going to get them kids or what?" the man in front of her asked.

"Okay," she said. "I'll go get them and come right back."

"Not a chance, lady. I'll send one of my men with you." He turned to wave at the truck. "Carson, get your ass down here."

As soon as the man turned, Martha took off running.

If they had killed soldiers for those suits, then there was no telling what they would do to the kids. Martha couldn't help the children already in the truck, but maybe she could lead the men away from Micah and Emma.

"Stop!" shouted the leader, anger rising in his voice.

She jumped into the ditch and made a run for the fort of blackened trees at the bottom of a nearby hill. A gunshot rang out, the crack shattering the quiet of the afternoon. Adolescent screams followed. Martha looked over her shoulder to see a boy in a wheelchair in the back of the pickup truck. He was shouting at the so-called Sons of Liberty to stop, but they were ignoring him.

Muzzles flashed, and rounds lanced into the ground next to her. The trees were still a hundred feet away. She wasn't going to make it.

Martha began to raise her hands in surrender when a bullet slammed into her shoulder, forcing her to the ground so violently that it knocked the air from her lungs. She hit the dirt hard, red flashing across her vision.

The injury was bad; she knew it right away by the lack of pain. The helpless feeling of being hurt without knowing how badly filled her with dread. She gasped for air and slowly rolled to her left side. The air hissing out of her chest meant she might have a punctured lung.

She knew then the wound wasn't survivable.

If the bullet had hit an artery, she'd be dead in minutes. Even if it hadn't, she'd be dead long before any help arrived.

"Why'd you have to go and do that, lady?"

Martha blinked away the tears welling in her eyes and glared at the leader, who was towering over her.

"I told them not to shoot you, but I guess one of them missed. Confidentially, I'm starting to think my men are enjoying this whole end of the world thing."

Micah and Emma started yelling, their thin, high voices carrying on the chill wind.

"What…" Martha wheezed. "What are you going to do with them?"

"Don't worry, I'm not going to hurt them. They're *far* too valuable. The government will pay a pretty penny to get those kids back. Some of 'em are cripples, but even the defective ones are probably worth something."

He stood and clucked his tongue like he was lecturing a child. "We got to get out of here before those fires catch up. You want a bullet in the head? It's all I can do for you now."

"No," she moaned, shaking her head from side to side. "Please, no."

He shrugged. "Your choice."

She watched the man slowly walk back down the slope to the road, leaving her there to die alone as the flames to the west slowly crept toward her.

— 1 —

Two Days Later

Estes Park Police Chief Marcus Colton stood in the chilly morning wind at the barricade blocking Highway 7. Several volunteers flanked him, all of them looking out over the highway in silence. They now knew why there weren't any refugees and stranded tourists staggering up the road.

They were all dead.

The radiation zone started about thirty miles to the south, and things were worse out there than anyone had predicted. Five days had passed since the North Korean attack. In that short time, several residents of Estes Park had lost their lives to the Tankala brothers. The police department, with the help of Major Nathan Sardetti and Sam 'Raven' Spears, had dealt with the serial killers, but justice had come at a high cost for the town of Estes Park, Colorado.

Colton had lost his best friend, Captain Jake Englewood, and Officer Rick Nelson was in the intensive care unit at the Estes Park Medical Center. He'd been trying to stop three junkies from robbing a grocery store pharmacy and gotten a brick to his skull for it. Detective Lindsey Plymouth and Raven Spears were tracking the assailants down while Colton waited at the roadblock for an update from Patrol Sergeant Don Aragon.

An hour earlier, Colton had sent Don south along Highway 7 in Raven's Jeep wearing a CBRN suit to scope out the area. He hadn't checked in, and Colton was growing impatient.

He pushed the radio to his lips and said, "Don, do you copy? Over."

There was a long pause, followed by static, and finally Don's Western drawl. "Lots of interference, but I can read you, Chief."

"You got a SITREP?" Colton asked. "Any survivors?"

"Negative, Chief. Everyone out here is dead."

Colton sucked on his cigarette, careful not to waste any of the precious tobacco. His hand was shaking when he pulled it away—a combination of PTSD, nerves, and early-onset arthritis. Colton cursed under his breath. He'd been looking forward to retiring in a few years, spending more time with his family. Instead, he was trying to hold the town together while the rest of the country fell apart.

"All right, head out just a bit farther and then report back," Colton said. He clipped the walkie-talkie back on his duty belt and gave a nod to Rex Stone. Colton had found the Stones' missing daughter, Melissa, murdered just before the EMP attack. Rex stood now in the bed of a pickup truck with a Springfield bolt-action rifle trained on the road.

"Didn't find anyone?" Rex asked in a gruff voice, his eyes fixed straight ahead. Five days ago, he'd been an easy-going, soft-spoken man. The initial shock of losing his daughter seemed to be turning to anger—an anger without a target. It was a dangerous combination. Colton wasn't so sure putting Rex to work was a good idea, but his old friend had insisted.

Colton shook his head and walked to the shoulder of

the road to wait for Don. The lack of refugees at least solved the growing dispute between Colton and his new second-in-command about whether to let more people into town.

Twenty-four hours earlier, not long after Colton had returned from Prospect Mountain with Jake's body, he had instructed his officers and armed volunteers to continue turning away refugees unless they possessed a specific skill that could benefit the town. People like doctors, engineers, mechanics, and police officers were highly needed. But since the storms had dumped radiation over southern and central Colorado, there hadn't been anyone to turn away, and Colton was beginning to wonder if there was anyone still out there.

He studied the snow-brushed mountains as they waited. Winter was near, and he wasn't sure he could get Estes Park through the cold without Jake. Even with the unexpected help of Raven, Colton didn't have enough manpower to get through the challenges Estes Park would face in the next few months.

First on Colton's list was to find the bastards that had put one of his officers in a coma. Raven and Lindsey were already working on that, but even if they did catch those responsible, there wasn't room in the small Estes Park jail to hold them. Theo, the thug that had started a shootout at Raven's house, was already locked up, along with several citizens who'd been caught looting.

"Got a vehicle inbound!" Rex shouted.

Colton looked up from his cigarette to scan the highway for Raven's Jeep. Instead, the growl of a diesel engine echoed off the bluffs. He reached for the grip of his Single Action Army Revolver, but he kept it holstered when he saw it was Lindsey driving Jake's red 1952 Chevy pickup. Raven sat in the passenger seat, and Nathan was in the bed with a rucksack over his shoulders.

Colton took one last drag and stomped the butt out before walking down the road to meet the truck. Lindsey pulled onto the shoulder and waved.

"Mornin', Chief," she said.

Raven hopped out and went to the lift gate to let his dog out and help Nathan down. The new K9 unit and the battered pilot walked over, Creek's tail wagging as he trotted next to the men. Nathan's broken arm was in a cast, and his skin was covered in lacerations and bruises. He and Raven had both taken a hell of a beating on Prospect Mountain in the battle that had left Brown Feather and Turtle Tankala, as well as Jake, dead.

"Major, you look like you got run over by a car, then a bus, then a train," Colton said. "When are those Marines coming to get you? I thought Secretary Montgomery was sending them out to pick you up."

Nathan shrugged. Even that seemed to hurt. He winced and looked out over the road. "I haven't heard anything, but they must still be looking for my nephew. I thought I might get a better signal out of the valley, just in case my sister tries to reach me."

Colton still couldn't believe the pilot was the brother of the Secretary of Defense. He also had a bad feeling that the Marines searching for Nathan's nephew weren't going to find anyone alive at the Easterseals camp in Empire, Colorado.

Lindsey pulled off a pair of aviator sunglasses and met Colton's gaze. The past five days had etched new lines around her eyes.

"Any luck?" he asked.

"We canvassed several folks on Black Canyon Drive,

including the Arnettes," she said. "They think they saw the suspects running across Devils Gulch Road yesterday."

"You think they could be hiding out in a house there?" Colton asked.

"That's my guess," Lindsey said.

Raven ambled over to them. A bandage masked the gash on his cheek and bags hung below his dark eyes, but despite his injuries he seemed in high spirits. Colton snorted. Give Raven something to chase and he'd be happy in hell itself.

"Lots of people live up that way, Chief," Raven said. "They could be anywhere. My suggestion would be to send a message to folks up there to keep an eye out and send word if they see anything."

"Can't risk it," Colton replied. "Remember, our suspects are addicts, and when their pills run out, they will be looking for a new source. No telling what they'll do to get more."

"The Chief is right," Nathan added. "You need to find them before they hurt someone else."

"What do you want us to do, Chief?" Lindsey asked. Her shoulder-length red hair fluttered in the wind. She was in her early twenties—too young, it seemed to Colton, to experience the horror of the past several days. He'd fought alongside men and women her age or even younger in Afghanistan. It changed them. Hell, it had changed him, too.

"Take Creek and see if he can pick up a scent. Maybe we can narrow down their location. If you locate our suspects, I want to know before you move in," Colton said.

Lindsey nodded, and Raven touched the bill of his

baseball cap.

"Good luck," Colton said. He went to pat Creek, but the dog was already darting after Raven. The Akita might be designated as a K9 unit, but he was loyal to one man and one man only.

Colton was reaching for another cigarette when his radio crackled.

"Chief, you copy?"

Colton plucked the radio off his duty belt and brought it to his lips. "Go ahead."

"I found a survivor," Don heaved. "A woman. She's in bad shape, sir. Looks like—" Static crackled over his voice.

"Come again," Colton said. "You're breaking up."

"She's—" Static. "Shot."

The word sent a chill through Colton. He lowered the radio and pivoted back to the Chevy.

"Hold up, Lindsey!" he said. "Move the barrier. I'm heading out, too."

Rex and the other men holding the road stared at him without moving.

"Do it," Colton said.

Several of the men began shifting the concrete blocks.

"You sure that's a good idea?" Raven asked.

"Don found a survivor on the road. Sounds like she's been shot," Colton said. "We're going to pick her up."

"Without suits?" Lindsey asked, leaning out of the truck's window.

Colton cursed. He had forgotten about the radiation. He raised the radio back to his lips.

"Don, can you get that woman back to town on your own?"

White noise crackled from the speakers, a long delay

19

before the reply. Don spoke in a low voice as if he didn't want to be overheard.

"Sir, I don't think she's going to make it. Even if I get her back to the hospital, we're already low on medical supplies. We have to look after our own."

Colton almost cursed a second time. He had set a dangerous precedent by ordering his officers to turn people away. But never once had he told any of them to abandon someone who needed medical attention.

What would Jake have done?

That answer was an easy one. Colton knew his best friend would have carried the wounded stranger on his back, if need be.

Colton clicked the radio. "We're not in the business of leaving people out there to die. Bring that woman back to town."

"But sir, I thought we agreed—"

"That's an order."

"All due respect, but this is a waste of time and resources," Don said.

Everyone on the road was staring at Colton now, the tension palpable around him. Some of the volunteers probably agreed with Don, but this wasn't a democracy. Colton called the shots, and he had to show everyone that he was still in charge of Estes Park.

He pressed the radio button again and said, "Do your job, Sergeant!"

There was no response, just the buzz of static.

"Good call, Chief," Nathan said. "That guy is a piece of work. You better watch your back around him."

"Get going," Colton said. "I'll handle this. You find those junkies. I want them locked up by nightfall."

"Okay, Chief," Lindsey said.

Colton folded his arms across his chest and looked back out over the mountains, recalling the night of the attack when he and Raven had found Melissa Stone's body. He'd known when the jets crashed and the lights went out that it was the start of something larger, but he'd had no idea that in five short days he would be the one deciding who lived and who died. With a heavy sigh, he jammed another cigarette in his mouth and went back to work.

***

Ty Montgomery coughed into the gas mask strapped to his face. The world smelled like burning cedar and plastic. His hands were zip-tied to the armrests of his wheelchair. There was no use in fighting the restraints. Even if he could slip out of them, there was nowhere to go. He was trapped with the other kids in the back of a pickup truck. There were four of them from the camp, all around his age, plus the new kids, Micah and Emma.

This was the second time they had been moved in the past two days. They had spent last night in a warehouse. A couple of the campers were autistic, and the constant chaos was hard on them, but the men didn't care. They just shouted and pushed the kids around.

Ty's best friend at camp, Alex, was right to have hidden when the soldiers came. If Ty had been able to, he would have done the same thing, but he had been captured along with these other kids, and the men were treating them like animals.

Sometimes, it seemed like this was all a bad dream. Except that it smelled too nasty and hurt too much to be a dream. He tried again to process the events of the past five days. First the massive explosion that had sounded like a volcano erupting. Then the fires. His friends had all been taken to different locations at the camp where they had taken shelter from something called radiation. After the rain had stopped, the Sons of Liberty soldiers had shown up with guns. Then they shot Mr. Barton and Mr. Gonzalez. That's when Alex had limped away and hid.

Ty shivered at the memory. Mr. Barton and Mr. Gonzalez had been his friends. He just hoped that Alex was okay, but deep down, Ty had a bad feeling that he wasn't. Alex had a minor form of cerebral palsy, and Ty was worried he wouldn't be able to take care of himself. He wished he'd gotten to say goodbye.

"Up there!" shouted a muffled voice.

The truck slowed and the soldiers all stood in the bed of the truck. Most of them didn't talk much around him and the other kids. The only nice one was a young man with a pimply face named Tommy. His arms and neck were covered in tattoos like the others, but he never shouted.

Ty listened whenever the men did talk where he could hear them. They called themselves the Sons of Liberty, and their leader was the General. He had a smooth voice and squiggly scar on his head, like Harry Potter. The General kept saying the time had come to take back the country from the corrupt government and restore it to what it was meant to be back when the nation was founded. The other men always cheered.

Ty didn't understand. His mom was in the government, and she was brave and kind. Why did they want to take it back from people like her?

These men weren't like any soldiers Ty had ever met. They certainly weren't like his Uncle Nathan or his mom.

These men all wore funny looking space suits, and instead of helping people, they kidnapped children and shot that old lady in the back.

She wasn't the first person they had killed along the road.

A jolt rocked the truck, and Ty grabbed the armrests of his wheelchair. His blindfold slipped down enough that he could see Tommy and another man named Carson standing to his left.

"Pull off," Carson ordered. He patted the roof of the cab.

The pickup crawled to a stop, and Carson jumped out onto the road. Tommy remained behind.

"It's okay," he said to the kids. "We're just stopping for a few minutes."

The muffled voices of the other soldiers sounded from all directions. They piled out of the vehicles in front of the convoy. Ty bowed his head to see better over his blindfold.

On the shoulder of the road, under a canopy of evergreens, stood a man and woman. They were both wearing backpacks stuffed with camping gear. The man waved to the Sons of Liberty, and a beaming smile spread across his face.

"You guys sure are a sight for sore eyes. My girlfriend and I were starting to think we were the last people on Earth!"

"We haven't seen anyone for over a day," the woman said. She wrapped her arms around her chest, shivering.

Ty wanted to tell them to run, but it wouldn't do any good. They wouldn't make it far.

Two of the other soldiers, Joshua and Bernie, strode toward the couple. They were both thickly built with bushy beards, shaved heads, and tattoos. They approached with their guns lowered toward the ground. The General joined them a moment later.

"Where are you two headed?" the General asked. Despite the breathing apparatus he wore, Ty could still clearly hear his smooth voice, like the narrator of a show on the Discovery Channel.

The young man looked to the west. "We're trying to get away from those fires."

"You sick?" Joshua asked.

The woman nodded.

"Can't use 'em," the General said casually. He walked back to the truck, leaving Joshua and Bernie in the street.

"What? What do you mean?" the young man said.

"He means you're fucked," Joshua said with a laugh. He turned with Bernie and followed the General.

"You can't just leave us here!" the man said, reaching out. "Please—"

His girlfriend ran past them, grabbing the General by the sleeve before they could stop her. Bernie and Joshua both raised their rifles.

"Get the hell back!" Bernie shouted.

The woman held up her hands. Her boyfriend did the same thing and slowly got in front of her to shield her body with his own.

"Whoa, whoa, we don't want any trouble," he said.

The General stood his ground and calmly said, "Give me your backpacks."

The woman looked at her boyfriend, who nodded back at her. She unslung her pack and handed it to the General, who then tossed it over to Bernie.

"Yours, too," the General said.

"But this is all we have. How are we supposed—" the

young man began to say when the General threw a right hook. A flash of metal glimmered in the sunlight as his fist connected with the man's jaw. A crack rang out, metal on bone.

The woman let out a scream and dropped next to her injured boyfriend.

The men laughed as the General held up the brass knuckles he liked to wear on his right fist over his glove.

The General crouched in front of the couple and tilted his head.

"People just don't listen," he said. "Now, I'm going to ask you one more time to give me your packs."

The woman helped her injured boyfriend pull off his pack. He let out a moan as she pulled it from his shoulder. The General grabbed the bag and glanced back at the truck, meeting Ty's gaze for a moment.

"Take note, kids. *This* is how we survive in the new world."

He stood and walked back to the truck, but Joshua remained by the couple. "Hey General, I got an idea. How about we take this lady with us?"

"She's sick," the General replied. "But hey, if you want her, be my guest."

The injured man pushed himself to his feet and stood in front of his girlfriend, one hand clutching his jaw.

"Run, Sarah," he said.

"Stay where you are," Joshua ordered.

The injured man pulled a small knife from a sheath on his belt and held up the blade in a shaky hand. "You'll have to go through me."

"Don't do it," Tommy whispered from behind Ty. "C'mon, man. Just let 'em go."

Joshua let out a bellowing laugh. Instead of shooting

the man, Joshua lowered his rifle. Ty let out a sigh of relief.

Tommy looked down at Ty and then tugged the blindfold back over his eyes. The last thing Ty saw was Joshua pulling his own knife. The woman screamed. Cheering and laughter from the soldiers followed. Then came the grunts and cries of pain from the young man, topped off by his girlfriend screeching in agony. It was over in less than a minute, but it felt more like an eternity to Ty. Tears welled in his eyes. One of them streaked down his filthy cheeks, and he couldn't even lift his hands to wipe it away.

No. Don't you cry. You're stronger than that, he thought.

If his mom were here, she would probably have told him it was okay to cry, but she was in Washington, D.C., working like always. He loved his mom more than anyone in the world, but he was mad at her, too. Why hadn't she come to rescue him?

The sobs from the other kids rose into a wailing cacophony. One of the soldiers told them to shut the hell up. Tommy tried to calm them down in his quiet, nasally voice.

"It's okay," he kept repeating.

A gunshot sounded, followed by two more. The woman stopped screaming.

"I told you not to waste bullets, Bernie. Those two were already as good as dead," the General said. "Were you this stupid in Iraq? If so, I'm surprised you made it back in one piece."

Several of the men chuckled. Ty tried to move his hands, but even if he could loosen the restraints, he couldn't exactly run away. Frustrated, he tugged harder on the zip-ties.

"Kid, don't do that," Tommy said. "It'll go better for you if you just hold still."

Ty froze. Tommy was right; he needed to be good until his mom came to get him.

"Let's move out!" the General shouted. "We're almost back to the Castle."

The doors to the other vehicles opened, then slammed, and then the convoy rolled forward. His wheelchair jolted, and although he couldn't feel anything below his waist, pain lanced up his spine from the impact. He let out a muffled cry and held onto the armrests.

Tommy tried to keep the wheelchair in place with his firm grip. A few minutes into the drive, his voice spoke softly next to Ty's ear.

"It's okay, kid. Just hang in there," Tommy said.

"Shut up, Tommy. I told you not to talk to those kids," Carson said. "Half of 'em probably can't understand you anyway."

Ty stayed silent and thought about his mom. She would come find him soon. And when she did, the Sons of Liberty were going to pay.

***

Lieutenant Jeff Dupree sat in the belly of a Sikorsky UH-60 Black Hawk helicopter, trying to get his thoughts in order. It was the third chopper he'd been on that day, having been transferred from a Sikorsky SH-60 Seahawk to a Sikorsky HH-60 Pave Hawk, and finally to the Black Hawk that his team was hitching a ride on now. Logistics since the North Korean attack had been a nightmare, and finding working aircraft and equipment had been a huge hassle.

He had a dozen things on his mind, but today he needed to focus on saving the son of the new Secretary of Defense. Knowing his own kids were safe in Key West with his ex-wife helped alleviate some of the stress of the mission, but it hurt to know they were better off with her than him. He wasn't the best dad—he knew that, he accepted it, and he kept saying he would make up for it.

He'd already missed too many birthdays. Once this mission was over, and Ty Montgomery was back in his mother's arms, Dupree was going home. It might be too late to patch things up with his ex, but maybe there was still time to be a father to his boys.

During his last tour in Iraq, he'd saved the lives of a dozen men. He had expected the airstrike he'd called in to kill him, and it nearly had. His left side, left arm, and part of his chin had scars from the blast. But while his men called him a hero, his wife just called him a lousy deadbeat dad.

The earpiece inside his helmet transmitted a message.

"LT, we're coming up on Cedar Rapids. It's pretty bad down there. That high-rise to the east looks like it swallowed a passenger plane."

Dupree joined the other men as they maneuvered in their tight-fitting CBRN suits for a better look at the city. Tendrils of smoke rose from the skyline. He quickly saw what the pilot was talking about. The wing of a plane stuck out the charred side of the building like a fin on a shark.

"That city is cookin' like bacon in a skillet," said Staff Sergeant Erik Emerson. "Good Lord, this shit is crazy."

"Keep us clear," Dupree ordered. "I don't want any survivors taking potshots at us. Not everyone is going to be happy to see a military helicopter."

"If there *are* any survivors," said Sergeant Dusty McCabe.

Dupree hadn't said it out loud, but he had wondered the same thing during their flyover. The view below was a constant reminder that life in the United States wasn't going to return to normal anytime soon. It was only five days after the North Korean attack, but civilization was falling apart. Riots, looting, violence, and radiation were killing hundreds of Americans by the hour. There was no telling when this place would be habitable again. Dupree scanned the highway snaking through the city. Cars and bodies littered the asphalt.

Corporal Nick Sharps let out a low whistle as the bird turned to the west. "Man, I would not want to be caught outside without one of these." He brushed off the shoulder of his CBRN suit.

"These suits will protect us, right, LT?" asked Emerson.

"Long as you got that shit on tight," replied Sharps before Dupree could answer. "You don't want to end up glowing in the dark. We'd hafta put you in the latrine as a nightlight, brother."

"Cut the crap," Dupree said. "Do you even know what radiation does? Do you shitheads have any idea what those people are going through?"

"Sorry, sir," Emerson said.

Dupree directed his gaze at Sharps. The man had given up a basketball scholarship at Duke to join the Marines after his brother was killed in Iraq. Dupree liked him, but Sharps was a jokester.

"No, sir," Sharps said a beat later.

"That's what I thought. Ever had a bad case of diarrhea?" Dupree said. "Add internal bleeding to that and gangrenous ulcers. You start puking up your guts, literally. Then it's going to be a race to see what kills you first: blood loss or a terminal coma, assuming you don't go crazy from delirium and blow your head off first."

Sharps looked at the floor, and everyone else in the troop hold fell into silence. The mind-rattling thump, thump of the rotors was the only sound as they pulled away from the city, but the quiet didn't last long.

"So those people are screwed?" Sharps asked. He pointed to the interstate cutting through cornfields. It took Dupree a moment to find the ancient boat of a Cadillac weaving through the minefield of abandoned vehicles scattered across the road.

"Wonder where they got a working ride?" McCabe said.

"How about some peace and quiet?" Dupree said. "We got a mission to focus on. Chances are we're going to find a bunch of…" He stopped himself short of saying exactly what he expected to find.

"Bunch of what?" Sharps pressed.

"This is a camp for disabled children, and Command said we need to prepare for the worst," Dupree replied.

Each helmet dipped in acknowledgement. They were all business now, prepared to do what Marines did best—save lives.

If there are any left to save, Dupree thought.

"How are we doing on fuel?" he asked over the comms.

"Good, sir. We'll stop for a drink after we secure our targets," the primary pilot replied.

Dupree grabbed a handhold and stood in front of his men. It never hurt to go over the mission one more time. "Remember, our orders are to locate Ty Montgomery. If the boy is still alive, we will bring him back to the USS *John C. Stennis*. If he's not, we'll at least be able to give his mother some closure."

"Sir, yes, sir," all but one of the men said in unison.

Sharps gave Dupree a cockeyed look.

"You got a problem, Sharps?"

"No, sir."

"Spill it, Sharps," Dupree ordered.

"Sir, it's just..." Sharps hesitated for a moment. "What's so special about this one kid? I mean, we all got families out there. I'm worried about my little bro and sis, you know?"

Dupree had prepared to give Sharps a dressing down, but the kid had a point. If he could, Dupree would have turned the bird around and flown straight to Florida to check on his boys.

"Life's not fair, Sharps," Dupree said, his voice raised so that everyone would hear him over the rotors. "This mission comes directly from President Diego. Our job as Marines is not to question orders. It's to follow them. Got it?"

This time every helmet dipped in acknowledgement.

Dupree turned his attention to the checkered fields below. It was easy to get bored with the view, but it was a welcome and peaceful distraction. Iowa looked like flat, empty land, but it was important to the country's economy. He came from a long line of farmers, and he knew that land was ideal for growing staple crops. Iowa was number one in corn, soybeans, hogs, eggs, and ethanol. The radiation would kill most everything down there.

Another hour or so passed before they saw the snowy tips of the Rocky Mountains. McCabe gave the order, and in seconds the other men were doing their final gear and weapons checks.

"Remember, your CBRN suit is your lifeline," Dupree said. "One tear could kill you, so be careful once we hit the ground."

Dupree did a quick once-over of his own suit and then pulled a magazine from the vest he wore over it. He palmed the mag into the rifle, but didn't chamber a round. The only time he'd used his weapon stateside was during training, and this sure as hell wasn't a training mission. Killing enemies in Afghanistan and Iraq was one thing, but he couldn't imagine firing on an American citizen.

"All right, listen up, everyone," he said after the men had finished their prep. "We're splitting up into three teams. Sharps and Emerson, you're on me. We'll take the dormitories. McCabe and Rodriguez, head east. Snider and Runge will go west."

"Target in fifteen minutes," said one of the pilots.

"Remember, Ty Montgomery can't walk, so be prepared to carry him out of there. If he's alive, he's going to be scared. Try not to give the poor kid a heart attack," Dupree said. "His mom gave me a password to use: *Falcon*. You got that? The first word out of your mouth should be 'Falcon'."

"What about other survivors?" asked McCabe.

"We will take as many children as we can," Dupree said.

"Ooh rah," Sharps said.

A light rain pattered against the aircraft as the pilots flew toward the mountains. Dupree nodded at Crew Chief Joshua Locust. The man hadn't said a word the entire flight, and he silently opened the troop hold door now, revealing a sea of green trees shifting in the wind. The cornfields were long gone, replaced by a forest of ponderosas blanketing the mountains.

They passed over another road blocked by several abandoned vehicles. Nothing looked out of the ordinary—if you could call the apocalypse ordinary—until he spotted several crumpled bodies in the center of the lane a few hundred feet from an overpass. Something about the way they were sprawled pinged his curiosity. Dupree brought his scope up to his visor just as the voice of the main pilot came over the open channel.

"You seeing this, Lieutenant?"

"Get us closer," Dupree said.

"Radiation must be really bad here," Sharps said. "Poor bastards."

Dupree scanned the road as the pilots hovered. A pool of blood surrounded one of the bodies.

"Damn, you weren't kidding, LT," Emerson said. "Those people really bled out!"

He centered his red dot sight on a man lying on his back. As he zoomed in, Dupree saw the bloody hole in the middle of the dead man's forehead.

Radiation hadn't killed him after all.

"Get us the hell out of here!" Dupree yelled over the thumping rotors. He lowered his gun to scan the road with his own eyes. There weren't any hostiles visible, but he couldn't see into the shadows beneath the bridge.

The pilots craned their helmets from the cockpit. "Come again?" one of them said.

"NOW!" Dupree screamed.

The bird pulled up and away from the road, jarring the Marines in the back. Dupree grabbed a handhold, but remained at the open door. It was possible that the man had shot himself rather than face a slow death from the radiation, but Dupree hadn't seen a gun anywhere at the scene. And those other bodies, all haloed with blood...no, something bad had happened down there. Something worse than radiation poisoning. He'd seen too many ambushes in Iraq and Afghanistan to miss the signs. Those people had been executed—and whoever had done it might still be around.

The Black Hawk leveled out, and Dupree found himself reaching for the charging handle of his M4. He chambered a round and put his weapon on safe as he watched the road below. He'd hoped to make it through this mission without having to etch more crossbones on the barrel of his rifle, but it looked like war had followed him home to the United States of America.

— 2 —

"Thanks for the ride, Detective," Nathan said as he climbed out of the back end of the pickup. Raven had offered him a hand, but the Major was too proud for help.

And a major pain in the ass, Raven thought.

"See ya around," Lindsey said with a wink and a toss of her red hair.

Raven rolled his eyes. First his sister, now Lindsey? What did all these women see in Nathan Sardetti?

"Good luck out there," he said to Raven.

Raven reached through the window and shook Nathan's hand. "Just in case your flight comes before we get back."

Nathan smiled. At least Raven thought he did; it was hard to tell with how bruised his face was.

Lindsey pulled away from town hall. By early afternoon the sun had poked through the dome of gray clouds, covering the terrain with a golden glow. Raven watched the mountains in silence on the ride out of town. It wasn't that he didn't want to talk to Lindsey. Normally, he would have jumped at the chance, even though she was a cop. Red hair, feisty, funny: she was practically his dream woman. They were only about nine years apart, which wasn't terrible. Or so he kept telling himself. He hadn't been sure which way she swung, but she had definitely been flirting with Nathan.

Cut it out, Raven. You got assholes to track down.

He snuck another look at her cute profile. How was a man supposed to concentrate with a woman like her around?

"No, I don't have a boyfriend," she said suddenly. "And I'm not interested in one, either."

Raven felt his cheeks warm. "What?"

"For a former Force Recon Marine, I'd have thought you would be a little bit more subtle when checking me out."

"Lady, I ain't—"

"Detective. And save it, Sam. You're not fooling anyone."

Raven smiled and turned back to look out of the passenger window. At any other time, he would have enjoyed the banter, but today he didn't feel much like his charming self. It wasn't because he was exhausted and covered in bruises and cuts from the showdown against Brown Feather. The events of the past five days had changed Raven. The injuries to his body were going to leave scars, and the horror inflicted by the wannabe Water Cannibals would stay with him forever. The stories from his childhood had given him nightmares for years. Seeing them come to life was enough to make him crave a stiff drink.

Too bad he'd quit drinking.

The old Raven would have tried to drown the memories in a bottle, but he didn't do that anymore. He had a family to protect—hell, thanks to Colton, he now had a whole town to protect. Sandra and Allie, along with the rest of Estes Park, needed him sober. And at the moment, they needed him to track down the junkies who had put Officer Nelson in the hospital.

"You okay over there?" Lindsey asked. "I didn't hurt your feelings, did I?"

Raven straightened his Seattle Mariners baseball cap and tried to sound convincing. "Lady…" He corrected himself when she glanced in his direction. "I mean, Detective. It takes a whole hell of a lot more than that to hurt my feelings."

"I'm just giving you shit." She met his gaze for a moment before looking back to the road. "I heard what you did up on Prospect Mountain, and I'm glad to have you with me. With us, I mean. The Estes Park police force."

Raven felt his smile return. He wasn't used to being flattered. Especially by a cop. And never by a pretty cop.

"Creek and I are happy to help."

"I just wish I'd been up there with y'all. Maybe I could have saved Captain Englewood."

Raven's smile folded to a frown. He was sorry for Jake and his family, but the man's sacrifice had helped save Sandra and Allie. There was no telling what Brown Feather would have done to them if Jake and Nathan hadn't shown up.

"The Stanley sure is a blessing," Lindsey said after a long pause.

"Huh?" Raven eyed the red roof of the iconic hotel in the distance. "Oh. Right. How many people are staying there?"

"Hundreds, I think. I've lost track. There are over one hundred and fifty rooms, plus there are other buildings on the property, but we still don't have enough space for everyone. We've moved some of the stranded tourists to other hotels and resorts. I can't imagine how they're feeling, stuck here and away from their homes and family."

Raven wanted to ask her about her own family, but this wasn't the time or the place. He continued to look out the window at the Stanley. It was amazing how things had changed nearly overnight.

"I always thought it would take longer for society to collapse," he said.

"Without power? Without smartphones?" Lindsey lifted a brow. "I'm surprised we're not hearing about more shootings."

"Like the one that Don found? I bet there are more cases like that. We just aren't hearing about them."

"Yeah," Lindsey said. "You're probably right. And you know what else? I really don't like the way Don talked to Colton. It's been a long time coming though, to be honest."

"How do you mean?"

"Colton and Don have always butted heads, ever since I got hired. Jake was the buffer between the two. Now that he's gone..." She shrugged, never taking her eyes from the road. "I don't think Mayor Andrews likes Colton much, either. I wouldn't be surprised if the administration tries to push Don into the Chief of Police position."

"I never liked that little prick," Raven replied. "He wanted to toss me in jail and throw away the key when I got arrested for poaching."

"Yeah, I know."

Raven rubbed his forehead and smirked. "Then again, I didn't really like Colton at first, either. He's kind of a prick, too."

Lindsey chuckled and shifted the aviators higher on

her freckled nose. "He means well. The man has a big heart, but he's one of those old-school, hard-ass cops. I hope I never get like that."

"Really?" Raven said. "Because I already think you're kind of a hard-ass. You're definitely a firecracker. Pretty terrible combination, if you ask me."

"Very charming, Sam." She laughed and turned onto Devils Gulch Road. The engine rattled as the truck shot down the open road. Fences separated the shoulder from grassy fields, and the houses were fewer and farther between out here on the edge of town.

To the west, bluffs dotted with Douglas firs, aspens, and ponderosa pines separated civilization from the wilderness. There were a few stalled cars ahead, but the only person Raven saw was a guy walking his dog along the shoulder. They were lucky the radiation had mostly passed them by up here, and people could go outside without fear of being poisoned.

"Any idea where we should start?" Lindsey asked.

"I say we canvass some more folks," Raven said. He pointed to the man walking his dog. "Starting with the guy in the Estes Park hoodie."

"That's Allen Dixon. He's a retired school teacher and a pretty nice guy," she said, bringing the vehicle to a stop.

Creek jumped up in the bed of the pickup and barked at Allen's Golden Retriever. Raven rolled down his window and told Creek to be quiet.

"Afternoon, Mr. Dixon," Lindsey called out.

Allen strode over to the vehicle and pulled down the hood of his sweatshirt, revealing a weathered, bearded face.

"Afternoon, Officer Plymouth and... I'm afraid I don't know your name, son."

"Raven Spears, sir." He stuck his hand out the window to shake.

"Nice to meet you," Allen said. "What brings you this way?"

"We're looking for three people who assaulted an officer," Raven said.

"Two men and a woman," Lindsey said. "Guys were both around forty years old and between five-ten and six feet tall. The larger man was wearing an Old Navy sweatshirt, and the thinner man had on a red poncho. The woman is probably five-five or shorter and about one hundred pounds. She had on a flannel shirt when she was last seen."

"They're all tweakers," Raven added.

"Tweakers?" Allen asked.

"Addicts," Lindsey corrected.

Raven nodded. "Yeah, addicts would be the fancy terminology. You seen anyone like that?"

Allen scanned the road like he was looking for them. As he turned, Raven spotted the grip of a pistol holstered under his sweatshirt.

"I heard about them, but I haven't seen anyone matching that description," Allen said. "Do you think they came this way?"

"Possibly," Lindsey replied. "We're encouraging everyone to use caution. Don't approach these people yourself."

"I'll walk into town if I hear or see anything," Allen said. He patted the door. "Sorry to hear about Captain Englewood. He was a good man and an old friend."

Lindsey nodded. "We're all taking it hard."

Allen started to walk away and then paused. "You know, I haven't heard anything from the Whites for a few days. I thought it was odd, but figured they were just keeping to themselves after all that's happened."

"Where do they live?" Raven asked.

Lindsey looked through the windshield. "Just three houses up. Right, Allen?"

"Yes, ma'am."

"We'll check it out. Stay safe out here," she said with a smile.

Creek barked at the Golden Retriever again as Lindsey pulled back onto the road. This time Raven let it go. He was fine with his Akita telling the other dogs who the boss was in Estes Park.

"The Whites have one hell of a house," Lindsey said. "Makes sense our suspects went there."

"Lots of these folks have nice houses."

"True, but the Whites' is one of the biggest."

"Maybe we should go get some backup, like the Chief said…"

Lindsey rolled her eyes. "Really?"

"Hey, I'm just trying to follow the rules for the first time in my life."

She laughed at that. "I think we can handle this."

"You're the boss."

"Don't forget it." Her dimpled smile was hard not to admire, but Raven forced his gaze back to the terrain.

Lindsey steered around a brand-new Dodge Ram with oversized wheels stalled in the middle lane. The next hill provided a view of the valley for several miles. A stone fortress was tucked inside the forest, overlooking the magnificent panorama.

"I'm assuming that's the house?" Raven asked.

"Yup. I'm going to drive past and park near the trees on the east side."

Raven pulled his Glock 22 and checked the ammo. He wasn't taking any more chances, especially if he was going to be raiding houses. A crossbow against an armed chase in close quarters was not his idea of a fair fight.

Lindsey tucked the truck behind a wall of ponderosas a quarter-mile from the border of the property. After killing the engine, she checked the magazine in her Beretta 92F and then tucked it back in the holster.

"No shooting unless I give you the order," Lindsey said.

"All due respect, but I was fighting in Iraq when you were still in grade school."

She crinkled her freckled nose. "And all due respect to you, but I'm the police officer. You're here to assist me."

Raven dipped his head and opened the door. Walking to the back of the truck, he grabbed his bow and then let the tailgate down for Creek to hop out.

"You okay, boy?" Raven asked, crouching beside his dog.

Creek wagged his tail and licked Raven's face. He seemed just fine, despite being tossed into a tree the day before.

Raven loaded a bolt in the groove of his bow and scanned the property while Creek relieved himself on a bush. The main house was two stories high with windows along the east side. A carriage house and a barn were positioned on the south side of the land.

"You take Creek around back. I'll take the front," Lindsey said. "I'm going to do this the old-fashioned way and knock. You keep out of sight unless you see something, got it?"

"Hold up," Raven said. "What do you know about the Whites? Does Mrs. White sit at home and knit while Mr.

White reads? Or are they card-carrying members of the NRA who would have no problem taking a pot shot at a handsome American Indian?"

Lindsey shook her head and smirked. "Laurel and Steve are both retired lawyers from Denver. They're quiet and keep to themselves. I don't think you need to worry about getting shot, especially if you stay out of sight." She paused and added, "That's what you did in the Marines, right?"

"Very funny," Raven said. He tucked his pistol into the holster at his back. This time he wasn't carrying his hatchets. One of them was still jammed in Brown Feather's head up on Prospect Mountain, and the other was in his gear bag.

"Come here, boy," Raven said. He bent down to give Creek a sniff of a hat one of the suspects had dropped when fleeing the Safeway parking lot. The dog took in the smell and sat on his haunches, tail wagging, ready to hunt.

"Good luck," Lindsey said.

"You too."

Raven followed Creek through the woods on the eastern edge of the property. He cradled his crossbow comfortably as he crept over the beds of fallen pine needles. Through the gaps in the trees, he watched Lindsey approach the circular drive. When she was halfway there, he emerged from the protection of the woods and ran toward the house. He stayed low, keeping out of view from the windows.

Creek followed him, sniffing the air. The dog took off for the backyard, but Raven didn't call after him. His furry best friend was smart enough not to walk into a trap.

Raven hugged the side of the house and crept under

the large windows. A crow cawed in the distance, but otherwise it was quiet.

In the Marines, he had been connected to his squad by a comm link and a variety of other modes of communication. That had all changed after the EMP attack. Raven had gone back to what he learned growing up on the Rez. That meant trusting nobody but Creek, and relying on nothing but his own senses.

The rap of Lindsey's hand on the front door sounded far too loud in the silence.

Raven stopped and waited for voices, but there was only Lindsey's as she asked, "Mr. White, Mrs. White. Is anyone home?"

Overhead, the sun peeked out of the clouds, illuminating the meticulously groomed backyard. There were stone paths, a fire pit and a fountain, and shrubs pruned into the shapes of animals. It put Raven's humble abode to shame, but he still liked his house better.

He took another moment to listen and then peered around the back corner at a pair of French doors. Drapes blocked his view of the inside. A staircase led up to the deck on the back of the house. There was another set of doors at the top. Creek was already there, sitting on his haunches.

Raven scanned the sprawling backyard one more time before heading up the steps. Although his dog thought the coast was clear, Raven still kept his finger along the trigger guard of his bow.

At the top of the stairs, he slung the weapon over his back and drew his pistol. He waved Creek away from the door and approached slowly, careful not to make too much noise on the creaky decking. Past the gauzy drapes, he could just make out the kitchen. The surfaces were all clean of dirty dishes and food, which told Raven his chases likely hadn't been here. Drug addicts weren't exactly known for cleaning up after themselves.

He readied his Glock with one hand and grabbed the sliding glass door with his other hand. The door was unlocked. While it was possible the Whites would leave their expensive house unlocked, it wasn't likely. Raven listened for Lindsey's voice, but heard nothing. The silence was disturbing. Where the hell was she?

He kept to the side of the door, out of sight, as he waited for her to come to the backyard, but the minutes ticked by. Eventually, he decided to move.

Raising his gun, he swept the muzzle over one of the biggest kitchens he had ever seen and slowly crossed the room with Creek by his side. The space opened into a living area with vaulted ceilings, a stone fireplace, and oak bookshelves lining the walls between the large windows.

The white couches and carpet were all immaculate— no sign of squatters here. To his right, French doors led to a study. Inside, he found a gun cabinet. His heart hammered when he saw the shattered glass forming a skirt around the base.

The weapons were gone.

Raven slowly stepped back into the living room to look for Lindsey. Something was wrong. She should have showed up by now.

He motioned for Creek to follow him toward the front door. Halfway there, a gunshot cracked outside the house. The sound sent his heart hammering even harder against his ribs.

Lindsey!

He rushed over to the front door, swung it open, and raised his Glock. A flurry of movement in the woods caught his attention. He holstered his gun and pulled his crossbow instead. As he brought the scope up, the red Chevy pickup screeched out onto the road. The truck backfired with another crack.

The noise he had heard inside wasn't a gunshot after all—it was just the damn muffler. He stood there staring, shocked that Lindsey would leave him. Then he saw she wasn't driving. She was in the bed of the truck, flanked by two men who were holding her down.

There was only one thing Raven could do. He aimed his bow at one of the tires and let a bolt fly.

***

Dressed in a CBRN suit, Colton sat in the back of Raven's Jeep Cherokee, pressing down on the dressing covering the woman's gunshot wound while Don raced toward the hospital. The wound wasn't fresh, but blood still seeped out.

"Hang in there, ma'am," Colton whispered. Her head was on his lap with her knees up against the other side of the Jeep. She squinted up at him like she was trying to see his face. She hadn't said a word since Don had picked Colton up at the barrier on Highway 7.

She moaned, and the whites of her eyes showed as they rolled up into her skull.

"Stay with me," Colton said.

The woman was about his age, with strands of silver in her hair and crow's feet around her eyes. Plastic garbage bags held together by tape covered her clothing, but he'd removed her scarf and goggles now that they were inside the safe zone. The bags had apparently saved her from the radiation, but dehydration and blood loss were slowly killing her.

"Where did you find her?" Colton asked.

"About thirty-two miles south. I almost ran her over, for Christ's sake. She was crawling down the road." Don looked up in the rearview mirror. "She's not the only one out there, Chief. You know that, right?"

Colton knitted his brows. "I thought you said you didn't find any other survivors."

"I didn't, but there were more gunshot victims. You've heard about the violence on Highway 34 over the radio. That's going to hit us eventually. We can't save everyone."

"I'm not leaving people to die out there if we can help them. I won't do it."

Don grunted and turned his attention back to the road. "She's probably contaminated, so we just risked the integrity of the vehicle by bringing her back."

"I'll have it hosed down and scrubbed." Colton touched her wrist to feel for a pulse. It was weak and irregular.

"Faster," Colton said. "She's hanging on by a thread."

The engine hummed as Don raced toward Estes Park, passing the lake and the first of the hotels that surrounded the town. He honked the horn at several teenagers walking in the middle of the road. One of them threw a pop can at the Jeep.

"Damn kids," Don muttered.

"Help," croaked the woman.

Colton glanced back down at her. "We're going to help you, ma'am. Just hold on."

"Where...where am I?" she said in a strangled voice.

"Estes Park. You're on the way to our medical center."

Don squealed down another street, jarring Colton so

that his hand slipped off the dressing. The woman grabbed his arm tightly and mumbled something incoherent. He had to keep her talking before she slipped back unconscious.

"Ma'am, my name is Marcus Colton, and I'm the chief of police. Can you tell me your name?"

"Doc—" She gave up and wheezed before she could get any more out.

Colton shook her gently. Maybe having her talk was a bad idea.

"Stay with me," he repeated. The medical center was just around the corner, and he would be damned if she died in his arms before they got her there.

She choked again and coughed up a mixture of blood and saliva that ran in a sheet down her chin. She choked, wheezed, and struggled for air. Her eyelids fluttered and then closed. A moment later she went limp in his grip.

"Ma'am," Colton said. He waited for her next breath, but it never came.

"Don, hurry up!"

Don's eyes flitted up in the rearview mirror, but he didn't reply.

Colton took off his helmet and leaned down, preparing to give her CPR.

"Chief, you could get contaminated!" Don protested.

Colton ignored him and pumped her chest, then breathed into her mouth.

No response.

"Come on," he said. He pushed harder, gave her air, and continued the process.

The vehicle jolted to a stop outside of the medical center.

"Go get help!" Colton said between breaths.

On the next compression, he pushed so hard he heard a pop. When he went down for another breath, her eyelids snapped open and she drew in a gasp.

Colton moved back to give her some space. Her eyes widened at him and she squirmed away. The movement set off another coughing fit.

"It's okay, ma'am. Don't try to move," he said. "You're okay."

Despite his assurances, she still reared back in fear. She held up an arm to shield her face.

"Ma'am, I'm not going to hurt you."

"Stay back," she said. "Get away from me!"

Colton held up his hands and scooted off the seat. He opened the door and moved out onto the pavement. Doctor Duffy was already rushing outside with a nurse named Julie. Don followed them outside.

"Make sure you're careful with her. She's been exposed to radiation," Don called after them. He took his helmet off and set it on the concrete.

Colton couldn't believe it when he saw Don shove tobacco into his mouth. If he was so scared of contamination, why would he…

"Stay away," the woman said. Inside the Jeep, she was breathing heavily with her back to the opposite door. She tried to open it, but the door was locked.

"Calm down, ma'am," Colton said. He moved out of the way for the medical team.

"I'm a doctor and I'm going to help you, okay?" Duffy said, seemingly undeterred by the threat of contamination.

The woman slowly lowered her hands, but her eyes continued roving from face to face, stopping on Colton. She glared at him like he was the devil in the flesh. As the adrenaline faded from her body, she slowly began to relax, her eyelids drooping. Julie and Duffy reached into the Jeep and helped move her onto a stretcher. Don joined Colton near the sidewalk while they moved her.

"You brought her back, Chief. Pretty impressive, but I don't see how delaying the inevitable is a good strategy moving forward," Don said. He spat a glob of tobacco onto the sidewalk.

Colton pivoted to face Don and poked him hard in the chest. "If you ever pull that shit again, we're going to have major problems. I'm the chief of police. Don't you forget that."

***

Sandra Spears was still rattled to her core from the events on Prospect Mountain. The return of Brown Feather and his brother, Turtle, had reopened wounds that had never quite healed. She thought that being cut off from the rest of the world in Estes Park would protect her from men like Brown Feather and her ex-husband, Mark, but not even the end of the world had kept her family safe.

It seemed like nowhere was safe anymore.

The people who had cracked Officer Nelson's head were on the loose while he crashed on the table in the emergency room. The swelling in his brain was getting worse, and without the help of life support equipment, it was almost impossible to stabilize him.

"Sandra!" Newton shouted. "Get in here. We're losing him."

She slipped on her gloves and pulled up her facemask. Despite everything that had happened, and as much as Sandra wanted to crawl into her bed and cuddle Allie, she was needed at the medical center.

"Heart rate is increasing," Doctor Newton said. "We're at one hundred and thirty."

"Blood pressure is seventy-six over fifty," Jen, one of the other nurses, said.

Newton bent down to examine the tube that was draining fluid from one of the burr holes he'd drilled into the patient's head.

"It's not draining at all now." Newton looked over his shoulder. "Where the hell is Duffy? We're going to have to drill another hole."

"I think he's with Teddy," Sandra said.

"I thought Jen was in charge of Teddy," Newton snapped.

Jen shook her head. "Doctor Duffy rushed outside to help a gunshot victim and told me to come in here."

"We don't just leave our patients, dammit!" Newton shouted.

Jen gave Sandra a meaningful, exhausted look. They were all tired, but Newton had been here for days. He was starting to lose his cool.

Rick's raspy breathing pulled them back to the table. All three of them moved into position as his muscles started to spasm.

"Sandra, grab his legs, Jen, you take his arms," Newton ordered.

Sandra was careful not to hold Rick down too hard at first, but he continued convulsing and jerking violently, forcing her to hold him tighter. Blood-tinged fluid dripped from his ears. His eyes rolled up into his head a moment later. Sandra could feel the life slipping away from the officer.

"Jesus," Newton said. He checked the dressings over

the man's matted hair. Blood was running freely from the bandages, and his breathing was shallow.

"Someone get me a BVM," Newton said.

Sandra reached for the bag-valve mask with her left hand and continued holding Rick's legs with her right. A kick knocked her grip away. She grabbed the BVM, handed it to Newton, and then grabbed both of Rick's legs. He kicked and jerked harder in her grip.

Newton placed the mask over Rick's face and started pumping air into his lungs. The officer kicked so hard it sent Sandra stumbling backward.

"Sandra!" Newton snapped. "Do your job!"

She rushed back to her position as Rick's eyes suddenly popped open. Newton slowly pulled the BVM away, and Rick took in a long, deep gasp of air. Dazed, but seemingly aware, he looked at Newton and then at Sandra.

Blood seeped from the holes in his head, running down his forehead like red tears. His lips moved, but no words came from his mouth.

"Officer Nelson, can you hear me?" Newton said.

Rick closed his eyes, and his body seemed to relax on the table. Sandra reached out for his wrist.

"Doctor Newton, I'm... I'm not feeling a pulse."

Newton pressed his stethoscope to Rick's chest, but after a moment of listening, Newton shook his head.

An eerie silence passed over the room. Without the usual chirp of medical equipment, the lack of noise was beyond unsettling.

Sandra put her hands on Rick's chest. She looked to Jen and Newton, and shouted, "Somebody help me!"

Jen grabbed the BVM mask and gave Rick air while Sandra pushed down on his chest. They fell into a steady rhythm to resuscitate him.

"Come on," Sandra said. "Come on."

Rick's eyelids remained closed, but they twitched with every push on his chest. Newton stood watching with a solemn look. He might have given up, but Sandra was not going to let him die without a fight. He had a wife and baby girl at home, and Sandra knew all about being a single mom. That child needed her father.

Newton finally moved back to the table and checked Rick's pupils while Sandra and Jen continued CPR.

"His pupils are fixed and dilated," Newton reported. "It's over."

Despite the signs of what likely was a brain herniation, Sandra continued pushing, over and over. A minute passed. Then two. Her hands were numb, but she kept pumping in hopes of restarting his heart. Jen continued to help, but she was watching Sandra like she was crazy.

"Sandra," said a voice.

She felt a hand on her shoulder but shook it away.

"Sandra," Newton said again, louder and firmer. "He's gone, Sandra. We can't do anything for him, I'm sorry."

Jen pulled the mask off Rick's face, but Sandra made one final push on his chest. Bloody fluid continued to ooze from Rick's ears and the burr holes.

She finally let out a sigh of defeat. Tears blurred her vision. One plummeted onto the table, mixing with blood.

— 3 —

Charlize Montgomery raised her binoculars at the coastline from the bridge of the USS *John Stennis* aircraft carrier. Dressed in a loose-fitting Air Force sweatshirt and sweatpants, she felt more like a college student preparing for an all-night study session than the new Secretary of Defense. Albert Randall, her longtime bodyguard, stood next to her. He still hadn't changed out of his charred and filthy Air Jordans.

"Are you okay, ma'am?" he asked when she stumbled slightly.

"I'm fine." She pressed the binoculars to her eyes. They had finally reached Florida, but the sight of the Sunshine State didn't cheer her up. Her mind was halfway across the country with the unit of Marines searching for her son. They still hadn't radioed in with any information, and she was growing impatient.

I should have gone myself.

Covered in sores from her extensive burns, Charlize knew she wasn't in any shape to travel. She had only just begun recovering. The doctors had her on a strong dose of antibiotics, and they were hopeful that they'd be able to counter the effects of the radiation she'd been exposed to. But the burns would take time to heal, and required constant attention.

Albert reached out to help steady her as she wobbled again.

"Did you take your pain meds?" he asked.

"Yes," she lied. The pain continued to make even minor tasks difficult, but the alternative was worse. The pills made her so tired she could hardly function. She was the Secretary of Defense now, but she was spending more time in the hospital than the command room.

"Ma'am, I really think you should..." Albert began to say.

She turned toward him, frowning. A sharp reply was on the tip of her tongue, but she held it back. Clint, her chief of staff, had died not long after the chopper had airlifted them from the ruins of Washington, D.C. With her son missing and her brother stuck in some godforsaken town in Colorado, Albert was her only real friend here.

"I want to say goodbye to Clint before the ceremony tonight," she said. "Will you see if you can arrange that?"

Albert hesitated.

"I'm fine, really," she said.

"Okay, ma'am." Albert turned to leave, but he shot a concerned look over his shoulder before ducking through the open hatch.

All around her, sailors were working at their stations. She felt like she ought to be doing something, too. Waiting to hear about Ty was torture. There was nothing worse than being helpless to protect your child, and this was the second time she had failed him.

Get it together, Charlize. You can't lose it now.

She pressed the binoculars back to her eyes, trying to focus. The aircraft carrier was two miles east of Palm Beach. Cars were zipping down the road as if nothing had happened. The coordinated EMP attack that had knocked out electronics in most of the continental United States hadn't reached southern Florida. After the devastation she'd witnessed at the nation's capital, Charlize had never expected to see a thriving American city again.

"Sight for sore eyes, isn't it, Madame Secretary?"

Charlize lowered her binoculars to find Lieutenant Janet Marco standing next to her. The XO jerked her long chin toward the porthole windows.

"Seeing civilization, I mean," Marco said.

"Funny, I was just thinking that."

Marco folded her arms across her uniform. "Someone waking up from a coma in Palm Beach might not even know the rest of the country was under attack. There's still power, police officers, and working vehicles. A hundred miles north, it's complete chaos."

"So I've heard," Charlize said with a sigh. "How about an update on the North Korean sub?"

The Lieutenant hesitated and then said, "We think there are two out there, but they're very hard to detect. They must be relying on battery power and are managing to come to snorkel depth where we're not looking for them. We lost several of our satellites during the attack, so that leaves us with airborne radar. Except we're also low on aircraft. What wasn't fried by the EMP is being used for evacuations and supply drops on the mainland."

"Our priority is finding those subs and stopping another attack," Charlize said. "We need to reallocate our aircraft and create multiple Helicopter Maritime Strike squadrons. Get someone on the horn who can make that happen. Those North Korean subs can't evade detection forever."

"Yes, ma'am," Marco said with a grin. She turned to leave, but Charlize grabbed her arm.

"Wait. I've spent too much time recovering from my

injuries and not enough being briefed. I want a better picture of what's happening in Florida."

"Absolutely," Marco said, gesturing for Charlize to follow. She led them to a station with dual monitors. Several officers stepped away as Marco spread a map of Florida across the surface.

"The cutoff line is here," she said, drawing a line south of Orlando. "The grid is down everywhere north of that line. We've deployed resources to all major highways and are concentrating on holding back refugees here and here."

Marco pointed at Highways 95 and 4 south of Orlando. "We're hearing some pretty ugly reports. There have already been thousands of deaths on the highways."

Charlize picked at her bandaged hand while she listened. The country was under martial law, and although President Diego was ultimately in charge, he had tasked Charlize with directing the men and women out there trying to keep law and order. So far, she felt like she hadn't been able to do anything to help.

She studied the map and said, "When I was deployed to Iraq and Afghanistan, I saw a lot of things from the sky—crumbling infrastructure, highways clogged with refugees, and despicable violence. But I never thought I would see it back home. I don't see how we can come back from this."

Marco narrowed her eyes slightly like she was trying to figure out if Charlize was being serious.

"This is the United States of America, ma'am. Not Iraq or Afghanistan. We will recover, just like we have from every other attack since the founding of our great nation," Marco said.

"You're right," Charlize said, feeling a little

embarrassed. She shouldn't have expressed her doubts. "We will come back from this stronger than before."

A smile beamed across Marco's face. "Yes, indeed, ma'am. I'll go make that call about those HSM squadrons."

Charlize nodded and moved away from the maps. She walked with a renewed sense of energy and a thirst for answers. She reached up out of habit to tuck her hair behind her ear before remembering that it had been cropped to almost masculine shortness. Instead, she straightened her sweatshirt and walked over to the man in charge of the ship.

"Good afternoon, Captain," Charlize said.

It took Captain Dietz a second to turn from the view, but when he did, he offered a half smile. "Secretary Montgomery, how are you feeling today?"

"I'm fine," she lied. "Have you heard anything about my son?"

"No, not yet, but rest assured, I sent our best team to find him. Lieutenant Jeff Dupree is spearheading the mission. Man's a hero. If anyone can find him, it's Dupree."

The name meant nothing to Charlize. She huffed in frustration. "That fire team was deployed yesterday, right? When can I expect a SITREP?"

Dietz paused, his wind-weathered forehead creasing in deep thought. "My family is out there, too. In the radiation zone in Virginia."

Charlize clenched her jaw, realizing how she had sounded. She wasn't herself today. Constant worry and the pain from her injuries had her on edge.

"I'm monitoring the situation and will let you know as soon as we hear something from Lieutenant Dupree,"

Dietz said. Behind them, Marco was gesturing for the captain to pick up his headset.

"Ah, maybe that's him now," Dietz said.

She took a step back and waited as he listened to the incoming message. His features suddenly hardened, and he glanced up at Charlize. He cursed under his breath as he pulled off the headset and stood.

"Everyone, listen up. We have a contact detected on the sonar. Sound the alert, Lieutenant, and order the evacuation of all top-level officials."

Marco nodded and turned to another officer to carry out her orders.

"We're evacuating?" Charlize asked. "Is that necessary?"

"Our anti-submarine warfare officers have picked up more pings on the sonar, but they still haven't been able to get a lock on whatever craft is out there. Admiral Luke has made the decision to—"

The wail of an emergency siren cut him off. It was the same sound she had heard right before D.C. had been hit by the nuclear warhead. On the flight deck, crews ran toward their aircraft. Rotors fired on a pair of Seahawks and an Osprey.

"We need to move, Madame Secretary," Albert said. Somehow, he'd managed to reappear by her side right when she needed him. Just as they were about to leave the room, Marco waved at Charlize.

Albert gave his approval with a nod. He followed her over to the Lieutenant's station. Marco held up a finger as she listened to her headset. Albert tapped his right burned Air Jordan on the ground nervously. A moment that felt more like an hour passed before Marco slipped the headset off. Her features remained stern.

"I have bad news about your son, Madame Secretary."

She could barely hear the XO over the sirens, and at first she hoped she'd misunderstood. Then she felt Albert's gentle hand on her shoulder.

"Tell me," Charlize choked out.

Marco hesitated. It was the first time she'd ever seen the eager young officer balk at following an order. "Lieutenant Dupree's team has reached the Easterseals camp, ma'am, but they haven't found any sign of survivors."

***

Dupree was having a hell of a time not throwing up in his CBRN suit. He bent down to examine another body. The young woman lay face down in the dirt outside one of the lodges that served as dormitories for the campers. Her exposed skin was covered in blisters and sores. One of the blisters had recently popped, oozing out a trail of pus.

Over his career he had seen a lot of nightmarish scenes, but dead children with radiation poisoning was a new level of horror.

He bumped the comm link in the helmet to report the death to the pilots, who would relay the info to Lieutenant Marco on the USS *John Stennis.*

"Black 1, this is Fox 1 confirming another casualty," Dupree said. "Still no sign of Falcon."

"Copy that, Fox 1."

Dupree looked over at Sharps and Emerson. The two Marines stood guard with their M4s cradled across their chests as they scanned the surrounding area for anyone that might still be alive. The odds of that were growing slimmer by the minute. They had searched the camp for an hour without locating a single survivor, and they were running out of places to look.

To the east, McCabe and Rodriguez exited another lodge. McCabe stood on the porch and motioned for Dupree to join them. He glanced down at the dead woman one more time. Leaving her out here alone seemed wrong, but they didn't have time to bury these people.

"Clear this lodge," Dupree said to Emerson and Sharps. The men nodded, but they didn't look eager. The scene was taking a toll on all of them. He jogged through the central gathering area and past a large fire pit ringed with benches. Branches shifted in the warm breeze, reaching for the bluffs that flanked the camp like medieval guard towers.

"No sign of Falcon," reported Snider over the comms.

"Have you searched those sheds we saw on the way in?" Dupree asked.

"Yes, sir," Snider said. "Runge just cleared both of them."

Dupree cursed. Where the hell was this kid? They had found several dead counselors and staff members over the past hour, but the numbers weren't adding up. It appeared many of the children were missing, including Ty Montgomery.

Had someone beat his team here and evacuated the others?

He jogged the rest of the way to the other lodge, where McCabe ushered him inside.

"Sir, I think I found the kid's bunk. Come take a look."

Dupree jogged up the ramp that led to the cabin, and Rodriguez opened the swinging door to let them inside.

The room was furnished with about a dozen beds, some of them set up for special needs children. Toys and stuffed animals were scattered on the floor. Dupree stepped over a blanket crumpled on the floor. The mess was yet another sign of a quick and possibly chaotic evacuation.

But if these kids had been evacuated, where were they now?

McCabe walked down the aisle separating the bunks. Dupree followed him to a bed with wheelchair access and the name "Montgomery, Ty". A model F-15 fighter jet lay on the sheets.

"Check out the inscription," McCabe said.

Dupree picked up the model and read the bottom.

To Ty - Dream big and someday you will soar to reach your goals.

"Where the hell is this kid, LT?" McCabe asked. "And where are all the other kids?"

Dupree set the model jet back down gently. "Good question."

They met back outside where Rodriguez was waiting. To the west, Emerson and Sharps emerged from the lodge where Dupree had found the dead woman.

"Snider, Runge, give me a SITREP," Dupree said into his mini-mic.

"About to enter the main lodge for a second pass, sir. Stand by," Snider said.

"The kids have to be here somewhere," Dupree said. He wasn't sure if he was talking to his men or himself. He waved for Sharps and Emerson to join him near the fire pit with Rodriguez and McCabe.

"Found a few dead kids back there, LT, but not our target. The kids were hiding in a closet," Emerson said.

"I've never seen anything like this."

"Jesus in heaven," McCabe said. He made the sign of the cross over his CBRN suit.

Dupree remained silent, using the time to think. A drop of rain pelted his visor as they waited. He stared out at the outside world like a fish inside of a bowl. Within minutes, the sky opened up, sending sheets of rain over the camp.

"What is this black shit?" Sharps asked, holding up a glove covered in what looked like wet ash.

"People, trees, buildings..." McCabe said.

Sharps eyes widened. "What do you mean?"

"It's what's left over when the world burns," Dupree said.

"Is it toxic?" Sharps asked.

"Could be, but our suits will protect us," McCabe said. He craned his helmet toward Dupree. "Right, sir?"

The comm link fired before Dupree could reply.

"Sir, I've got movement inside the cafeteria," Snider reported. "Looks like we have a survivor!"

"On our way," Dupree said. He jerked his chin, and his men quickly fell in behind him. They fanned out, moving slower than normal in the downpour. An armada of angry storm clouds had rolled in from the west. They bulged like overflowing garbage bags, swollen with ash and smoke from the forest fires.

He flashed hand signals to his men as they approached the main lodge, running through the camp layout he'd memorized during the long flight. There was a cafeteria and several community rooms inside this building, but nothing to indicate a shelter or basement.

"Sergeant McCabe, on me," Dupree said. "Sharps, you and Emerson hold security outside."

Dupree made his way up the wide stairs to the front doors. He strode into the main seating area, which looked like it had seen a stampede, not an evacuation. Chairs were upturned, and rotting food had splattered on the ground. He stepped around a paper plate cemented to the floor by what looked like mashed potatoes.

"Sir," McCabe said, pointing toward the center of the room.

Dupree moved around a long table to find another dead camp counselor. He was curled up in a fetal position, his hands gripping his stomach, which told Dupree he had died of radiation poisoning.

McCabe approached slowly, looking up every few feet to scan the entrances to the other community rooms for contacts.

"Snider," Dupree said. "Did you see the body in the cafeteria? Bearded guy, red hat?"

"Yes, sir. I thought I reported it already."

"No, you didn't," Dupree said.

"Holy shit," McCabe said as he bent down next to the body. "This guy was shot."

"Shot?" Snider asked over the comm.

Dupree moved around the side of a table and saw the small pool of blood under the corpse that he hadn't noticed before.

"Shit," Dupree said, bending down. A sloppy grouping of three rounds to the chest had taken this man out. He stood and raised his rifle at the crack of shattering dishes in the kitchen. A flash of motion came from the entrance, and a figure limped into the mess hall. Dupree lowered his muzzle when he saw it was just a boy.

"Stop!" Snider shouted. He ran out into the mess with Runge right behind. The kid halted in the middle of the room as the Marines closed in around him. His eyes darted back and forth like an animal being surrounded by wolves.

"Stay back," the child said. He tried to escape, but only staggered a few feet before Snider tackled him to the ground.

"Get off!" the boy screamed.

Runge bent down to hold his legs.

"Kid, stop fighting," Snider said. "We're not going to hurt you."

"Liar!" the boy yelled. He bit at Snider's suit and clamped down on the sleeve. Snider brought a hand up to smack the kid, but Dupree caught his wrist in mid-air.

The boy, suddenly silent and lying on his back, glanced up at Dupree. Black hair matted his forehead and rashes marked his cheeks and chin. He reached up with a curled right hand.

"Get off him," Dupree said.

Snider and Runge loosened their grips. Dupree slung the strap of his rifle over his back. He bent down, forcing a smile that the boy returned with a scowl. It wasn't all that much different from the look Dupree's sons gave him when he would show up late to a birthday party or sporting event—if he showed up at all.

"We're here to help you," Dupree said.

The boy scooted backward across the floor. "That's what the other soldiers said."

"Soldiers?" McCabe asked. "What other soldiers?"

Dupree waited for the boy to respond, but the kid averted his gaze.

"We're the good guys," Dupree said. He reached into his vest and pulled out a sealed bag containing a chocolate bar. He had brought it along just in case they found survivors and needed bait to get them to leave the camp.

The boy licked his cracked lips and held out a hand, suddenly not so scared. "I'm really hungry, but they told us not to eat anything because of the rad nation."

"Radiation," McCabe corrected, chuckling.

Dupree shot the sergeant a look that told him to back off.

The boy reached for the bag again, but Dupree held it just out of his reach.

"What's your name?" Dupree asked.

"Alex Stephens."

"My name is Lieutenant Jeff Dupree, and I'm going to help you, but first you need to tell me what happened here. Who took your friends and where did they go?"

Alex swiped the sweaty black hair from his forehead. "The soldiers said they were going to take us somewhere safe, but I could tell they were bad men so I ran. I ran and I hid."

"Did they say where that safe place is?" Dupree asked.

Alex shook his head, and Dupree finally handed him the bag. The boy unsealed it and wolfed the chocolate bar down, eyes flitting from face to face like he still wasn't sure if he could trust them.

"Call in our ride, Sergeant," Dupree ordered. He helped Alex to his feet, but the boy was having a hard time walking. He was weak and sick, but it was more than that. The boy appeared to have cerebral palsy or something like it. As they crossed the room, Alex stumbled, and Dupree reached out to help.

"No touching!" Alex shrieked. Dupree quickly took his hands away from the boy.

By the time the group moved out of the building, the

Black Hawk was flying over a bluff to the north. It set down in a soccer field on the edge of the camp. Sheets of rain fell across the path to the helicopter.

"Go get Alex a suit," Dupree said.

McCabe ran to the Black Hawk while Dupree took a knee next to Alex.

"Is there anything else you can tell me about what happened? Did you see Ty Montgomery?" Dupree asked. "He would have been in a wheelchair."

Alex lowered the bottled water they'd given him after he'd finished the chocolate. "Ty's my best..." He staggered slightly from side to side, like he couldn't find his balance.

Dupree reached out to grab him, but held back at the last moment. The kid did not like to be touched, and he reminded himself to be patient.

"It's okay, buddy," he said helplessly. As bad as he was at talking to kids, he was even worse at lying to them.

"I'm really sick, aren't I?" His teeth chattered as he looked at Dupree.

"We're going to give you medicine to make you feel better."

Alex shivered and lifted his curled hand to his face.

"I know it's hard, but can you please tell me what else you saw? Ty is counting on you, buddy," Dupree said.

"They put him and the other kids into trucks and drove off. I wanted to help Ty, but I couldn't..." Alex whimpered. "I couldn't help him."

"It's okay, we're going to help him," Dupree said. "But I need to know where they went."

Alex shivered violently. He reached up and pointed to the south with a shaky hand. "They went that way."

"Where's that suit?" Dupree shouted. He glanced over

his shoulder and saw McCabe running back toward the building. In the split second that it took for Dupree to turn, Alex collapsed. This time, Dupree reached out and caught the boy in his arms.

— 4 —

The sound of violence echoed through Estes Park. Colton rushed out of the station to listen, but he couldn't pinpoint the source of the gunshots. Don stood on the sidewalk next to Officer Tom Matthew. Both men had their hands on the grips of their holstered weapons like they were preparing for a shootout.

"I don't hear anything else," Colton said. He walked over to the other officers and stood in front of them. "Did you—"

Pop. Pop.

Colton heard that. The sound was distant but unmistakable. "Where the hell are those shots coming from?"

"Devils Gulch Road, maybe," Matthew replied. "You think it's someone out hunting?"

"You'd have to be pretty stupid to try to bring down an elk with a 9mm," came a rough voice. Nathan was limping toward them through Bond Park, wearing his rucksack. He had been sitting there waiting for his ride, but the Marines still hadn't shown up to evacuate him.

More distant pops echoed west of town. Colton looked in that direction, past the restaurants, t-shirt shops, and ice cream parlors. He fully expected citizens to be outside hunting for food, but Nathan was right. This was small arms fire, and it was coming from the direction he had sent Detective Plymouth and...

"Raven," he muttered.

"You think they ran into trouble?" Don asked.

"Sure as hell sounds like it," Colton said. He faced his men with a scowl. "Matthew, get the Jeep. Don, grab our rifles."

Both officers took off running in opposite directions.

"Goddammit, I should have given Lindsey my walkie-talkie to stay in touch with Margaret," Colton said. "If Raven is shooting it out with another damned debt collector, so help me..."

Nathan remained silent, his bruised face turned toward the mountains.

Another flurry of gunshots rang out, followed by the boom of a shotgun. The popping of a pistol quickly replied.

"Sounds like a battle," Nathan said.

Colton paced the sidewalk. Every passing second was one closer to losing control of the situation. He couldn't—*wouldn't*—see any more of his people hurt.

Squealing tires sounded from the other side of town hall. Matthew sped out of the side parking lot in the Jeep, the sides still dripping wet from being hosed down earlier. He brought it to a halt in front of the sidewalk. Don hurried over with a pair of Colt AR-15s and ammunition.

"Let's go," Colton said.

Nathan moved to follow, but Colton blocked his way. "Not you, Major. You need to stay here with the radio in case those Marines come to get you. I've got this."

The pilot hesitated and then held out a hand. "If I leave before you get back, good luck."

"Likewise," Colton said. He shook Nathan's hand and then jumped into the Jeep with Don. Matthew stomped the gas pedal as soon as they were buckled in. He tore away from town hall and turned onto the street leading up to Devils Gulch Road. People on the sidewalks turned to watch the Jeep fly by at fifty miles an hour.

Colton didn't bother telling Matthew to slow down.

"Are you all wearing your vests?" he asked.

"Yes, sir," Don said.

Matthew didn't answer.

"Officer Matthew?" Colton asked.

"I took mine off earlier," Matthew said, keeping his eyes on the road. "Sorry, sir."

No matter how many times Colton harped on his officers about wearing ballistic vests, someone always decided not to bother.

"Jesus," Colton said. "My vest saved my life yesterday. When are you guys going to start listening to me?"

"Sir, I'm sorry. I usually —"

"Just stay low," Colton said. "I have a feeling we're about to walk into a firefight."

Matthew nodded, and Colton turned to watch the trees race by on the side of the road. With the windows down, it wasn't hard to pick up on the distant pop of gunfire. Each shot made Colton tense. The cool breeze carried the familiar, calming scent of cedar, but it did little to settle his nerves.

Constant violence was the new normal. Colton would have to deal with it, just like he had in Afghanistan. He pulled out his revolver and snapped open the empty cylinder. Then he plucked rounds from his father's old duty belt and loaded his weapon. Would one of these bullets end a life today?

"That gunfire stopped," Don said.

Colton looked up from his pistol, trying to listen past the wind rushing into the vehicle. All was quiet again. He cursed under his breath.

Matthew turned the Jeep onto Devils Gulch Road. He eased off the pedal as they approached a big truck blocking the center lane. The Jeep rolled up and over a hill that provided a rolling view of the terrain beyond. Several houses were nestled along the south side of the street. A natural border of rocky bluffs protruded over the trees to the north.

"Where the hell are they?" Colton muttered.

Matthew pointed down the road. "Is that Jake's truck?"

Colton leaned forward, squinting at the red vehicle parked in the grass on the right shoulder about a quarter mile down the road from the White estate. The passenger door was wide open, like someone had jumped out in a hurry. The back right tire was pancaked.

"Looks like someone shot an arrow into that tire," Matthew said.

"Not just someone. Raven and his damn crossbow," Don said. "But why?"

"Maybe he was trying to stop someone from taking the truck," Colton said. He shook his head. He didn't have time to make sense of the scene.

"Slow down and park over there," he said, pointing to the shoulder right outside the White estate.

Matthew eased off the gas and brought the vehicle to a stop. Colton ordered everyone to take up position behind the Jeep and then unclipped his walkie-talkie. He took a knee behind the bumper and scanned the road with the radio to his lips.

"Margaret, do you copy? Over."

Her prompt reply crackled from the speaker. "I'm here, Chief."

Colton turned the volume down and checked the truck and woods to the south.

"Anyone have eyes?" he asked.

"Negative," Matthew replied.

Don shook his head. "They must have taken off into the forest."

Colton brought the radio back up. "Looks like Detective Plymouth and Raven Spears ran into some trouble outside of Steve and Laurel White's house. There's no sign of either of them, but it looks like they may have fled into the woods to the southeast of the White property. Over."

"Roger that, Chief. I just heard—"

Static crackled from the speakers.

"Round up any available officers and send them this way," Colton said. "I'm heading out to find Raven and Lindsey." He glanced over at Matthew. "You stay here and wait."

"But—" Matthew began to say.

"That's an order, Officer Matthew."

The radio sputtered again. "Chief, there's something else you should know."

Colton stood and began to move around the side of the Jeep, raising his AR-15 with his right hand and keeping the radio close to his lips.

"Go ahead," he said.

"I have some bad news about Officer Nelson."

The world seemed to slow. Static buzzed from the speakers as he watched the wind sway the branches of ponderosas under a sky full of clouds that looked like bullets.

"Rick passed away about thirty minutes ago," Margaret said. "I just got word from the hospital. I'm sorry, Chief."

Colton drew in a long breath, grief washing over him. He tucked the radio in his vest and gripped his rifle with both hands. Two officers had died in the past twenty-four hours. He refused to lose another.

***

"Where are we?" Ty asked. His voice seemed to go on and on like they were in some sort of tunnel. It was warmer here than the last place the Sons of Liberty had taken them, and it smelled damp, like a basement. They still hadn't removed Ty's blindfold, although they had taken his mask off. The air didn't taste burned anymore, which was good, but his back hurt and he felt like he might throw up. Someone had pushed his wheelchair up a rocky path for a while, every bump rattling his teeth and making his tummy feel queasy, before moving him and the other kids into this building.

"You're safe," Tommy said.

Carson grunted and spat on the floor. "I don't get why the General wanted us to grab these cripples."

Tommy didn't reply, but Ty snapped at the word.

"I'm not a cripple. You're going to be sorry you said that. My mom is coming to get me, and when she does–"

"Shut up, kid," Carson replied. "Your mommy isn't coming."

Raised voices sounded in the distance, reverberating off the walls. Ty's heart was racing, partly from anger, and partly from fear. What if Carson was right?

She won't give up, he told himself. *She's the bravest, toughest mom in the whole world, and she will find you and beat these guys up.*

And if his mom couldn't find him for some reason, his

uncle would. Uncle Nathan was probably in his fighter jet right now, looking for him. The idea made him feel better, but he was still mad. Hadn't anybody ever taught these men it was rude to call someone names?

"Stay quiet, kid," Tommy said. He brought the wheelchair to a stop, and Ty heard the smooth, deep voice of the General issuing orders.

"Max, I want these kids sprayed down and evaluated by Doc Rollins as soon as possible," he said.

"Sir, what should I tell Rollins if these kids have severe radiation poisoning? He'll want to know if he's authorized to treat them."

The approaching footfalls abruptly stopped not far from Ty.

"I've already told the old man not to waste medical resources," said the General.

The rap of boots hitting the ground continued onward. Ty gritted his teeth and waited. When the footfalls sounded like they were about to pass, he did exactly what Tommy had told him not to do.

"Hey, over here. You see me?" Ty tried to wave his bound hands. "My mom is going to come here and she's going to put you all in prison."

Laughs rang out from all directions.

"Go ahead and laugh," Ty said. He was used to being teased, but his mom had taught him to draw strength from it instead of shame. Ty had survived just about the worst things that could happen to a kid, and he was still strong. Nobody could take that away from him with stupid, mocking laughter. "You'll be sorry when my mom gets here. She's friends with the president. He'll have you all arrested."

A finger snapped, silencing the chuckles like a switch

being flipped. A single pair of boots tapped the ground and stopped directly in front of his chair.

"What did you say?" asked the General.

"I said you'll be sorry when my mom comes to find me."

Under his blindfold, he could see muddy boots in front of his wheelchair. They stepped closer.

"After that, kid."

"I said my mom knows the president—"

"President of what?"

"The United States of America," Ty said proudly. "She's a United States Senator and she—"

The blindfold was stripped off Ty's face. He blinked at the bright lights hanging from cords overhead. It took him a moment for his eyes to adjust, but he quickly realized he was somewhere underground in what kind of looked like a cave. The walls and ceiling were rough rock, but the floor was concrete. Crates of supplies and large orange barrels were stacked against the walls.

The General was crouched in front of his wheelchair. He was still wearing the space suit, but Ty could see his blue eyes behind the visor. The squiggly scar on his forehead caught Ty's attention.

The man pointed at it. "You like my scar? This is what happens when you get captured in enemy territory. You should have seen what I did to the monsters that did this to me. Sometimes you have to become the fiercer monster to survive, kid."

Two overweight men with long beards chuckled behind the General. They held large rifles and wore black baseball caps with snake symbols. Every inch of exposed skin below their necks seemed to be covered in tattoos.

The General held up a hand for silence. "My name is

Dan Fenix. General Dan Fenix, but you can call me Fenix." He paused a moment, licked his lips, and leaned closer. "What's your name, son?"

"You don't scare me, mister. None of you do," Ty said.

"Kid, I couldn't care less if I scare you or not. I told you and your friends that we came to help you at the camp, remember? If it weren't for us, you'd be dead."

"Then why are my hands tied, and why did you shoot Mr. Barton and Mr. Gonzalez? They didn't do anything to you."

"They got in my way," Fenix replied. He let out a short sigh like he was getting frustrated. "And we tied your hands because…"

He looked back at his men and raised his voice. "Why did you guys tie this poor boy's hands? Carson, did you do it?"

Carson nodded. Ty saw his tormentor clearly for the first time. He had a shaved head and greasy black eyebrows. A big, ugly eagle holding a flag was tattooed on his neck.

"Well untie him, damn it," Fenix snapped. He crab-walked closer to Ty and put his gloved hands on the armrests of the chair. For the first time since the gunshots on the road, Ty felt a paralyzing fear grab him. There was something wrong with this man. It wasn't just that strangers weren't supposed to touch his chair. His eyes were so cold and flat. His words sounded nice, but his eyes gave him away.

Ty remained silent, terrified that if he did talk, he would stutter. His mom always taught him to never show his fear.

Fenix stood and clasped his hands behind his back.

"Fine, you don't want to talk to me? I guess I'll just have to ask one of your little friends. I might even have to hurt them. Is that what you want?"

"My name is Ty."

"Ty what?" Fenix turned halfway with one ear in his direction.

"Montgomery."

Fenix's cold eyes lit up as he turned back to Ty. "You're Senator Charlize Montgomery's son?"

Ty nodded proudly, although something felt wrong about doing so. Maybe he shouldn't have told Fenix his mom's name. Maybe... but no. His mom would come find him, and she would make these men pay for what they had done to Mr. Barton and Mr. Gonzalez.

Fenix clapped his hands. "Hot damn. See? I told you guys this plan was golden. We got ourselves a real valuable hostage. We're going to be able to buy enough ammunition to take over Colorado and purge it of the filth. Nobody is going to be able to rise up against us."

Everyone in the tunnel, even the other kids, stared at Ty like he was some sort of celebrity. His stomach ached, and he reached down to grip his belly. He gagged, and swallowed the acid boiling up his throat.

"I think I'm going to be sick," Ty mumbled.

The words wiped the smile off Fenix's face. He snapped his fingers at Tommy and Carson. "Get this kid showered off and take him straight to Doc Rollins. Anything the old man needs, tell him it's authorized."

Fenix leaned down in front of Ty and gave him what appeared to be a genuine smile. "We can't let anything happen to little Mr. Ty Montgomery."

— 5 —

"They took him, Nathan. They took Ty."

The words crackled out of the speakers of the analog radio. Nathan's heart hammered his rib cage. For a moment he didn't respond. He couldn't.

He was sitting at a picnic table in Bond Park outside of town hall, trying to make sense of what his sister had just said. The gunfire to the west had ceased, but none of the police officers had returned. There was no one here to see him if he broke down, but he had to hold it together for Charlize and Ty.

"Nathan, are you there?" his sister asked.

He brought the receiver to his lips. "Yes, I'm here. I'm sorry, there's a situation here in Estes Park."

Charlize continued like she hadn't heard him. "Some soldiers took Ty and the other kids from the camp."

"But he's alive?"

"I'm... I'm not sure. Oh God, how is any of this happening?"

"Charlize, I know this is hard, but you have to calm down," Nathan said. "Start over and tell me exactly what happened."

There was a short pause and what sounded like Charlize taking a few deep breaths on the other end of the line.

"The Marines I had deployed to the camp found a boy named Alex. He said soldiers shot two of the counselors and took several of the children."

Nathan nodded, recalling the boy's name from Ty's enthusiastic tales of his time at the camp. He kept the receiver out, holding back his questions. Right now, he needed to listen.

"He said he saw the soldiers load Ty into a pickup truck and take him away."

"Where?" Nathan asked, unable to hold his questions any longer.

"I… I don't know. Lieutenant Dupree is combing the area from a Black Hawk, but they don't have much fuel left, and they have to take Alex to a hospital. They aren't going to be able to come get you right now, either."

There was commotion on the other line, a humming of some sort and then the unmistakable sound of helicopter rotors.

"Are you going somewhere?" Nathan asked.

"I'm being evacuated. The North Koreans still have subs in the water."

Nathan cursed. "I'll go find him, Charlize. You just get somewhere safe."

"No," she replied without hesitation. "The roads are dangerous. The briefings I've gotten…it's chaos out there, Nate."

"Which is all the more reason I should be out there looking for Ty. Especially if Dupree has to return to base."

A male voice sounded in the background. "We have to move, Madame Secretary. We can't delay any longer."

"Hold on, Albert," Charlize said. Wind crackled over the channel, followed by the chop of a helicopter taking off.

"All due respect, Sis, but I'm going out there."

A hard pause passed over the channel. Nathan wasn't sure if it was because she was considering his request or because she had run out of time.

Static came over the channel, followed by his sister's voice. "Do you still have access to a CBRN suit and a working vehicle?"

"I'm sure I can get both," Nathan said.

"What time is it there?"

"Five or so in the afternoon."

"It's too late to leave today," Charlize said. "Give Dupree one more shot at this. If he doesn't find Ty by morning, you have my authorization to search for him yourself."

Nathan thought about it for a moment. He was only eighty-six miles away from the Easterseals camp. He didn't like waiting any longer, but the roads would be worse at night. He looked over his shoulder at town hall as the doors creaked open. Margaret, the police dispatcher, stepped outside. She seemed to be crying.

Charlize's voice pulled him back to the radio.

"Is there someone who can go with you tomorrow?" she asked.

"I'll be fine on my own."

There was another short pause.

"Keep that radio with you. I'll call you with an update as soon as I can. I love you, Nathan."

"I love you, too. Everything's going to be okay, I promise. Now go get on that bird and fly somewhere safe."

Nathan lowered the receiver and shut off the radio to save the juice. After packing it up, he limped across the grass toward the station. First thing he had to do was get the CBRN suit, a rifle, and then a vehicle.

Margaret pulled her hands from her face and looked up at him.

"You okay?" he asked.

"No, I'm not. Officer Rick Nelson just passed away."

Nathan looked at his boots, then back to Margaret. "I'm really sorry to hear that, ma'am."

"He won't be the last," she said gravely. "Things are getting worse by the minute. Chief Colton's out there looking for Raven and Detective Plymouth right now. There's been some sort of a shootout. I can't get my head around all this violence. We've lived in peace for so long."

Nathan tried to think of something else to say, but couldn't find the words to comfort her. He looked to the west. The Estes Park police department and Raven were on their own this time. Nathan had his own mission to prepare for.

As soon as Colton got back, Nathan was going to do what he should have done all along. He was going to head south. Not in the morning, not in six hours. As soon as he had a vehicle and a weapon, he was heading out there to find Ty.

***

Raven worked his way through the trees, steady but fast, following the trail—a crushed sapling here, a few drops of blood on the ground there. His best friend trotted to the east, sniffing the ground. Creek was in his element, following the scent of the bastards that had tried to steal the pickup truck and kidnapped Lindsey. They weren't far ahead, but they were armed with a shotgun and Lindsey's pistol.

After firing an arrow into the Chevy's back tire, two

men and a woman had bailed and opened fire on Raven. He was only able to get off a few shots before they had fled into the woods with Lindsey. A shotgun blast had almost taken off Raven's head, ponytail and all.

He kept low and raked the barrel of his Glock over the terrain as he pursued his chases. His view had transformed into a two-dimensional grid. Scanning it systematically, he looked for the bright blue of the Old Navy sweatshirt that the man with the shotgun was wearing.

Snapping and crunching branches sounded ahead, followed by a raised voice.

"Keep moving, bitch!"

Raven moved around a tree and crouched next to a boulder covered in orange moss. There, to the southeast, he finally spotted Lindsey's uniform through the gap in the trees. He bolted for another rock.

A thin man with a red poncho had a gun pointed at Lindsey's back—her gun, Raven realized. The cuffs around her wrists were hers as well. How these idiots had gotten the drop on her was going to be a matter of discussion over a cup of coffee at some point, but first he had to get her out of this mess.

The second chase, a frail woman with wild red hair and a red flannel shirt to match, followed the group through the woods. She was gripping her shoulder where Raven had clipped her with a round back on the road.

"Look at me again and I'll shoot you!" the man with the poncho said to Lindsey.

She glared at him and tried to speak, but there was something jammed in her mouth. A sock or glove, maybe. The guy with the shotgun was leading the group. He stopped at the bottom of the slope and looked in

Raven's direction.

Raven ducked back down. His plan was to take that guy out with his bow, but now that they had Lindsey's weapon, he was going to need to get closer and bring them down swiftly. He would need Creek's help.

With a flash of his hand, Raven ordered Creek to flank the group. Then he took off running for the cover of a massive ponderosa. The kidnappers were moving down a ridgeline that led toward the town. Raven knew this area well. He had guided an illegal hunting party here. The rich idiots had paid extra for the night vision goggles and suppressed rifles. The night hunt was supposed to end with a trophy bull elk. Instead, they had gone home empty handed. Raven had a bad feeling this hunt wouldn't end the same way.

Someone was going to die. He just had to make sure it wasn't him, Creek, or Lindsey.

Keeping low, he ran for the crest of the hill that overlooked Estes Park. His body ached and the slash to his chest burned, but the adrenaline made him forget the pain.

He ducked under a branch and crouch-walked over to the side of a tree to look out over the lush valley below. Smoke swirled from chimneys into the sky. His chases were getting closer to town. A shootout in the forest was one thing, but in a residential area it could result in innocent casualties.

Raven hugged the ground as he scanned the woods down the slope. He could hear two voices and more snapping twigs somewhere to the southeast.

He slung his bow over his back and pulled out his Glock. Then he slipped around another tree and moved his finger from the outside of the trigger guard. Creek was somewhere out there and moving into position.

The woman in the flannel shirt and the man in the red poncho emerged in the dense trees below. Lindsey was walking between the two, but where the hell was the guy with the Old Navy sweatshirt?

Raven swung his Glock toward a flash of motion to the southeast. He ducked just as the boom of the shotgun sounded. The blast slammed into the tree behind him, and splintering wood rained down onto his head. It was the second time he had almost lost his brains in the past hour. He wouldn't get so lucky a third time.

He dropped to his stomach and squeezed off two shots at the center of the Old Navy logo. Both rounds went wide, punching into the bark of an aspen tree to the man's right.

Another shot kicked up dirt to Raven's left. He rolled away and pulled the trigger as soon as he had the sights lined up. This time the round hit the man's shotgun. He stumbled backward, crazed eyes looking down at his weapon. The shock quickly passed and he brought it back up to fire.

Gunfire cracked to the southwest—not handguns, but rifles. The shots distracted the man long enough for Creek to attack. A ball of fur slammed into his side and knocked him to the ground. The bastard screamed and jerked his arm as Creek tore at his sleeve.

"Good boy," Raven said with a grin. He pushed himself up and looked to the southwest, where Colton and Don were moving in with their AR-15s shouldered.

The man in the red poncho got off a single shot with Lindsey's pistol before a volley of 5.56mm rounds tore through his chest. He slammed into a tree and slid down the trunk, blood streaking down the bark in a sheet.

The woman screeched in a primal voice and took off running for Colton. Lindsey stuck out her foot and tripped her. She landed on the ground face first, her flannel shirt a mess of mud and pine needles.

Don strode forward with his rifle aimed at her head.

"Stay down!" he shouted.

Colton went to check the man in the red poncho. He had slumped to the dirt, unmoving. Colton kicked the gun away and then walked back over to Lindsey and uncuffed her. The detective rubbed her chafed wrists, scowling at the woman on the ground.

"You're lucky they showed up!" Lindsey shouted, kicking at the dirt. "I would have killed you."

"Detective Plymouth, go pick up your weapon," Colton ordered. She hesitated and Colton arched his brows. That got Lindsey moving. She walked away from the woman, who was now crying while Don cuffed her.

Satisfied that they had the situation under control, Raven jogged over to Creek and the third kidnapper. The Akita stood over him, snarling, with a chunk of the man's shirt in his maw.

"Call him off," the man begged. "Please!"

Raven grabbed the shotgun off the ground and waited a few more satisfying seconds before ordering Creek to stop. By the time the dog obeyed, Don had the woman cuffed and Colton was running over toward Raven with Lindsey.

"You okay, Raven?" Colton asked.

Lindsey grunted. "So much for having my back."

"*What?*" Raven said. "I just saved your ass. I mean, these guys helped, but it was mostly me."

"Cut the shit. Both of you. All that matters is everyone's okay and that we got these sons of bitches,"

Colton said. "Detective, you're lucky to be alive at all."

"I know," she said quietly. "They were using me as a hostage, but I have no doubt they would have killed me if you guys hadn't shown up."

Creek let out a low whine and brushed up against Raven. He reached down and the dog proudly presented him with the ripped cloth from the man's sweatshirt.

"It's okay, boy, you did good. You did really good."

The soft fur of his best friend usually helped calm Raven's nerves, but his pulse continued to throb across his scratched, bruised body.

"Thanks, Raven," Lindsey said like she actually meant it. She bent down to pet Creek. "And thanks to you, too, handsome boy."

Raven had to chuckle. Even his dog had better luck with the ladies than he did.

***

Colton opened the back door of the Jeep outside the rear entrance to the police station.

"Get out," he snarled.

Milo Todd and his sister, Cindy, scooted across the seat and out onto the pavement with their hands cuffed behind their backs. Colton could smell their body odor from where he stood. They were both filthy, and Cindy was bleeding from her shoulder.

"I need a doctor," she said.

Lindsey laughed. "Get in line. There are plenty of people in need of medical attention right now that haven't killed police officers."

Don parked Jake's pickup truck in the stall to the right of the Jeep, giving Colton a view of the corpse in the back. Eric Thornton, a friend of Milo and Cindy, lay in the back of the truck. The man's red poncho was soaked with blood from the bullet wounds that had ended his life.

Colton refrained from spitting on the body. He needed to be a role model in front of his officers, but it was hard to stay professional. These people had killed a good man, not out of self-preservation or some misguided cause, but simply to feed their addiction.

He grabbed Milo under the arm and pulled him away from the Jeep. "Let's go, asshole."

"Hey!" Milo protested.

"Shut up," Colton growled.

Officer Matthew directed Cindy toward the building. Nathan, Lindsey, Raven, and Creek stood watching them lead the prisoners across the parking lot. Behind them, a small crowd of citizens had gathered on the street outside Bond Park.

"Keep them back!" Colton shouted.

Detective Tim Ryburn and Officer Sam Hines hurried over to the park.

"Take them inside, Don," Colton said.

As soon as the door shut behind them, Colton stalked through the parking lot away from Bond Park. He needed a moment to breathe and a moment to think alone. He passed the H1 Hummer and moved around the side of the station, where he had a view of Prospect Mountain. What he really wanted was a cigarette, but he'd smoked the last one when they were putting the spare tire on Jake's pickup truck. With the nation's infrastructure broken, there wouldn't be any more cigarettes delivered. Maybe it was just as well.

"Chief? Can I have a word?"

He sighed. Colton should have known better than to think he would have a moment of peace and quiet. Nathan limped around the corner, holding his cast with his good hand.

"I'm sorry about Officer Nelson," Nathan said. "I wish I'd been able to stop what happened that afternoon."

"Me too," Colton said. "It's time I start realizing that evil doesn't give you a second chance."

Colton eyed the aerial tramway at the top of the mountain. He still hadn't fully dealt with the events that had occurred there, and he wasn't sure if he would anytime soon. Throughout the day, he found himself wanting to ask Jake's opinion or share a joke, and then he'd remember all over again that his best friend was dead.

"I've got a favor to ask of you, Chief," Nathan said.

Colton stiffened and faced Nathan. "What's that?"

"Remember that gear you promised me?"

"Yeah," he said slowly.

"I'm going to need it. Some soldiers took my nephew before the Marines got to the Easterseals camp."

"What do you mean they took him?"

"Apparently some soldiers showed up, shot two camp counselors, and went off with a bunch of the kids."

Colton wiped his forehead with a sleeve. He was so goddamned tired. It was hard to think. "Why would they...unless...do you think they knew who your nephew is?"

"I highly doubt that, but it's possible. Either way, I'm heading out to track Ty down."

Colton's day kept getting worse. They were already stretched thin on resources, but Nathan had risked his life to help him catch Brown Feather and Turtle. He couldn't let the pilot down now.

"Hold here a minute," Colton said. He walked back to the corner and looked around the side of town hall. Raven and Creek were still outside the back entrance to the police station with Lindsey.

"Raven, come here a second," Colton called out.

Raven trotted over with Creek in tow. "What's up, Chief?"

"I've got another mission for you and Creek."

— 6 —

After years of being poked and prodded by doctors in hospitals, the sight of needles no longer bothered Ty. He watched Dr. Rollins insert the needle into his upper arm without even flinching.

"Tetanus shot," Dr. Rollins said. "Just to be safe. The General wants to make sure you're as healthy as a horse."

A bank of lights overhead illuminated Ty's skinny legs dangling over the elevated bed. His skin was so pale he could see his veins. Sometimes his legs didn't feel like a part of him, and other times he could almost feel them. Today was one of those days. He willed them to work, to stand up and run away from this man.

Dr. Rollins forced a smile full of yellow teeth. "Almost done," he said.

Ty looked out the open door into the main medical facility. Several of the other kids were there sitting in chairs, waiting to be treated. Micah and Emma, the two kids from the road, were shivering together on a bench. He shared a room with them now. There were also Tim, Jack, Shana, and Rhonda from the Easterseals camp. The other children were being held in a different room than Ty, and the men wouldn't let him talk to them.

For some reason, the General wanted Ty to be looked at first. It wasn't the first time he'd gotten special treatment because of his mom, but he never felt good about it.

"Help them," Ty insisted, pointing at the siblings. Emma had already thrown up twice since they got to the Castle. "They need it, I don't."

"Soon, I promise." He shifted his glasses up to look at the other kids and then shut the door, sealing them inside the small room with a click.

Ty wanted to believe that Dr. Rollins was a good person. He didn't have tattoos or a shaved head like the soldiers. He decided to take a chance and ask some questions.

"What is this place?" Ty asked.

"Med ward," the doctor said, distracted by writing something down on a pad.

"No, I mean what's the Castle?"

Dr. Rollins looked at the window at the top of the metal door and then crossed to a glass cabinet. He pulled out several pill bottles, set them down, and looked over his shoulder at the window again.

"Your mom is really Senator Montgomery?"

Ty nodded. He waited for a response, but Dr. Rollins continued working. He counted out some pills onto a tray, grabbed a bottle of water, and returned to the exam table.

"Take these," he said.

"No," Ty said. "Not until you answer my questions."

Dr. Rollins glanced at the window again. A tattooed man with a sharp nose strode by the room and stopped just outside the door. Rollins turned back to Ty and held the pills out.

"Please, just take them," he said. There was fear and sadness in the old man's eyes. Ty knew then he wasn't bad like the other soldiers.

"I'll take them if you answer my questions," Ty whispered. "I promise not to tell anyone we talked."

Dr. Rollins waited for the man outside to walk away. "You're going to get me into trouble."

"I promise I won't tell. What is this place, and why am I here? I want to go home."

The doctor checked the window a third time. "You don't tell anyone this. Okay? I mean *anyone*."

Ty nodded firmly, and Dr. Rollins continued in a hushed voice. "The Castle is the Sons of Liberty's home base. General Fenix started building it and stockpiling supplies here years ago for his army."

"Army?" Ty asked. "So what do they need me for? I can't fight."

Dr. Rollins frowned. "You're not going to fight for his army, son. You're going to help him build it."

***

Charlize sat in the troop hold of a Seahawk helicopter, tucked between a team of Navy SEALs and Albert. They had just taken off from the roof of a hospital in Palm Beach after being diverted earlier that day. The pilots were taking them to a secure location President Diego had picked after the evacuation from the USS *John Stennis*.

On the horizon was the aircraft carrier. Clint's body was still on board, and they hadn't been able to hold a remembrance ceremony for him. Leaving without saying goodbye broke her heart—not that there was much of it left intact to break.

"That's not Clint down there anymore. His soul is in a better place, and if you have anything to say to him, he can still hear you," Albert said, as if he could read her mind. He put his massive hand over hers. "Try not to worry about Ty, either. I bet this is all just a misunderstanding and he'll be home soon."

"Hard not to worry, but thank you," Charlize said. She doubted Albert was right, but she had to hold onto hope that maybe this was some sort of mistake. Maybe it had been the Colorado National Guard or another unit who had picked up the kids. She could get a call any minute explaining the mix up.

Charlize reached up and dabbed her burned forehead with the medicated gel she kept in her pocket. The pulsing pain was really starting to bother her, resulting in a headache that had settled behind her eyes. The constant rattle from the rotors overhead didn't help. She should have taken her medicine before leaving the ship.

Albert watched her from the side, concerned but keeping quiet. He had severe burns too, and had never complained once. He had lost his entire family—his wife, two daughters, brother, and mother-in-law—in the blast that leveled D.C., and he had hardly said a word about it since. She could see he was hurting deep down, beneath the layers of muscle and grit.

"How are you doing, Big Al?" she asked.

He managed a smile. "I'm all right, ma'am."

"I'm so sorry about your family."

"Not your fault, ma'am."

"If you ever want to talk to me—"

"I know," Albert interrupted. It was his way of saying *not now*. He looked away to scan the interior of the troop hold. He was easily the biggest man there, but he wasn't a trained killer like the Navy SEALs. The men, in turn, all averted their gaze from Charlize and Albert. They were either anxious at the presence of the Secretary of Defense or else their minds were simply elsewhere. She had a feeling it was the latter. Her own mind was racing like the F-18 Hornets still peeling off the deck of the USS *John Stennis.*

Every head turned to watch the fighters scream away, one at a time, from the aircraft carrier. One squadron fanned out to sea while the other tore off to Palm Beach. The Seahawk was following a dozen other helicopters in the same direction.

Charlize eyed the Osprey carrying President Diego, which was sandwiched between the small fleet of choppers. The other birds buzzed around it like wasps protecting their queen. She cupped her hands over her headset as the F-18s roared past them.

"Aren't those Hornets going the wrong way?" Charlize shouted over the thump of the rotors.

Senior Chief Petty Officer Fernandez, a handsome Latino man with a graying mustache, looked in her direction with the hardened, non-judgmental gaze of a career warrior who had seen action all over the world.

"They're heading toward the line, Madame Secretary," he said.

"What line is that, Chief?" Albert asked.

"The line separating paradise from hell," Fernandez said without emotion.

"Florida has been cut in half by an invisible border just south of Orlando. The grid north of it is down," Charlize explained.

Fernandez nodded. "That line is a moving target. We've already had to fall back in several areas. We're headed to Highway 4 after we drop you off at Constellation."

"It seems to me they need men of your caliber for

more important missions than holding security on a highway," Charlize said, frowning.

"There are a hundred thousand refugees pouring in from the north, Madame Secretary. We're needed to help coordinate the units there," he said.

Charlize could feel Albert looking over at her, but he remained silent, too. He went back to tapping his burned Air Jordans, and Charlize lost herself in her thoughts.

The number of refugees was staggering, and it would only get worse. It was hard to picture when she looked at the city below. While the streets were busy, vehicles were still moving and the grid was still working. There was no sign of looting or riots, no sign of people suffering from radiation poisoning.

It won't last, she thought. The refugees would kill to get down here. It was all about self-preservation now.

Charlize shook her head. The country was collapsing after less than a week.

To the east, the North Korean submarines were watching it all unfold. They were hiding in their subs, but they would have to surface for fuel eventually, and when they did, she would nail them with the HSM squadrons.

But even with the North Korean threat eradicated, the country would still be tearing itself apart. Her job as Secretary of Defense was to try and hold it all together, and do it while she was losing her mind with worry.

"Madame Secretary," one of the pilots said over the comms. "Lieutenant Marco is on the line requesting to speak with you."

"Patch her through," Charlize replied. She pushed the mini-mic to her lips and tried to remain calm. The XO of the USS *John Stennis* was her lifeline to Nathan and Dupree now that she didn't have access to a radio.

"Ma'am," Marco said. "I have a SITREP for you. Lieutenant Dupree is heading southwest over Interstate 70. There's still no sign of Falcon. The pilots have about an hour of fuel left. Then they'll need to fly east to refuel and drop that sick boy off at Buckley Air Force Base."

Charlize wanted to order Dupree to stay out there as long as he could, but Ty's life wasn't the only one on the line. Alex was sick and needed help, too. Instead, she thanked the lieutenant for the update and went back to looking out the windows. She wondered if she had made the right call in telling Nathan to wait until the morning to leave Estes Park, but there was no turning back now.

For several minutes, no one said a word in the troop hold. Albert and the Navy SEALs all stared ahead blankly. Each of them had families to think about. There wasn't a single American alone in their misery. Of everyone here, she was the only one who got to pull rank, and she was starting to feel pretty awful for doing it.

The silence ended with another transmission from one of the pilots.

"We're ten minutes away from putting down," he reported. "Senior Chief Fernandez will escort you to Constellation by boat after we land."

"Take a look northwest," said the other pilot.

Charlize leaned to her right for a view out the starboard side window. Her headache was worse, and the pain behind her eyes blurred her vision. The tops of skyscrapers glittered and flickered across an unfamiliar skyline. Plumes of smoke rose among the buildings. Dozens of dots circled the city—helicopters, she realized.

"That's Orlando," the main pilot said. "Or what we're calling the Hornet's Nest."

Charlize could see why the city had earned the

nickname. The bird continued turning, providing a view of Highway 95. Cars were creeping down the southbound lane, so slowly she could hardly tell they were moving at all.

On the shoulder, a small convoy of Humvees and military trucks drove north like fish battling against the current to get backup river. In between the vehicles, a crowd of people were making their way on foot. From her vantage point, they blended into a single snake.

"My God, there are thousands of refugees down there," Albert said quietly.

"Hundreds of thousands," Charlize replied, remembering what Fernandez had said earlier. She hadn't wanted to believe it, but now she could see them with her own eyes. Even the pictures of refugees pouring out of cities in war-torn regions overseas didn't compare to what she saw below.

At least the American military was supporting these people. In Iraq and Afghanistan, fleeing civilians were killed by bombs and missiles, leaving scenes of carnage on the road. Charlize had been there to see one of them firsthand.

Fernandez patted his helmet and cleared his throat. "Listen up, men. After we get Secretary Montgomery safely to Constellation, we're heading down there. There are—"

"Looks like a skirmish on the highway," reported one of the pilots. "Someone just open fired down there!"

Charlize and Albert joined the Navy SEALs on the other side of the helicopter. Fernandez held up a hand to keep her back.

"Better to stay seated, ma'am," he said. "I don't want you getting hit by a stray bullet."

"That's why I'm here," Albert said. He crowded in front of Charlize with his hulking frame. Below, she could see a mob of civilians fanned out across the highway. More gunshots tore into the crowd, and those fleeing stampeded to escape.

"What's happening down there?" she asked.

Fernandez shook his head. "Who knows? Maybe someone wanted a bottle of water. The stories I've been hearing…hell, I heard about a guy that shot someone for a candy bar."

"Looks like the military is moving in," Albert said.

Humvees raced down the shoulder of the road even as the pilots pulled away from the scene. Charlize cupped her hand over her mouth when she saw the bodies on the highway they were leaving behind. Dozens of civilians had already been shot or trampled to death in the chaos.

"Our job is to stop shit like that from happening," Fernandez said to his men.

Charlize returned to her seat with Albert, still shocked by what she had witnessed. This wasn't supposed to happen here, not in America. It took her several minutes to get control of her breathing.

As the Navy SEALs finally moved away from the windows, she spied a landmark she hadn't seen in years. The rocket launch towers of the Kennedy Space Center rose like missiles above the horizon.

"Prepare for landing," one of the pilots said. He glanced back from the cockpit and said, "You're almost to Constellation, Madame Secretary, but this is as far as we can take you."

She watched the ground rise up to meet them as realization set in. Constellation wasn't some top-secret military base. It was somewhere at Cape Canaveral, the same place that had launched missions into space.

Years ago she had toured the facilities, first as an Air Force pilot, and then as a United States Senator. When she'd been a kid, she'd dreamed of becoming an astronaut for a mission to outer space, but those dreams were no more. She was the Secretary of Defense now, a role she'd never dreamed of taking on, and it was time to get down to work.

***

Raven had made a lot of promises lately. He'd promised himself and Sandra that he would protect his family and Estes Park from evil after he killed Brown Feather and Turtle.

He'd also promised to help Colton maintain law and order in whatever way Colton saw fit. Now the Chief was asking Raven to follow through with that promise by helping find and rescue Nathan's nephew, who also happened to be the son of the new Secretary of Defense. Funny how that little detail hadn't really come up much in conversation before now.

Raven crouched next to Creek and scrutinized the lawman and the pilot. He hadn't particularly liked Nathan when he'd met him the night of the North Korean attack, but Nathan had helped save Sandra and Allie. There wasn't anything less honorable in life than a man who refused to pay his debts, and Raven owed Nathan.

"I'll go with you to find the boy," Raven said, standing up and joining them.

"You sure your sister won't mind?" Nathan asked.

"Of course she will. That's why you're going to tell her we won't be gone long and that everything will be fine."

Nathan grinned. It looked like it hurt.

"I'm sure she'll understand," Colton said. "I'll make sure she's well looked after while you're gone, Raven."

"Promise?"

Colton nodded, and Raven shook his hand to seal the deal.

"Sandra might forgive me, but Creek isn't going to for leaving him here. Are you, boy?"

The dog looked up, eyes flitting from Nathan to Raven.

"I won't risk him getting radiation poisoning, and I don't guess there are any suits that will fit him," Raven said.

Nathan held down a hand for Creek to sniff, but the dog put his head back on his paws and snorted.

Good dog, Raven thought.

Around the corner of town hall came Patrol Sergeant Don Aragon. He pulled up his duty belt and jerked his chin at them. "Sounds like Cindy Todd's going to need stitches. She's bleeding pretty bad."

"You clipped her good, Raven," Colton said.

"Sorry," Raven muttered.

"I'm not," Don said. "I'm also not keen on the idea of wasting medical supplies on her. I say we let her bleed, but Lindsey told me to run it by you."

The words seemed to take Nathan by surprise. He turned to Colton. "You decided what you're going to do with her yet, Chief?"

"Need to talk to Mayor Andrews first before I do anything," Colton replied. "For now, get her stitched up."

Don rolled his eyes, but tipped his cowboy hat before walking away.

"I really don't like his attitude," Colton snarled.

Raven shrugged. "I really don't like him at all."

Colton shook it off and pointed at the VW van tucked between Raven's Jeep and the department's Humvee. "How do you feel about driving that?"

"You sure it can be trusted on the open roads?" Nathan asked. "Looks like it's slower than a donkey."

Colton laughed. "Not that slow." He reached into his pocket, pulled a key off the ring, and handed it to Raven. "I wouldn't feel right about sending you two out there in that swag mobile, so I'm going to let you take your Jeep."

"Mighty generous of you," Raven said with a grin. "Considering she's *mine*."

There was no trace of an answering smile on Colton's features. His mind was clearly elsewhere. Raven plucked the key out of his hand and bent down to check a dent on the back bumper. When he looked up, Colton had already turned away to look at the crowd on the sidewalk outside Bond Park. Fifty people were gathered there. Some of them were shouting, but Raven wasn't sure what they were carrying on about.

"I'm going to have to go deal with this," Colton said with a sigh.

Nathan set his rucksack down next to the Jeep. "And we better get moving while we still have light."

"Okay, but I need to swing by the hospital to drop off Creek and say goodbye to my sister before we head out. Otherwise, she *will* kill me."

Nathan grinned. "My sister is going to kill me too when she finds out I didn't wait until morning to head out there."

"It is very dangerous on the roads, but I've already told you so a dozen times," Colton said.

The back door to the police station opened, and

Lindsey stepped outside holding two large duffel bags. She brought them over to the Jeep and dropped them on the ground.

"Your CBRN suits, gentleman. I've also added a Geiger counter. I'd say good luck, but you're going to need more than luck out there. You're going to need one of these."

She unstrapped a third pack and pulled out a handheld GPS device and pair of night vision goggles.

"These work?" Nathan asked.

"Yup. Leroy Travis donated them to the department. Apparently Bill Catcher wasn't the only prepper in town with faraday cages. Leroy also gave us a digital radio that actually works."

"I'll be damned," Raven said, reaching out for the night vision goggles. The optics looked ancient, nothing like the advanced "four eyes" type he was used to wearing, but they would do the job.

"Detective Plymouth, I don't remember authorizing you to give out our supplies, but I suppose Nathan and Raven need them more than us right now," Colton said. He examined the optics. "They should help you drive in the dark with your headlights off. Might make the roads a bit less dangerous."

"That's what I was thinking," Lindsey said. She was clearly rattled from the incident just hours before, but she still managed a smile.

"I owe you a coffee when I come back," Raven said. He massaged the scruff on his chin. "Actually, now to think about it, I think you owe *me* one for saving your ass earlier today."

Lindsey rolled her eyes. "Wouldn't that make us even? Guess we don't have to get a drink at all."

"Wait, so I don't have a chance at all now?" Raven said, frustrated and kind of confused.

"Maybe if you cut your hair," she said, shooting him a sideward glance. "I don't date men with hair longer than mine."

Nathan let out a laugh, and Colton shook his head wearily.

"Go help Don with Cindy, Detective," Colton said. "Raven and Nathan, I'll meet you at the hospital after I finish talking to these people."

"You got it, Chief," Lindsey said. She walked back to the building, and Colton hurried across the parking lot and to Bond Park.

"Settle down, everyone," he said, hands raised.

A flurry of questions rang out all around him. Raven didn't envy Colton's job. He was trying to keep the town from falling apart, but between the shootout with Nile Redford's men, the brutal killings by the Tankala brothers, and the manhunt for the addicts who killed Officer Nelson, things were hanging on by a thread.

Raven listened to Colton try and reassure the crowd. Everyone had a question. Some people wanted to know about food, others about the killings, and others about military support. Colton didn't have many answers.

"Chief's going to need a lot of help up here," Nathan said quietly. "When you get back, I mean."

"Yeah, I know," Raven replied. He looked over at Creek. He hated leaving the dog, but he couldn't risk bringing him out there. For this hunt, he was going to have to sit on the sidelines.

"You take care of Sandra and Allie when I'm gone, okay, boy?"

Creek sniffed the duffel bags as Nathan opened them

and rifled through the contents. Raven bent down next to him to examine their gear. In addition to everything else Lindsey had shown them, she'd also included a medical pack. Raven opened the other bag to reveal food, water, and extra magazines for their Colt AR-15s.

They had everything they might need to track Nathan's nephew to hell and back. Raven just hoped they would find the boy alive.

— 7 —

Alex was dying inside the oversized CBRN suit, and there wasn't much Lieutenant Dupree could do about it. He held the boy in his arms as the other Marines stood at the open door of the Black Hawk. It was a sign of how bad off the kid was that Dupree was able to hold him at all. They were headed back to Buckley AFB, low on fuel and low on morale after failing to find Ty Montgomery.

Sergeant McCabe crouch-walked back to the seat next to Dupree.

"Sir, there's no sign of survivors down there," McCabe said. "Although we did see some recent tire tracks in the ash. Two vehicles appear to have been heading east not too long ago."

"That might be the kidnappers," Dupree said. "We'll start the search along this road once we re-fuel and drop Alex off."

"Are we going to be able to sleep at all, sir?" Sharps asked. "I haven't gotten more than two hours in the past two days. This chopper isn't the only thing running on fumes."

Dupree looked at each of his men in turn. Even with the visors obscuring their faces, he could see the exhaustion in their eyes. No, it wasn't just exhaustion—it was doubt.

Watching the country collapse had taken a harsh toll on the team. Everyone was worried about their own families, and while it wasn't a Marine's job to question orders, Dupree knew all of his men, and not just Sharps, were wondering what made Ty Montgomery so damned important.

"Everyone gets two hours of R&R when we get to Buckley," Dupree said. It wasn't much, but it was better than nothing, and his men needed the shuteye to function.

McCabe exhaled in his helmet. He reached down into his rucksack and pulled out a plastic sealed medical kit.

"Buckley AFB, ETA thirty minutes," one of the pilots said. "They've scrubbed the base pretty good, but we'll need to stay in our suits for now."

"I'm tired enough to sleep in this thing," McCabe said as he rummaged through the medical kit.

Dupree wasn't tired at all now. The adrenaline was still pumping through his veins, and he had a feeling it was because things were about to get worse. He gripped Alex tighter as the pilots pulled farther into the sky.

"Jesus, look at that," Sharps said from the doorway.

The change in direction provided a view of the horizon to the southwest. A black wall of smoke being fed by the burning forests choked the sky. Where there had been a gold and green ocean of trees, there was now only a bed of embers. If the rain continued, Mother Nature might have a chance of stopping what man had started, but Dupree had learned a long time ago not to hope for miracles.

"Close those doors," Dupree said.

Crew Chief Locust got up from his seat across the troop hold and closed off the view.

"Am I going to die?"

The voice came from Alex. He shifted his helmeted

head so he could see Dupree's face. Tears streaked away from the boy's filthy cheeks.

"You're going to be fine, kid," Dupree said. "We're taking you to get help right now."

"I want to see my mom and dad." Alex licked his cracked lips. "Can you take me to my mom and dad?"

He began to squirm in Dupree's grip. He nodded to McCabe, and the Marine pulled a syringe out of the medical kit.

"My friend Sergeant McCabe is going to give you something to help you sleep, okay?"

Alex glanced up at McCabe with bloodshot eyes and coughed. His small body practically vibrated in Dupree's arms. Saliva mixed with blood peppered the inside of Alex's visor.

"I want to see my mom and dad," Alex said again.

Dupree kept the kid talking while McCabe prepared the needle. "Where are your parents?"

"Richmond, Virginia, United States, North America, Earth," he rattled off in quick succession, his eyes briefly clearing.

Dupree held in a curse. Richmond was smack in the middle of another radiation zone.

"I want my mama," Alex whimpered.

"We're taking you to a hospital first. I'll talk to someone there and see if they can contact your parents."

"Okay," Alex said. Tears continued to fall down his face as he watched the needle.

"This might hurt," McCabe said. He pulled back Alex's sleeve to expose the skin without puncturing the suit and then injected the morphine. It only took a few seconds to kick in, and Alex relaxed in Dupree's arms. He was asleep a few minutes later.

"Help me," Dupree said to McCabe.

Together, they gently laid Alex on the floor of the helicopter.

"He's not going to make it, is he?" Sharps asked. There was empathy in the Marine's eyes Dupree hadn't seen before. War brought out a lot in men, and it wasn't always bad. He had seen Sharps grow into a man over the past few years, and even though he was still a jokester, he was as courageous as any Marine Dupree had ever met.

"Sir, I've got eyes on a working vehicle," Locust said from the door, saving Dupree from answering. "A Humvee...make that two Humvees heading east. Looks like a Colorado National Guard unit, sir."

Dupree checked Alex again to make sure he was still sleeping and then made his way to the cockpit. He motioned for McCabe to follow.

"How much fuel do we have left?" Dupree asked.

The main pilot checked the gauges. "Thirty minutes worth, maybe a bit more."

"And we're about twenty minutes from Buckley?"

"Yup," the pilot confirmed.

Dupree cursed. "That's a small window, and Alex is running out of time."

"Sir, all due respect, but that kid probably isn't going to make it no matter what," McCabe said.

Deep down Dupree knew it was true. He wasn't ready to give up on Alex, but their primary mission was to locate and evacuate Ty Montgomery from Colorado and return him to the Secretary of Defense.

"Alex said those soldiers loaded the kids into a pickup, right?"

McCabe nodded. "I believe so, sir,"

The Humvees zigzagged around the cars stalled along

the highway. There was no sign of a pickup or any kids, which suggested this wasn't related to their mission. Still, it was their first sighting of any military presence out on the road. To Dupree, it was worth checking out.

"Cut 'em off," Dupree said. "We have to make this fast."

Both pilots turned to look at him like he was crazy.

"That's an order," Dupree said. He moved back into the troop hold, adrenaline rocketing through him.

"Locust, get on the M240. The rest of you, lock and load. I want to ask those soldiers some questions and see if they have any info that could lead us to Falcon."

The fatigue plaguing the Marines seemed to evaporate. They snapped into action, checking their weapons and suits as Locust opened the door. The other Marines crowded around, their weapons cradled and ready.

The Black Hawk shot over a forest spared from the flames, the wind from the rotors whipping the tops of pines like ripples in a pond. Dupree brought the scope of his M4 to his visor. The Humvees trailed a black cloud of exhaust on the off-ramp and turned onto another road that snaked through the forests.

"They have to see us up here," McCabe said. "Why aren't they stopping?"

Dupree pushed his scope back to his eye. The Humvees' turrets were armed with M240s, but he didn't see anyone manning the weapons. They raced down the road without slowing. A bridge crossed a stream about a mile ahead. From the sky, this tiny sliver of terrain still looked beautiful, but everything down there was likely toxic. Bluffs coated with moss towered over the road on the other side of the bridge. Gangly trees protruded out of the rocks.

The Humvees stopped on the bridge. The doors opened, disgorging soldiers in green CBRN suits.

"Look like they finally got the message," McCabe said.

Dupree lowered his rifle and turned to the cockpit. "Put us down behind that minivan."

"Yes, sir," replied one of the pilots.

"McCabe, Emerson, and Sharps you're with me," Dupree said. "Everyone else, you stay in the bird and watch our back."

McCabe hesitated. "Sir, I got a bad feeling about this. What if those guys are the same ones that took Falcon?"

"I'm hoping they are," Dupree said.

Sharps chuckled. "Me too. I've been itching for some action."

Dupree shot him a glare. "Goddammit, Sharps, you're a Marine. A few minutes ago, I was actually thinking about how you were growing up. Do you still not see what the fuck is going on down there?"

The tall Marine glanced outside at the burning skyline and the road dotted with stalled cars.

"That shit down there is our new world," Dupree said. He let the words sink in and bent down next to Alex as the bird lowered into position. The boy was breathing slowly, lost in a deep sleep. Dupree was relieved to see he wasn't suffering.

"I'll be right back, kid," he whispered. He touched Alex's arm and then stood. At the door, he chambered a round in his M4 and turned the selector to single shot.

The rotors whipped up ash and dust below, spinning it in all directions. As soon as the wheels touched the ground, Dupree hopped out and ran at a crouch toward a minivan. The Humvees—and the men guarding them—were about three hundred feet away.

Wind from the rotors slammed into Dupree as he jogged away from the bird. McCabe, Sharps, and Emerson followed close behind. They fanned out in combat intervals, their weapons cradled.

"Eyes up," Dupree said over the comm link. He scanned the bluffs bordering the road and then counted five contacts dressed in ash-caked CBRN suits. They all carried M16s, but one man's was equipped with a grenade launcher attachment. He stepped away from the group with his weapon lowered toward the concrete.

Dupree motioned for his team to hold security here. He walked out to meet the man with the grenade launcher. They stopped five feet from one another.

"Lieutenant Jeff Dupree with the United States Marine Corps. Identify yourself."

"I'm Sergeant Jack Smith with the Colorado National Guard." He looked up at the helicopter, then back at Dupree.

"What are you guys doing out here?"

"Was about to ask you the same question. Sir."

Dupree didn't like Smith's tone, the slight and faintly sarcastic emphasis he'd placed on *Sir.*

"We were ordered to help evacuate any survivors and bring them to a refugee camp south of Denver," Smith finally said when Dupree didn't volunteer any information. "My unit split up about thirty miles west of here a few days ago after we were ambushed by some raiders. Bunch of skinhead fucks."

"Skinheads?"

"Aryan Brotherhood types," Smith clarified. "I've lost contact with two of my Humvees and a Bradley since the attack."

Dupree sucked in a breath. He'd fought Taliban forces

during the war, but even he was wary of the Aryan Brotherhood.

"We're on our way back to Denver now," Smith said. "Got more survivors suffering from radiation poisoning. Anyone out here is probably as good as dead, to be honest, and I fear my lost men are, too."

Dupree looked over Smith's shoulder. The other four National Guard soldiers were checking the bluffs. If Smith and his men were trying to trick Dupree, they were doing one hell of a job.

"How many civvies you got?" Dupree asked.

"Six, including a couple kids."

"Mind if I take a look? We might be able to airlift them out of here, but I don't have much time. We're low on fuel."

Smith gestured with a gloved hand. "Be my guest, sir."

The distant whoosh of rotors reminded Dupree that he had a half dozen rifles on his back, but that didn't relieve the anxiety swirling through his body. Even if these soldiers could be trusted—and his gut said they were on the level—his mission was falling apart.

Dupree motioned for McCabe and the other Marines to follow him toward the Humvees. His men kept their rifles cradled, but Dupree knew they were all on high alert. He still hated the idea of shooting Americans, but he wouldn't hesitate to kill the bastards that ambushed Smith's unit. Any coward that could do that deserved a round to the skull.

"Eagle 1 and Eagle 2, you got eyes on anything?" Dupree said into his mini-mic.

The pilots responded with a negative. Dupree relaxed slightly but kept his weapon at the ready as he approached the Humvees. Smith opened the back door of the first vehicle and Dupree halted, half expecting someone to pop out and shoot him in the head. But no one inside the first Humvee was going to be shooting anyone.

Two women were slumped against one another in the back seat, their skin red with rashes and shirts covered with vomit. A girl no older than nine was sobbing and clutching a doll to her chest.

"It's okay," Dupree said, holding up a hand. "I'm not going to hurt you." He slowly backed away and checked the other Humvee. Another woman and two men were resting in the back seat. The man was doubled over in pain, clutching his gut.

"They're in bad shape, and the roads ahead are going to be blocked once we get close to Denver," Smith said. "Think you can help get 'em somewhere safe?"

"There's plenty of room on our chopper."

"Thank you, sir," Smith said. This time, he sounded sincere.

"All clear down here," Dupree reported over the comms. "Requesting evacuation for six more civvies."

"Copy that, sir," replied one of the pilots.

Dupree motioned for Sharps and Emerson to help him. McCabe stood guard while they helped the guardsman pull the survivors from the Humvees.

"Hurry up," Dupree ordered the pilots. The bird circled once and then lowered back toward the highway. The two women from the first Humvee were in such bad shape, Sharps and Emerson had to carry them. They moaned as the Marines picked them up and slung them over their shoulders.

Dupree squeezed past and reached out to the girl in the back seat.

"It's okay, sweetie, we're going to get you out of here."

She clutched the doll tighter to her chest with one hand and brushed a hank of brown hair from her face. Several strands of hair came off in her fingers. That made her sob even harder.

Dupree reached inside the truck and grabbed her, repeating, "It's okay, sweetie."

The mantra didn't seem to calm her much. She struggled in his grip as he carried her away from the trucks.

"Good luck!" Dupree said over his shoulder to Smith.

Dupree didn't like turning his back on anyone with a gun, but he was out of time. He looked skyward as the Black Hawk began to descend.

A hot flash of panic rushed over Dupree when the pilots suddenly halted their descent, hovering overhead. The rotor drafts slammed across the road, wrinkling his suit and whipping the girl's hair around her head like a halo.

"Sir, we got eyes on a vehicle heading your way through the canyon. Looks like a pickup truck."

Before he could react, a crack sounded. Locust, who'd been on the heavy gun aboard the chopper, grabbed his gut before plummeting out the open door of the troop hold. He crashed to the concrete ten feet in front of Dupree, screaming all the way down. His bones shattered with a sound like the boom of a shotgun.

"AMBUSH!" McCabe shouted.

Dupree ducked down with the girl as a bullet whizzed past his helmet. He set her gently on the ground and turned to fire his M4 at the guard soldiers. Damn it all to hell. He'd believed they were all right. What the fuck was this country coming to when one soldier couldn't even trust another?

Just as Dupree centered the muzzle on Smith, the man's visor exploded outward. The exit wound formed a crater where his nose had been, making it look like he had two mouths. He crashed to the ground in front of the Humvee.

A few feet away, Emerson fell to his knees, gripping his neck. Blood streamed through his fingers and sheeted down his CBRN suit.

All around Dupree, Colorado National Guard soldiers and Marines scrambled for cover. Two of the guardsmen fired M16s at the bluffs.

Smith's men weren't con artists leading the ambush after all, Dupree realized. They were caught right in the middle of it, just like the Marines.

Dupree snapped into action. "McCabe, Sharps, covering fire!" He pulled the girl back to the relative safety of the Humvees. "Someone, get on the M240!"

The bark of 7.62 mm rounds sounded a few seconds later, and Dupree caught a glimpse of Snider manning the big gun in the sky. The tracer rounds lanced into the bluffs. Whoever the bastards were, they were dug in. Dupree couldn't see a single hostile from his position.

He shielded the girl with his body and reached for his rifle. It lay on the ground a foot away. A round ripped through his hand, and he pulled it back like a kid that had touched a hot stove. Blood gushed out of a hole in the center of his knife hand.

Dupree reached for the Beretta M9 on his holster instead. He pulled the pistol with his left hand. The pain in his right was severe, but it was already turning numb. He peeked around the bumper for a target just as the other two guardsmen collapsed to the ground, their bodies riddled with bullet holes.

It was just Dupree, McCabe, and Sharps now. The other two Marines hid behind the Humvee to his right. Sharps was gripping his right shoulder where he had taken a round. Three of the civilians were there, too, eyes all wide with terror.

"Give us covering fire!" Dupree shouted over the comm.

Snider, Runge, and Rodriguez were firing from the open door of the Black Hawk, but it wasn't enough to deter their attackers. Automatic gunfire replied from the bluffs. Dupree still couldn't see any of them.

"It's too hot to land, sir!" yelled one of the pilots.

The other pilot yelled back. "We can't leave them down there!"

A hard pause passed over the channel that felt like an hour. Dupree raised his M9 and searched for a target. Rounds punched into the concrete, pushing him back.

"Dupree, you got fifteen seconds to get to the troop hold," one of the pilots said.

Fifteen seconds, Dupree thought. Fifteen seconds stood between life and death. He looked down at the girl. She was staring blankly at nothing, catatonic.

"McCabe, grab this kid and get her to the chopper. Sharps, you and I are going to lay down covering fire." He pointed his bleeding hand at the other civilians. "You three, run as soon as we start shooting!"

Sharps met his eyes. There was fear in his gaze, but Dupree could see he was prepared to give his life in this moment. Dupree spared a precious second to nod at the young Marine.

"Ooh rah!" Sharps shouted.

Dupree yelled back, "Give these bastards hell!"

The moment Dupree stood to fire, he was hit by a round in the side. The bullet seized the air from his lungs. He grabbed the wound with his bleeding hand. Stars floated before his vision from the intense wave of pain.

Dupree looked up to a rocky outcropping and spotted the shooter. He lifted his M9 in his shaky left hand while the man who'd shot him pulled a magazine from his rifle. He tried to duck down, but there wasn't cover.

In the stolen moment, Dupree squeezed off three erratic shots. The first streaked into the sky, the second hit the rock in front of the man, and the third hit the tree to his right. Overwhelmed by pain, Dupree fell to one knee and dropped his pistol.

Above, the man stood and aimed his rifle.

So this is it. This is your last moment.

He was never going to see his boys or his ex-wife again. The extra salt on the wound was not knowing if she would even care. He had been a bad husband and a lousy dad, but he had to hope she still loved him to some degree.

To the side of his blurred vision, he saw Sharps running and screaming. The former basketball player was zigzagging like he was about to put up a layup. The fancy moves drew the attention of the man aiming his M4 at Dupree. He shifted the muzzle just as Sharps shouldered his rifle and fired a burst into the man's chest.

Sharps turned to run again, but he took a round from another shooter on the other side of the bluff. The bullets knocked him to the ground. He pushed himself up, but a second bullet ripped through his back, forcing him to the pavement. Lying flat, he looked over at Dupree wearing a mask of terror. The sniper finished the job with a shot to

Sharps' forehead.

Dupree tried to shout, but all that came out was a muffled grunt. He picked up his pistol, stood, and staggered out into the street to distract the remaining snipers. There were two left that Dupree could see.

"Snider, two o'clock," he gasped into the comm.

Snider directed the M240 fire on a short man perched on a rock to the north of the road. The rounds took off his arm.

Dupree turned slowly, looking for other targets. As he spun, he saw the carnage on the road. Sharps and Emerson were both lying in puddles of blood. The guardsmen were all sprawled out and leaking red. Three of the civilians were also down.

But some of them had escaped.

McCabe carried the little girl to the chopper as the pilots lowered to the ground. Two of the women had managed to limp away under the covering fire from Snider, Rodriguez, and Runge.

"Hurry, sir!" McCabe shouted.

Dupree tried to move toward the Black Hawk, but he only made it one step before he crashed to the ground, his legs giving out.

Over the crack of gunfire, Dupree made out what sounded like an engine. A pickup truck was racing toward the bridge. The men standing in the bed were already firing at the chopper.

"Get out of here," Dupree said.

"Sir!" McCabe shouted back. "I'm coming, just hold on."

"No!" Dupree yelled, his voice cracking. "Get Alex and those civilians to safety..."

"We can still—"

"And tell my wife…tell my ex-wife I love her and the boys."

The chirp and crack of gunfire sounded all around him. A round bit into the ground to his right. He lifted his head to watch the chopper pull away before collapsing to his stomach. Ribbons of red swarmed his vision. Dupree closed his eyes so he didn't have to look at Sharps.

At least some of them got away, he thought. Dupree found he was okay with dying, knowing that he'd done his best.

He opened his eyes to watch the Black Hawk traverse the skyline. He took in a breath of air that crackled in his chest. Blurred shapes flickered across his vision.

"Which one of you idiots shot this Humvee?" snarled a voice.

Dupree gripped his pistol and tried to lift it as a pair of boots stopped right in front of him.

The man kicked the gun from Dupree's grip, then bent down close enough that Dupree could see a squiggly scar on his forehead.

"You killed several of my men…" he said in a smooth, deep voice. He flicked the tag on Dupree's chest. "Lieutenant Dupree."

"Who are you?" Dupree managed to whisper.

"Who am I?" The man pointed at his chest and looked back at his men. "Who am I, boys?" He laughed and leaned back down.

"The General of the Sons of Liberty!" The men behind him raised their fists into the air.

"That's right," the man said. "I'm General motherfucking Fenix. I've been waiting years for something like this to happen. Ever since I got back from that sand trap shithole in the Middle East." He spread his arms out to point at his men. "*We've* been waiting."

He licked his lips, leaving them glistening. "The government has failed us. From one soldier to another, you already know that the tree of liberty must be refreshed from time to time with the blood of patriots and tyrants. I will lead the Sons of Liberty to take back what's ours."

"Fuck you," Dupree snorted. "Don't quote a Founding Father, you psychotic piece of shit."

"Man," Fenix said, his smile widening. "I was going to give you a swift death, but you just pissed me off. Let's go, boys. I want to get these vehicles and weapons back to the Castle before dark."

Dupree tried to raise himself up. He'd made his peace with dying, but he wasn't going to do it at the feet of some White Supremacist jack-off with delusions of grandeur.

Fenix watched him with an amused smile still plastered on his face. After a moment, Dupree collapsed back to the pavement, his strength gone. He reached out in vain for his pistol, which lay several yards away, his fingers raking through the mess of ash and blood.

The man mimed a gun with his thumb and forefinger, like a kid playing cops and robbers. "Bang, bang," Fenix said, chuckling to himself, before walking away.

8

"You're lucky he didn't shoot you in the head," said Sandra Spears.

Cindy Todd sat on the hospital bed in front of Sandra, both hands cuffed to the rails. The bullet had grazed her right shoulder. From what Sandra could see, the damage appeared to be limited to the epidermis and outer dermis.

The wound wasn't nearly as bad as the other gunshot victim, Martha. The woman Colton and Don had brought in from Highway 7 was lucky to be alive. It was remarkable, really. She should have been dead after the exposure to radiation, dehydration, and blood loss.

Some people are survivors, Sandra mused. *And some just get lucky, whether they deserve it or not.*

She continued cleaning Cindy's wound to prepare it for Doctor Duffy. When she had finished, he began stitching up the skin. That task became increasingly difficult every time Cindy opened her mouth. Sandra wanted to slap her—or worse—and Duffy didn't seem much more enthusiastic about treating their latest patient.

"The pig killed Eric. That piece of shit killed him!" Cindy said. She yelped in pain as Duffy yanked on a knot. "C'mon, at least gimme something. This fucking *hurts.*"

Sandra reached for the nearby cart for a topical anesthetic, but hesitated when Duffy shook his head.

"Chief Colton said no pain meds."

"What? That's barbaric!" Cindy protested. "I need

them. Those pigs shot me!"

"My brother shot you," Sandra said. "He's not a police officer."

Cindy looked away from the wound to meet Sandra's gaze. Sweat dribbled down Cindy's forehead and snot dripped from her nose—signs that she was suffering from opiate withdrawal. Sandra had seen this hundreds of times in patients. She had also seen it in both her ex-husband and Brown Feather. There was nothing like first-hand experience to identify an addict.

Without the opiates, Cindy would continue to crash until she was debilitated from a fever and terrible pain. It was like having the worst cold imaginable for weeks straight. Normally Sandra would have shown empathy, but she felt none for this woman. She was glad they weren't wasting medicine to treat her. Part of her wished Raven had finished the job.

No, you're both better than that.

Thoughts of Officer Rick Nelson and his family filled her mind as she waited for Doctor Duffy to finish stitching up the woman's shoulder. Did Cindy have any idea what she had done? Could she comprehend how her actions had ruined lives?

"You're lucky you didn't hurt my brother," Sandra said, unable to hold back her anger.

"Whatever, bitch," Cindy said.

Duffy shot Sandra a glare that told her to back off. She took a step away from the bed and watched as he continued to stitch up the wound. Cindy wiggled and squirmed against her restraints.

"Hold still," Duffy said. He paused and waited for Cindy to relax, then continued with the stitches.

A knock on the door interrupted him on the last loop.

Sergeant Aragon stepped inside the emergency room. He fixated on Cindy, his nostrils flared like an enraged animal. It seemed Sandra wasn't the only one who wanted to give Cindy a good dressing down.

"Miss Spears," Don said, his gaze shifting to her. "Your brother is outside in the parking lot and needs to talk to you."

"About what?" Sandra asked.

Don shrugged. "Didn't say." Sandra shook her head. If Raven was in trouble again, so help her...

"I'll finish up here," Duffy said.

Sandra didn't bother saying anything else to Cindy on her way out. Nothing she could say would have an impact on a delusional, addicted mind.

Sandra tossed her gloves into a wastebasket and reached for the hand sanitizer in her pocket as she followed Don into the hallway. He pushed open the double doors that led to the intensive care unit, where the smell of bleach filled her nose. White partitions separated beds from one another in the open space.

She tried to slip by unnoticed, but Doctor Newton called after her. "I need some help with Martha when you have a moment. Meet me in the isolation ward."

"I'll be back in a few minutes," Sandra said. She hustled through the room but slowed when she saw the drape cordoning off Teddy's bed was partially open. He was sitting up, blond hair ruffled in all directions, concentrating intently as he tried to figure out how to open a water bottle with only one hand.

"Hi, Teddy," Sandra said, waving.

He smiled, his cheeks dimpling. "Hi, Nurse Spears."

Seeing the boy smile was a miracle in itself, but watching him struggle with a small task like that made her heart ache. Children were resilient; even Allie was recovering just a day after being kidnapped and threatened by Brown Feather. But neither of them was out of the woods yet. It was going to take a lot of therapy to help Allie, and Teddy needed constant medical support.

Sandra left the ward, promising to bring Allie for a visit later, and jogged toward the lobby. Her daughter came running over from her seat next to Marie Brown, Teddy's mother, who'd become her usual babysitter during Sandra's shifts at the hospital.

"Mama, Uncle Raven and Creek are outside," Allie said, extending her hands.

Sandra hugged Allie, but kept her eyes on Raven in the parking lot. He was talking with Colton and Nathan next to his Jeep. Creek was sitting on his haunches near the bumper, looking up at the open lift gate. Inside were bags of gear and two CBRN suits.

"Allie, stay here," Sandra said.

"But Mom—"

Sandra hunched down in front of her daughter. "Baby, I'll be right back. Okay?"

Eyes downcast, Allie nodded solemnly. Sandra walked over to the doors, palmed them open, and strode out into the cool breeze.

"Raven, you want to explain all that gear in your Jeep?" Sandra said.

"Hey, sis," he replied gingerly.

She could tell by his sheepish grin that he was nervous.

"Where are you headed?" she asked.

Raven looked at Nathan and then Colton for support, but Sandra snapped her fingers to draw her brother's attention.

125

"Don't look at him. I asked you a question, Sam."

Nathan limped forward. His features were so swollen Sandra hardly recognized him. Her brother didn't look much better. The three men remained silent, none of them wanting to answer her question.

"Well?" she asked, moving her hands to her hips.

"I asked Raven if he would help track Nathan's nephew," Colton said. "I can't send any officers out there with them, and Raven's skills are perfect. If anyone can find Ty, it's—"

Sandra interrupted with a huff. "I thought a team was sent to find this boy?"

Nathan squinted as if he was in pain, probably because he was. The pilot had been through the meat grinder over the course of the past few days. If it were up to Sandra, he would be lying in a hospital bed.

"Ma'am—" he began to say when she cut him off.

"I told you not to call me ma'am."

Nathan sighed. "Sorry, Sandra. Someone took my nephew and killed two camp counselors. My sister is going crazy with worry."

Sandra brought her arms up and folded them across her chest. The cold bit through her scrubs, but it wasn't the wind that had just given her the chills.

"Who would do such a thing?" she asked. All trace of anger had slipped from her voice.

"We're not sure, but I'm hoping we will find out with your brother's help," Nathan said.

"Creek's going to stay here to look after you and Allie," Raven added, finally remembering how to speak. The dog stood and let out a low whine. "It's okay, boy. I won't be gone long."

Sandra shook her head in disbelief. "I don't

understand how either of you think you're in any shape to go out there. You both look like shit. Do you know what will happen if you get an infection, Raven? Without antibiotics, you could die from a cut. And Nathan, you have a broken arm, for God's sake."

"All due respect, but I'm trained for this sort of thing," Nathan said.

Raven nodded in agreement. "Same here. Have you forgotten I was a Force Recon Marine?"

A beeping sound came from the back of the Jeep. Nathan limped back over to his gear.

"That's probably my sister," he said.

A female voice sounded over the channel, but it didn't sound like the one Sandra had heard on Prospect Mountain.

"Major Sardetti, do you copy?"

Nathan pulled the radio from his rucksack and brought the receiver to his lips. "Roger that, this is Major Sardetti."

"This is Lieutenant Marco of the USS *John Stennis*. Secretary Montgomery asked me to get in touch with you to relay a message."

Nathan clicked the receiver. "Go ahead, over."

"Lieutenant Dupree's team was attacked on Interstate 70 about fifteen minutes ago. The Black Hawk managed to escape with half the team, but Lieutenant Dupree and several other Marines are MIA, presumed KIA."

Nathan cursed and lowered the receiver.

"Secretary Montgomery was moved to a secure location, but has given you the green light to head out and find her son."

A voice pulled Sandra back to the medical ward.

"Allie, get back here," said Marie Brown.

Sandra turned to see Allie walking into the parking lot. Marie stood in front of the building, lipping *sorry* to Sandra.

"Come here, sweetie," Sandra said. The girl buried her head in the crook of Sandra's arm.

"Major, do you copy?" Marco said over the radio.

Nathan held the receiver out in hesitation, then brought it back to his lips. "Tell my sister I'm heading out right now."

***

Raven watched Creek run after the Jeep in his side mirror. He almost slammed on the brakes to pick up his dog. For the past eighteen months, they had been best friends. Inseparable, even. Creek never talked back, always had Raven's back, and was a hell of a companion. That's exactly why Raven wouldn't risk bringing him. He simply couldn't ensure the dog's safety in the radioactive landscape.

He gunned the engine on the road out of town, leaving behind his dog, his family, and the town he now called home. This wasn't goodbye—it was just see you later.

Or so he kept telling himself.

Sandra was going to be pissed at him for a while, but he owed Nathan. Raven was the only one who could help the pilot right now.

"Still got a couple good hours of sunlight," Nathan said. "We should be able to make it most of the way before it gets too dark."

"Where was Dupree last seen?"

Nathan draped a map over his knees. "Somewhere

around this area on Interstate 70."

"Okay, then that's where we're headed," Raven said.

"Normally it would be quicker to take US-36, but I have a feeling those roads will be packed with refugees." He studied the map for several minutes. "Yeah, let's take Highway 7. It turns into 72 and then 119 intersects with Interstate 70."

Raven looked up as they passed Prospect Mountain. Brown Feather and Turtle were still up there.

Let them rot.

He slowed as he approached the roadblock on Highway 7. John Palmer, the firefighter turned soldier, was manning the barriers. He lowered his rifle and walked up to the driver's side window, eying the Jeep and their CBRN suits quizzically.

"Headed south?" Palmer asked. "Chief Colton approved this?"

"Yeah," Raven said.

Palmer looked to the south, then back at Raven, shaking his head.

"Good luck," he said, patting the Jeep. He motioned for his men to move the barriers out of the way.

As the Jeep growled away from Estes Park, Raven steeled himself for the road ahead. The men who had taken Ty weren't his only concern. From the sound of it, they were going to run into bodies. Lots of bodies.

He looked over his shoulder at his gear bag. The empty back seat made Raven sigh. He already missed Creek. Nathan was checking his Colt AR-15. He pulled a magazine from his rucksack and palmed it in the gun. Then he chambered a round with a click. He rested the gun next to him and pulled his M9. He placed the loaded pistol on the dashboard.

"I'm going to charge your rifle, too," Nathan said.

Raven reached out to stop him. "I'm good with my crossbow."

"No," Nathan said firmly. "You're not taking a knife to a gun fight. Whoever took out half of Lieutenant Dupree's team are very well trained."

"How do you know?"

"You don't know who Lieutenant Jeff Dupree is— was—do you?"

Raven shook his head.

"He was awarded a Silver Star for gallantry in Iraq several years ago."

"What did he do?"

"Called an airstrike on his position to save a dozen Marines," Nathan said. "I know this because one of the pilots who nearly killed Dupree is a buddy of mine."

"So he survived the airstrike but then got murdered by a bunch of American assholes back at home. Jesus Christ, that is awful."

Nathan grabbed the other Colt AR-15 from the back seat. "Don't worry, we're going to avenge Lieutenant Dupree, but you're going to need to pack some heat, brother."

Raven wasn't sure what surprised him more—the fact Nathan had called him "brother," or the fact he'd said, "pack some heat."

"Whoever ambushed Dupree and his men know what they're doing. We have to be smart. There's only two of us," Nathan added.

"Fine," Raven said. He focused back on the road while Nathan prepared their weapons and pulled out the Geiger counter.

The road wound through the hills outside of Estes Park. Abandoned vehicles were sporadic here. Most of them had already been pushed off to the side of the road, allowing Raven to gun the Jeep. He punched the gas down, speeding through the winding roads at sixty miles an hour.

They passed the remaining homesteads bordering the town, but there was no sign of people out here. No refugees, no raiders—nothing but open road surrounded by rolling hills dotted with pine trees. They climbed out of the valley, leaving civilization behind for a view of the fires to the southwest. A fortress of smoke drifted over the mountains.

"That looks bad," Nathan said. "I hope we can get through."

Raven took in a breath of filtered air and studied the fires in the distance. There was no way to tell exactly how far away they were. In the mountains, it was always hard to gauge distance. What looked like two miles could end up being ten.

They drove in silence, Raven using the time to think. As his Jeep continued the climb, he couldn't help but feel like he had somehow climbed out of the hole he had dug himself into after leaving the Marines. He had a purpose again, a mission, thanks to Colton. Raven hadn't realized how much he'd been drowning without that. He still felt the weight of responsibility on his shoulders because of the disastrous raid in North Korea his squad had been part of, but he realized now that there had probably been countless factors leading up to the attack. In a way, the bombs had given him a fresh start—a chance to prove the man he was.

"So, what's next?" Nathan said. "How do you plan on

finding my nephew?"

Raven pulled his thoughts back to the present. "Growing up on the Rez, I was taught two ways to hunt animals and people. The first you already know. You look for tracks, broken vegetation, droppings, or some other sort of trail. You listen for any sounds the chase might make and pay attention to your other senses. The smell of a campfire, for example."

"And the other way?"

Raven cracked a grin. "You let your chase find you."

"Sounds like a terrible plan to me."

"Most of mine seem to be pretty bad at the beginning," Raven said with a chuckle. "But they have a roundabout way of turning out all right."

His smile faded when he saw the lumps on the road ahead.

"Look like bodies," he said, easing off the gas. "Better check for radiation."

Raven scanned the area as he drove up the steep slope. To the left of the road, a metal barrier separated them from plummeting over the side into the valley below. To the right, ponderosa pines and aspen trees grew out of the sandy brown dirt. Farther up the hill, boulders and trees speckled the terrain.

There were hundreds of places for people to hide. His eyes were working in overdrive, flitting across the canvas for contacts. Anyone out here would be a potential hostile, especially if they were suffering from radiation poisoning—desperate, delusional, and violent.

At the top of the road were two bodies, a male and a female. Both were wearing blue ponchos and blue jeans. He slowed on the approach, one hand on the wheel, the other on the handle of the Glock he had holstered on a strap around his right leg.

The Geiger counter ticked to life, and Nathan held the device up. The crackling told Raven they were entering a red zone.

"It's bad," Nathan confirmed. "Really bad."

Raven's suit suddenly seemed to tighten around his chest, and he found it hard to breathe. "How long do these filters last?"

"Don't worry, we have plenty," Nathan said.

Raven killed the engine and slipped the key inside his tactical vest. He joined Nathan in the street after grabbing the other Colt AR-15. Side by side, they swept their rifles over the landscape.

"Check them," Nathan said, pointing at the bodies.

Raven gripped his rifle as he made his way toward the corpses. Gusting wind swept across the bodies, rustling their ponchos. Nathan raked his rifle over the trees, paused, and then continued roving the muzzle over the terrain. He gave the all clear with a hand signal.

"She's dead," Raven said. He looked down at the woman's features. They seemed to be frozen in agony. Her mouth was agape, and her eyes were wide open. He checked the man by rolling him over while Nathan continued up the road.

"Raven, come check this out," Nathan called.

He left the corpses and hustled up the hill, stopping at the crest to stare at one of the grimmest sights he had ever seen in his entire life.

Plumes of smoke billowed away from Longs Peak like a volcano had just blown its top. Hundreds of thousands of trees burned to the southwest of Rocky Mountain National Park.

"I can't tell if the road goes through those fires, but

there's no way we'll make it through if it does," Nathan said.

"What other options do we have? We could go around, or you could wait for your sister to find you a ride via helicopter. But by then it could be too late for Ty."

Nathan continued to stare at the smoke as if he was searching for something.

"Come on, let's get back to the Jeep," Raven said. He stopped at the two corpses to shut their eyes and then hurried back to his vehicle.

Nathan climbed in the passenger seat and exhaled. "Let me see if I can reach anyone on the radio who might know how the roads are east of here. Maybe we can backtrack and take the other route."

He pulled out his radio and scrolled to the channel he had been using to contact his sister.

"Lieutenant Marco, this is Major Sardetti. Do you copy? Over."

The reply of static hissed out of the speakers.

"Pull over for a sec," Nathan asked.

Raven eased to a stop and looked out over the valley. Nathan fiddled with the antennae, and then opened the door.

"Stay here, I'll be right back," he said.

Raven kept one hand on the steering wheel, and the other on the gears. He tried to listen to Nathan talking outside, but the stuffy helmet made it difficult to hear.

A few minutes later, Nathan jumped back into the Jeep.

"So?" Raven asked. "Did Lieutenant Marco—"

"I couldn't get through to Marco. I tried my contact at Cheyenne Mountain though, and he said the roads to the east are…not an option." Nathan paused, and then explained, "They've been overtaken by raiders. Our only option is to continue south."

Raven tapped the steering wheel and put the vehicle in first gear. "All right, girl. Into the gauntlet we go."

9

Colton walked toward Bond Park with his wife and daughter. Their hands felt so fragile against his calloused skin, but his girls were tougher than they seemed. He tightened his grip, thankful that he could still hold them. Rex and Lilly Stone would never be able to hold Melissa's hands again. Parents had lost children and children had lost parents. Officer Rick Nelson's little girl wouldn't even remember hearing her daddy's voice.

That was the new reality. America wasn't at war—they'd already lost it. The battle they faced wasn't for victory but survival.

But tonight they weren't gathered in despair. Despite everything, they were gathered in celebration. Estes Park had avoided the radiation that had blanketed the region to the south, Brown Feather and his brother were dead, and Milo and Cindy Todd were in jail. For the first time in days, people weren't afraid to leave their homes.

Colton forgot some of his worries as the scent of barbeque drifted through the heart of the town. The torches burning around the perimeter of Bond Park cast a glow over platters of food the local restaurants and stores had donated. The display stacked on tables made his stomach growl. He had a feeling this was going to be the last time he would see this much food for some time.

"What do we do when it's all gone?" Kelly asked.

"You better start liking elk," Colton said. "You, too, kiddo."

Risa looked up at him, curious eyes meeting his own. "We can't eat Rudolph, can we?"

Kelly and Colton both chuckled.

"Rudolph is a reindeer, sweetie. Elk are a different type of animal," Kelly said.

"I'm already putting together hunting parties. We have a good supply of wild game up here." Colton lifted his chin at the tables. "Plus, that isn't the only meat in town."

He looked over his shoulder to make sure no one was listening, then whispered, "I had Officer Hines take several loads up Trail Ridge Road and store the reserves in a meat locker we built. The rest I decided to have cooked up before it goes bad."

"Good thinking," Kelly said. She brushed her braided hair over her shoulder and smiled warmly at him. Colton still hadn't told his wife about Martha, or the violence on the road, but he wasn't going to spoil the mood now by scaring her.

"I'm hungry," Risa chirped.

"Okay, okay," Colton said. "Let's go grab some plates. Tonight, you can eat all you want."

Risa skipped ahead to join a growing crowd. Kelly hurried after her, but Colton took his time, enjoying the smiles and listening to the friendly conversations. For a moment, it almost seemed like a normal night in Estes Park—until he saw Detective Lindsey Plymouth, dressed in uniform, jogging over to him.

"Chief, we just got a report of a break-in at the coffee shop on MacGregor Avenue," she said. "I've also got some more bad news."

Colton wanted to sigh, but instead he jerked his chin for Lindsey to follow him away from the crowd. Neither of them spoke as they moved through the locals. He tried to hurry past the picnic table where Mayor Gail Andrews and Tom Feagen, the town administrator, were sitting, but they spotted him.

"Hey, Chief," Gail called. "Can I have a word?"

Jim Meyers, the owner of the Stanley Hotel, sat down at the table and nodded at Colton, but Tom merely shoved a spoon of beans in his mouth and looked back down at his food.

"How's the Stanley?" Colton asked.

Jim shrugged a shoulder. "Could be worse."

Gail tapped a finger on the table. "Colton, do you have a few minutes?"

"I'll be right back, Mayor."

Colton didn't wait for the inevitable protest. He put his hand on Lindsey's shoulder and guided her away from the table. This time they didn't stop for anyone until they got to the street. Looking back over the celebration, Colton had a feeling the chance to enjoy a barbecue with his family had just slipped away.

"I always thought I was lucky working up here. I was insulated from politics," he said.

Lindsey raised her eyebrows. "Insulated from most everything else, too," she said.

"I did get a little bored, but at least we had peace and quiet," Colton admitted. He shoved his hands in his pocket and said, "Spill the bad news."

Lindsey didn't hesitate. "Officer Matthew is checking out the report of the break-in on MacGregor, but this is the third one today, Chief. We've been seeing vandalism across town. So far it's been limited to a few broken windows and spray paint, but I'm worried it will get worse."

Colton shook his head. "We don't have enough officers, damn it."

"I know, which is why I thought I'd make a suggestion…"

Lindsey looked over Colton's shoulder at the citizens gathered in the park. He turned to see what she was checking out. Then he realized what she was thinking.

"No," he said.

"But Chief, there are thousands of people in town who don't have a damn thing to do but wait for help to come. And think about all those tourists stranded here."

"I'm having them all vetted. If we find any police officers, then I'll gladly deputize them if they want to join our department."

Lindsey flicked her nose with a thumb like a rapper about to bust a rhyme. Colton really hated it when she did that.

"Just say it," he said.

"You've got to start trusting people, Chief. I know you have issues with Don, but that's exactly why we need more help. I about got killed today, and things aren't getting any better out there."

Damn it, she was right. Jake was gone, Raven might not make it back from the rescue mission, and Don was about as trustworthy as a snake.

"I know a few former soldiers that could help us keep things under control…for a small price," Lindsey said cautiously.

"A mercenary force," Colton muttered. He shook his head warily. "If this is going to happen, then I want you in charge. Not Don. Okay?"

Lindsey smiled. "I got your back, sir. Don't you worry."

She jogged back to the station, and Colton returned to the barbecue. He spotted Kelly and Risa eating at a table with several of their neighbors. His mouth watered when he passed a platter of chicken wings. Before he could start loading up a plate, Mayor Andrews called out for him again.

Colton let out a short sigh to prepare for what would likely be worse than a grilling in front of a congressional committee. Every face looked up from their meals with the same skeptical gaze.

Gail set her fork down neatly on her plate. "I heard you gave a large amount of our gear and the Jeep to Sam Spears and Major Sardetti."

"Yes, I did, Mayor. It's Raven's Jeep."

"No, it *was* his," Tom cut in. "Just like this food *used* to belong to the stores in town. Things changed when those bombs dropped. If we're going to survive the winter, we need our resources, Marcus."

"Chief," Colton corrected. "And if we're going to survive the winter, you need to get off your ass and start doing something other than complaining and eating free chicken wings. Raven and Nathan helped me kill Brown Feather and Turtle, and now they're off trying to find the lost son of the Secretary of Defense. What do you plan on doing?"

Tom wiped barbeque sauce off his lips with a napkin and stuttered, "I—that's hardly—"

"Listen, Chief," Gail said mildly. "I think Tom's point is that we need to be careful with valuable resources. For example, the woman you brought into town today." The mayor looked at those around her and then back at

Colton. "I was told she was nearly dead."

"But she pulled through," Colton said. He didn't know where Gail was getting her information, but he was starting to lose his patience.

"But what will it cost to keep her alive?" she asked.

"Ma'am, if you think I'm going to let innocent people die, then we need to have a very serious talk. I'm all about securing our town and having a vetting process on who we let in, but part of my job is protecting those who can't protect themselves."

Gail rubbed her forehead. "We can't save everyone, Chief."

"It's us or them," Tom said gravely.

Colton mastered his temper with difficulty. "Martha was *shot*, Mayor. That's different. Did you just expect me to let her die on the road? What if that was your mother, or sister, or daughter?"

"But she isn't from Estes Park," Tom argued.

"I'm making the best choices I can in a bad situation," Colton said, trying to sound reasonable. "It's my job to make those calls."

Gail looked at him over her green-rimmed glasses. "Your own officers are questioning your orders."

Several other families enjoying their meals turned to listen to the conversation. Colton clenched his fist. Now he knew where she was getting her info. Don was worse than a snake; he was a weasel.

"Ma'am—" Colton began to say.

"Do you really think Raven and Major Sardetti are coming back?" Gail interrupted. "Raven is hardly reliable. How many times has he been in and out of jail?"

"Excuse me?" snapped a voice that Colton knew all too well. He turned to see Sandra Spears standing nearby with Allie by her side.

"What did you say about my brother?" Sandra said.

Gail looked Sandra square in the eyes. "I'm only expressing an opinion held by many of my constituents."

"My brother is coming back, and I worked all afternoon to make sure Martha does make it. Turns out she's a doctor, someone this town really needs, and Colton saved her life. You should be thanking him," Sandra said.

Gail smiled warmly. "I'm grateful to hear she might pull through, Nurse Spears, but we need to figure out—"

"Hey!" Tom shouted, cutting her off. He stood and pointed as Creek darted away from the table with a barbequed rib in his mouth.

"That stupid dog took my food," Tom said.

Sandra let out an impressive whistle. Creek trotted over, his prize still clutched in his jaws. She pointed at the ground. The dog reluctantly dropped the bone and sat on his hind legs.

"You're wrong about Raven, Mayor. He and Major Sardetti will both return. With that Jeep," Colton said confidently. "Now if you'll excuse me, it's been a long day and I'm going to have dinner with my family."

Gail nodded curtly. "Good night. I'll see you in the morning."

Colton didn't return the formality. He strode away with his hands in his pockets and his head down. He didn't want to talk to anyone else but Kelly and Risa.

"Wait up, Chief," Sandra called after him. "Do you mind if we join you for supper? I just got off a fourteen-hour shift, and they told us to come down here to get some food."

Colton didn't have the heart to tell her no. He smiled

and gestured at the table where Kelly and Risa were already seated.

"How's Martha doing?" Colton asked.

"She's a tough lady, but she wouldn't be here if it weren't for you," Sandra said. "You did a good thing, performing CPR. Did you get checked out for radiation exposure afterward?"

"I'm fine," Colton said. "Don't tell my wife about that, by the way."

They reached the table and Colton made the introductions.

Kelly stood and wiped her lips with a napkin, then held out a hand. "Nice to meet you. I've heard a lot about you and your brother."

Sandra scowled. "I get that a lot."

"No, mostly good stuff," Kelly said. She hid her lie with a smile.

"Sweetie, you remember Allie, right?" Colton said.

Risa nodded and offered Allie some of her potato chips. Creek looked like he wanted to take her up on the offer, but Allie pushed her face against Sandra's side. He didn't remember Sandra's daughter being so shy, but she'd been through a lot recently.

"Please, have a seat," Kelly said.

"We're going to grab some food first," Sandra said. "You stay, Creek."

The dog sat next to Colton, looking up with dark, pleading eyes.

"Let me guess, you're starving to death," Colton said with a grin.

"I made you dinner," Risa said proudly.

A hearty meal of chicken wings, mashed potatoes, and beans was lumped on a plastic plate in front of him, but

Colton was no longer hungry. Tomorrow would mark the sixth day since the attack. Things weren't getting better, and help might never come. Gail still seemed to think she was in charge of a quaint little tourist town in the mountains, but the truth was that Estes Park was in the middle of a warzone. People like Don, Gail, and Tom would never see the situation as Colton did: with a soldier's eyes.

His gaze swept across the park, taking in both familiar faces and strangers who'd been stranded in town. How many of them understood what was really going on? And how would they react when they realized things were never going to go back to the way they were?

Colton grabbed the plate and set it down in front of Creek. At least one of them was going home with a full stomach tonight.

***

A twelve-foot bank of grass bordered the circular island about the size of two football fields. The walls protected Charlize from the wind, and it also blocked the view from any tourists who might pass this way on a boat.

The island was too perfect to be natural. It was manmade.

She stood at the edge of the boat ramp, the only spot where she could actually see the ocean. Chief Fernandez and his Navy SEALs were climbing back into the boat that had dropped her and Albert off. He threw up a stiff salute and said, "Good luck, Secretary Montgomery."

"Stay safe, Chief," she replied.

She watched the boat zip over the waves toward the mainland. They were going back out there, but this time they weren't being inserted under the cover of darkness in some foreign country. Their duty was to hold security on an American highway used for decades by tourists traveling to Cocoa Beach, the Kennedy Space Center, and Disney World.

One of the Marines nearby called out to her over the whistle of the wind. He guided them across the island toward a blocky concrete structure. It towered over a group of soldiers. In the middle of the group stood a man in a blue uniform with a chest full of medals. He stepped out to meet them and offered his hand to Charlize.

"Welcome, Madame Secretary," he said. "It's good to see you again. As you may remember, I'm General Justin Thor. Please follow me inside."

His voice was rough, and his face was even rougher, with one brown eye recognizably larger than the other. The pain was making it difficult to think, but she only vaguely remembered this man. Her eyes flitted to his three-star rank, but nothing rang a bell. Usually she had a good memory, but the meds and constant anxiety had jumbled her mind. Charlize thought she might have met General Thor at a budget hearing on special projects, but before she could recall anything else, the screech of the blast doors derailed her train of thought.

"Thank you, General," she said, shaking his hand.

"This way," Thor said, gesturing for her to proceed into the hallway beyond the blast doors. Banks of lights guided them toward elevator doors at the end of the short passage.

"I certainly hope this facility was better designed than the PEOC," Albert said.

Thor looked over his shoulder and smiled. "It's the safest place in the world, in my opinion. I'm a bit biased, though, because I helped oversee the construction. You'll see why I'm so confident shortly."

Charlize was too tired and in too much pain to care much about the engineering that went into this place. She stepped into the elevator and rested her back against the wall. The bandages on her burned hand felt tight, pain pulsating down her forearm. She needed to have them changed soon.

The elevator chirped and began to descend. Beads of sweat dripped down her forehead. She used the sleeve of her sweatshirt to dab away the sweat, and with it the residue of the burn gel. The one painkiller she'd taken today had worn off completely. Her nerves prickled, and her breathing had become shallower.

"Are you feeling okay, ma'am?" Albert asked.

Charlize tried to arrange her face into an expressionless mask. "I'm fine." The truth was that she felt like she might start screaming if she had to be stuck in this tiny metal box a moment longer. She'd never been claustrophobic, but being trapped in the nightmarish remains of the destroyed bunker beneath the White House had apparently done more than just physical damage.

"We have a very good medical facility here, Madame Secretary," Thor said. "I've already spoken with our doctors, and they are prepared to continue your treatment."

"I want to get to the command room first. I assume President Diego is already there."

Thor offered a brusque nod. "He asked me to escort you to Command personally."

The elevator jolted slightly when they reached the bottom and the doors whisked open, revealing another hallway and a second pair of doors ahead. Two rigid Marines holding M4 carbines stood guard.

They both snapped to attention as she approached. The one on the right moved aside to allow Thor access to the control panel. This time the doors opened to reveal a short metal platform leading to even more doors. The seams of those doors parted, and Charlize saw what looked like a fancy subway car. A dozen white leather seats furnished the windowless space.

"What's this?" she asked, hesitating on the threshold. She wiped more sweat from her forehead.

"Our ride to Constellation."

"I thought this *was* Constellation," Albert said.

"Not yet," Thor said. "We're still two miles away. This train will take us underneath the ocean floor to the main facility."

Charlize followed him across the platform into the train car. She took a seat next to Albert, wincing at the pain that raced up her back. The panel of lights above flashed green after the door sealed behind them. She immediately felt as though the air was being sucked from the small, enclosed space. General Thor sat across from them and clasped his hands together, fiddling with a gold Air Force ring.

A soft vibration reverberated through the train. There was a jolt as they separated from the docking station, and then a series of smooth clicks. The train quickly picked up speed, and all sense of motion vanished.

Charlize took in short breaths, trying to manage the growing pain and anxiety. She was going to have to take another pill if she wanted to function today. There was no way around it now. She blinked several times and eyed the Marine sitting to Thor's right, who was cupping an earpiece. The younger man leaned over and said something to the general.

Thor looked up at Charlize and proudly announced, "Constellation is officially now the home of U.S. Northern Command and our recovery efforts. President Diego just gave the order."

Charlize sank into her seat. The news meant she was going to be here for a while.

"Do you have a family?" she asked him.

Thor lifted a brow. "Pardon me?"

"Do you have a wife and kids?" she asked. There was a reason for her question. She wanted to know right away if he was going to help her get Ty back.

"No, Madame Secretary. Live free and die free. That's the way I've lived my life."

Charlize couldn't help but nod. "Easier to focus on a war when you don't have to worry about kids. I get that."

"Indeed, ma'am."

He looked at his watch. "We should be under the ocean now and will reach Constellation in about ten minutes."

Charlize closed her eyes for several moments. When she opened them again, her vision blurred and her stomach churned.

"Ma'am, I think we should go straight to the medical facility," Albert said quietly.

"No," she said, stiffening in the leather seat. "Take me to the command center first."

He hesitated this time. "You said if I ever needed to talk to you, I could speak freely."

She glanced over and met his sad eyes.

"I can't protect you if you don't let me help you," Albert said. "You need to see a doctor."

"I know, and I will, right after the command center, I promise."

Albert moved his lips to the side and then nodded. "Fine, but right after that. Even if I have to carry you there."

"I promise." She managed a smile and considered talking to him about his wife, Jane, and daughters, Kylie and Abigail. Charlize was all too aware that he'd chosen to protect her instead of going to them during the attack on Washington. If he regretted his choice or resented her, he didn't show it. Then again, Albert rarely ever let any emotion show on his face. Sometime soon, they'd have to talk about what had happened.

But this was not the time or the place for that conversation. Instead, she closed her eyes to transport herself to a place where there was no pain or worry. She imagined the cockpit of her F-15 Strike Eagle, tearing over the ocean. Too soon, a hand on her arm brought her back to reality.

"We're here," Albert said.

He helped her stand with deliberate care. As soon as she was on both feet, the world began to spin. The green light seemed to flash in and out, and the white walls blurred. She blinked away the dizziness, swallowed, and drew in a shaky breath.

Albert helped her through the doors. Outside, Thor was talking to a Marine next to a sign that read *Level A*. He gestured for her to follow them down a windowless passage.

Boots pounded the tile floor behind them, the three Marines following. Charlize leaned on Albert. He was enough of a gentleman not to mention it, but his forehead wrinkled in concern. Movement flashed ahead in the first junction. A woman and man in white lab coats walked by with tablets in their hands. They glanced in her direction before disappearing around the corner.

The next hallway was filled with more people dressed in the white lab coats. Some of them chatted quietly, but others hurried to and fro with urgency. People flowed through the open double doors ahead.

"That's the cafeteria," Thor said. "There's also a large study, library, and entertainment center on this level. Barracks and restroom facilities are on Level B. Labs and the medical facility are on Level C."

"Labs?" Charlize asked. "I thought this was a bunker."

Thor smiled like he was happy she asked the question. "This is a research facility, ma'am. We built Constellation to house over three hundred people, mostly scientists. Over the past five days, we've brought in the brightest minds our country has to offer."

A flashback to the budget briefing years ago emerged in her mind. There had been a line item in that funding request for a top-secret facility. Was this it?

"President Diego wanted me to wait to give you the full tour," Thor said. "Come on, we're almost to Command."

He continued walking, but Charlize had more questions.

"What is the purpose of this facility?" she asked.

Thor looked over his shoulder. "Constellation was designed to help lead recovery efforts in case of a major disaster like an asteroid strike. Needless to say, it's also helped us hit the ground running with the response to the EMP attack."

Thor stopped outside a pair of wide black doors, where a pair of Marines came to attention. They pushed the doors open to reveal a two-level circular room with a domed ceiling. Monitors lined every wall, and a holographic map of the United States was projected in the air over a long table at the bottom.

President Diego stood in front of that table, his arm in a sling. Staff, scientists, and military personnel bustled around the room, the worker drones in the hive of the command center. Diego looked up when the doors opened and nodded to Charlize.

Charlize tried to focus on Diego's face, but it seemed to split into three overlapping images. She blinked several times until her vision returned to normal.

The president was smiling. "Welcome, Secretary Montgomery. Now that you're back on your feet, I'm hoping you can start to lead the war effort."

"Yes, sir, I'm ready." Charlize staggered slightly, and Albert reached out. She hardly felt the pressure on her arm from his grip. She pulled away, determined to stand on her own.

"Wonderful," Diego said.

"I'm anxious to get started, sir. We need to find those North Korean submarines before they can inflict more damage on our country," Charlize heard herself saying, but she felt strangely disconnected from the present moment. "I ordered HSM squadrons deployed before leaving—"

The migraine that had settled behind her eyes pounded, driving a spike of pain into her brain. A powerful wave of nausea and light-headedness followed, but she remained upright. Diego reached the top of the stairs. Once again, he blurred into triplets.

"Are you ready to help me take back our country?" Diego asked.

The room began to spin, and her knees wobbled.

"Madame Secretary," Diego said. He turned to Albert. "Is she okay?"

"No, she's not, sir," Albert said.

Charlize tried to protest, but the world suddenly changed orientation and she found herself staring at the domed ceiling. The white lights brightened into a blanket overhead, searing her eyes and igniting her migraine.

Albert's kind face moved into view above like an eclipse, and she felt her body rising into the air as he hoisted her up in his arms.

"Guess I'm carrying you to that medical ward after all, ma'am," Albert said.

10

It sounded like someone was being tortured in another room. Ty Montgomery wrapped his arms across his chest, shivering. He was trapped in a cell smaller than his cabin at camp. There were two beds, but three kids were locked inside. Micah tried the handle again and then sat down next to Emma on the other bed. Their hair was still wet from being hosed down.

"Why did they lock us in here?" Micah asked.

"We're hostages," Ty said. "They don't want us to escape."

His mom's bodyguard had gone over all kind of drills with him in case something bad happened, but Ty had forgotten Albert's rules when it mattered. He never should have told General Fenix his name. But if he hadn't, they might have hurt him like they were hurting someone right now.

The screaming stopped abruptly, but Ty continued shaking. Dr. Rollins had told him he was going to be fine, but now he was starting to wonder. The sweatpants and sweatshirt the men had given him were hardly enough to keep out the cold, and his stomach felt sour again.

Ty pulled the quilt up over his legs. Since he couldn't feel anything below his pelvis, it was vital to keep his legs and feet warm.

Emma started sobbing into her brother's shoulder when another scream reverberated down the hallway outside their room.

"It's okay," Ty said. "My mom is going to come get us out of here."

The light bulb dangling from a cord illuminated Emma's frightened, rash-covered face. She sat with her small legs hanging over the side of the bunk. Both her and her brother were younger than Ty by a few years, and he decided it was his responsibility to look after them.

"I want my mama," Emma cried.

"Mama and Papa are gone," Micah said. It sounded to Ty like it wasn't the first time he'd explained this to his little sister.

"I'm sorry for your loss," Ty said solemnly, just like his mother had taught him to say when someone was grieving.

Micah wiped the tears from his sister's face. She stopped crying after a few minutes, and her sobs were replaced by the plop of water from the ceiling into a bucket near the metal door. Water careened down the side of the rocky walls and collected in a puddle at the foot of Ty's bed. He wasn't sure where they were, but he guessed they were inside a mountain. Too bad there were a lot of those in Colorado.

"They called this place the Castle, right?" Ty asked.

Emma's eyes widened. "Like the kind with a prince and princess?"

"No. Not a real castle," Micah said, shaking his head at his sister.

"Why did they bring us here?" Emma looked at Ty for an answer.

Ty wasn't exactly sure, and he didn't want to scare the kids with his ideas. He still didn't understand what Dr. Rollins had told him about helping the General create an army. How was Ty going to help him with that? All he knew for sure was that most of these men were bad and they couldn't be trusted.

"Don't worry," Ty said again. "It's going to be—"

A long, pained screech split the air like someone was being burned with a hot iron. Micah and Emma's eyes both widened.

"Why are they hurting that man?" Micah asked, his lips trembling.

Ty tilted his head, trying to listen, but the screaming faded away, replaced with the plop, plop of water in the bucket and approaching footsteps.

"They got Joshua and Bernie," said a smooth, deep voice that had to be General Fenix. "How the hell did you fuck this up so bad, Carson? I thought you said it was the perfect ambush."

"They had a helicopter, sir."

"I know they had a helicopter," Fenix snapped. "I was in the pickup truck, but I should have been on those bluffs. Maybe then Joshua and Bernie would still be alive. You're a lousy shot, Carson."

The footsteps were growing louder. Micah and Emma moved away from the side of the bed, pressing their backs against the wall and huddling together.

"I-I'm sorry, sir," Carson stuttered.

Another scream rang out.

"I'm starting to think we'd have been better off with a vet or butcher, or even that lady from the highway you shot," the General said. "Are we sure that Rollins is a real doctor?"

Ty understood then. The man crying out wasn't being tortured after all. He was being operated on by Dr. Rollins.

"He really needs pain meds, or we're going to have to hear that for a while," Carson said.

"If he's not going to make it, then why would I do that?" Fenix said. "If he makes it, he makes it. But we need to save those meds for someone who has a better chance."

"Yes, sir."

"How about Tommy?" Fenix asked.

Ty's teeth were chattering from the cold. He locked his jaw so he could hear the next response. Aside from Doctor Rollins, Tommy was the only one of the men who had actually treated Ty decently since the men took them from the Easterseals camp.

The footsteps stopped outside the door.

"He took a bullet to the shoulder, but he should be okay," Carson said.

"Good, I need his help with something later," Fenix replied. "In the meantime, I'm going to pay a visit to our celebrity guest."

Ty pulled the quilt up around his chest as the metal door shrieked open. General Fenix stood in the entry with a toothy grin. He stroked the bottom of his beard several times as he looked at the kids with blue eyes colder than a glacier. Carson hovered behind Fenix, his beady eyes hidden by the bill of his black baseball cap. Tattoos—some faded, some bright black, lined his exposed hands, arms, and neck.

"So, you're really Charlize Montgomery's son?" Fenix asked. "I heard she just got a major promotion."

Ty decided he wasn't going to talk to the General this time. He sat on the bed, eyes downcast.

Fenix kicked the bucket of water near the door. It hit the wall with a crack, and water blossomed across the floor. Emma sobbed into Micah's shoulder.

"Stop crying, kid," Fenix said. He turned back to Ty. "You don't want to talk to me? I get it. I wouldn't want to talk to me either, but you're going to have to eventually. Because if you don't talk, Little Mr. Montgomery, then I might have to hurt someone."

Fenix looked back at Emma and Micah with a crazed grin.

***

The jagged mountains had swallowed the setting sun, but the magnificent glow from the forest fires in the next valley brightened the view atop the hill. Nathan watched the fires licking the terrain like the devil's tongue, spreading out to consume everything in their path. Pillars of smoke rising off the inferno clouded the dark horizon, blocking out the stars.

He had thought they would need the night vision goggles, but the fires provided plenty of light to see that the road was blocked below. He cursed and pounded the dashboard with his gloved hand. There was no way through. They had spent over an hour on a dirt road to get back to the highway, but now they were stuck again, close to the area where Lieutenant Dupree and his men had been ambushed. There wasn't a doubt in his mind that his nephew was somewhere on the other side of the blaze.

"Reminds me of the burning oil fields in Iraq," Raven said quietly, as if he was lost in a memory.

"We have to make a run for it," Nathan said.

"You nuts, Major?" Raven shot him a sideward glance, his dark brows arcing behind his visor. "We'll get cooked like jerky down there. It's already been hell just getting here."

"You heard what they've been saying over the radio," Nathan said. "This is the only way."

Raven looked back at the windshield. "I think I'd rather take my chances with raiders than fire. At least you can fight back against men."

Nathan reached for the door handle and opened the door before Raven could stop him. He was sick of arguing. For the past few hours they had bickered back and forth about continuing through the mountains and which routes to take.

"What are you doing?" Raven shouted. He grabbed at Nathan's uninjured arm, but Nathan yanked it away.

"Listen, Raven, I came out here to find my nephew. If it means I have to walk through those flames, then I will."

Raven slowly pulled his hand back and put it on the steering wheel.

"Jesus," he muttered, staring at the flickering glow. "I get it man, I do. I'd go through hell and back for Sandra and Allie. But this shit is crazy."

"The entire world has gone crazy, brother."

Raven tapped the wheel. "I know, believe me. But driving down this road is suicide. Our tires will freaking catch fire!"

Nathan pulled out his binoculars and scoped the valley. The flames had consumed half of the terrain, leaving behind a path of destruction. The fire was now engulfing the forest on the western and eastern sides of the highway. The jagged bluffs at the other end of the valley served as a natural barrier that seemed to be holding the fire from moving into the next ravine.

He felt like he was on a roller coaster that was about

to rocket through an oven. It was hard to imagine a situation where they would come out the other side unscathed.

Nathan zoomed in on the path, stopping on a bridge crossing a stream about a quarter mile from the bottom of the hill. Steam rose off the banks from the heated water.

The trees on the other side had been reduced to piles of embers, and several charred vehicles simmered on the asphalt just beyond the bridge. He centered the binoculars on the softened, deflated tires of a pickup truck. Raven was right; if they blew one of the Jeep tires, they were toast. But that didn't mean there wasn't a way forward.

Nathan looked at the stream snaking through the smoldering landscape one more time.

"I have an idea," he said, lowering his binoculars and closing the door. "I think we can get through if we keep to the right side of the road."

Raven pulled out his binoculars with one hand and brought them to his visor. He quickly lowered them. "I can't see shit with these."

"Try the night vision goggles," Nathan said.

Raven placed them over his helmet and raked them back and forth.

"Still can't see a way through, Major," he said a moment later.

"Just trust me. If we take a dip in that stream first, we have a shot of making it across the road."

"What if there's another fire on the other side of this valley?"

"Then we get in that water and wait it out. Our gas masks will protect us from the smoke as long as there is enough oxygen."

"Yeah, but not the heat," Raven said. "These filters remove the particles, but it doesn't cool the air. Our lungs will burn."

A sudden explosion flashed on the highway beyond the bridge. The gas tank of a pickup truck had burst into flames.

"That could be us in a few minutes," Raven said.

Nathan felt his heart catch in his chest. This was a risk, a really big one, but it was the only way forward. If they turned around, they would lose hours. It was a treacherous, slow path back to the turnoff, which would take them through territory that had fallen into anarchy.

"Please," Nathan said. "This isn't for me. Ty is just ten years old."

Raven let out a long sigh, tapped the steering wheel, and then shifted into gear.

"All right, sweet girl, time to show Major Sardetti what you got," he said to the Jeep.

He pushed down on the gas. Nathan fastened his seatbelt and watched the flames flickering across his vision. The headlights cut through the smoke drifting across the road at the bottom of the hill, capturing a graveyard of burned-out vehicles.

Flakes of ash and soot slowly coated the windshield. Raven turned on the wipers and sprayed the glass, but all it did was spread the ash into a streaky paste. Raven was leaning from side to side to see around the obscured view.

Just ahead, Nathan saw something lying in the middle of the road. "Don't hit that!"

"Shit, shit, shit," Raven cried. He tried to correct their trajectory, but that sent the Jeep on a crash course for another bulky object half-covered in ash.

"Watch out!" Nathan reached for the steering wheel, but it was too late.

The tires thumped over it with a sickening crack and squish.

"Oh God," Raven moaned. "That was a dead body, wasn't it?"

Nathan didn't respond. He grabbed the handle grip on the ceiling as the shocks jolted up and down again. Raven pushed down on the brakes, sliding across the road straight for a burning tree.

"We can't stop or we're going to catch on fire!" Nathan yelled. "Go left, go left!"

"Were those bodies?" Raven asked again. "Did I just run over bodies?"

"Yes, and there's another one at three o'clock!"

Raven turned left and fiddled with the windshield wipers, but that made things worse. The heat was rising inside the Jeep, making it harder to breath. Sweat beaded across his face.

"Ten o'clock!" he yelled.

Raven maneuvered past the corpse and swerved around a motorcycle lying on its side.

"Twelve o'clock!" Nathan shouted.

They came up on two charred vehicles framing the middle of the road. Raven squeezed through the gap, losing the passenger mirror in the process. He cursed, but kept the vehicle steady.

Nathan focused on the blaze. From this vantage point, the wall of fire looked larger than it had from the top of the hill. They weren't even in the thick of things yet, and the vehicle was already taking a beating. Even worse, the rising heat was almost unbearable inside the suit. He felt like he was slowly being cooked alive.

"Hold on," Raven said. He slowed and pulled onto the shoulder where there was a gap in the guardrail large enough to let a vehicle through. Rocks crunched under the tires as he drove toward the edge of the bank beside the stream.

Another body lay curled up at the water's edge below, a last and desperate attempt to survive the flames. Nathan looked away from the charred corpse and held on to his seat, preparing for the jarring descent. Nathan's bones rattled along with the chassis.

Raven steered around a boulder and pulled down the slope. The bloodied cow guard scraped against a rock before hitting the water. He drove out into the flow of mountain run-off. Normally the water was icy cold, but not tonight. Steam rose off the water where it lapped against the banks.

"My poor baby," Raven said, gritting his teeth.

He powered through the weak current, the water coming up over the tires. Nathan wasn't sure it would make much of a difference now that he could see the flames in the distance.

"You ready for this?" Raven said. He pulled up the other side of the bank and veered back onto the road, tires squealing over the pavement. The wipers finally cleared the windshield, providing a clear view of the fire eating the forest along the road.

Nathan gripped the handle tighter. Sheets of sweat poured down his face, stinging his skin. It felt like he was breathing inside a sauna.

"Punch it," Nathan said. It was the same thing he had said to his old wingman and best friend, 1st Lieutenant Mark Blake, a hundred times. He didn't know Raven well—and to be honest, he hadn't made much of an effort—but Nathan was suddenly glad to have a wingman again.

Raven pushed the pedal to the floor, the engine groaning in response.

"Come on, baby," he said.

Nathan leaned against the door to look at the front right tire.

"How's it looking?" Raven asked.

"Good... I think."

They swerved around a State Trooper's cruiser and sped between a pickup truck and cargo van, losing the driver's side mirror this time.

"Dammit," he cursed. "I'm so sorry, girl."

"Slow and steady, Raven."

Despite Nathan's warning, the speedometer continued to climb past fifty miles an hour. The inferno blazed like a tidal wave of fire. Nathan stared into it, determined. There was no turning back now.

Smoke seeped into the vehicle through the vents, squeezing past the towels they had covered them with. It swirled in the cabin, filling it with a black haze. The temperature continued to rise, too, and Nathan resisted the urge to take off his helmet and wipe his forehead.

This was it. They were almost to the flames.

Another pair of corpses smoldered on the asphalt just ahead. Raven twisted the wheel with calculated precision. Nathan tried to relax, but every muscle in his body was taut. He eyed the speedometer again. Sixty miles an hour.

The headlights cut through the smoke and hit a curve in the road ahead. Burning logs covered the path. Raven cut the gas and turned sharply, but there was nowhere to go but through the fire.

"Hold on!" he shouted.

The tires squealed. Fire licked the passenger side window, and Nathan reared back, gripping the seat with his broken arm. The Jeep tipped slightly, but then steadied out.

Nathan loosened his grip, pain setting in as Raven picked up speed again on the next stretch. Where there had once been a forest, there was now a cemetery of blackened timber and charcoaled boulders. Raven kept to the right side of the road, as far from the flames as possible.

Nathan twisted to see the terrain they had just passed through. The charcoaled cars, smoldering bodies on the ash covered road, and the flattened trees along the steaming river didn't seem real. He'd never seen anything like this.

He turned back to face the windshield as Raven drove up into the safety of the cliffs. It was hard to tell where the smoke ended and the night sky began. Both men were breathing heavily from the adrenaline rush and the heat. Nathan blinked away the sweat around his eyes and focused on the orange flicker rising over the gray rocks.

He already knew what it was before they'd reached the crest of the road. Raven brought the vehicle to a stop. He shut the Jeep off and stepped out onto the hot pavement with Nathan.

They grabbed their rifles and stared out over what looked like the epicenter of a nuclear warhead strike. He imagined this was how D.C. had appeared after the ground detonation.

"My God," Nathan muttered. He took a step forward, his boots crunching over debris scattered over the road.

"Winds are changing," Raven said.

"And keeping the smoke away from us for now."

"Yeah, but look at the way we came."

The shifting winds were spreading the fire behind them. They were trapped on a hilltop between two burning valleys. But at least the air wasn't as hot up here. He brought up his rifle and zoomed in on the bridge below. A burning Humvee blocked the road just in front of it.

Nathan backpedaled, his boots crunching over metal. He bent down and picked up a bullet casing, realization setting in. "Looks like someone ambushed that Humvee from up here."

Raven eyed the casing and then looked back down at the bridge. "You think those were Lieutenant Dupree's men?"

"I'd bet money on it," Nathan finally said.

"Come on, we better get back to the Jeep," Raven said.

They climbed inside and kept their rifles at the ready while the smoke rose off the fires all around them. It was hot, like sitting in a sauna. Nathan's clothes were soaked beneath his suit, but as long as the smoke and fires didn't shift, they would be safe up here for a while.

"You think anyone's still out here?" he asked.

"No way they could have survived the flames or the smoke." Raven squirmed in his seat. "Guess we're going to have to wait it out up here."

"The fires won't spread over the rocks, right?" Nathan asked, suddenly unsure.

Raven shrugged and closed his eyes. "You better hope so, Major. This was your bright idea."

"You're going to sleep, just like that?" Nathan asked.

He shrugged again. "We both need rest. I have a

feeling tomorrow's going to be a big day if we survive the night. You should try—"

A bloody hand slapped the passenger window and Raven let out a high-pitched scream. Nathan scooted back from the door.

"What the hell?" he muttered, staring at the blood streaks on the window.

Raven fumbled for his gun and Nathan grabbed the door handle. He pushed it open, throwing the person outside backward.

Nathan grabbed his rifle and aimed the muzzle at a soldier in a CBRN suit. He was doubled over, gripping his stomach.

"Help me," he said. "Please..."

Nathan lowered his rifle and got out of the truck. He approached the soldier carefully.

"What happened to you?" Nathan asked.

The man coughed and pointed toward the bridge. "We were ambushed down there."

Nathan glanced over his shoulder at Raven. He stood with his AR-15 aimed at the bluffs overhead, already hunting for threats.

A distant crack made Nathan flinch. The boom of thunder followed.

Nathan held up a hand toward the man. "What's your name?"

"Jeff," he said, his teeth chattering. "Jeff Dupree."

Raven and Nathan exchanged an incredulous look.

"Lieutenant Dupree," Nathan said. "I'm Major Nathan Sardetti... Charlize Montgomery's brother."

Dupree looked up, squinting behind his visor as if he was trying to see into the sun. He tried to talk, but blood bubbled out of his mouth.

Nathan took another step closer. "Let's get back to the Jeep so we can take a look at that wound."

Dupree allowed Nathan to help him back to the truck, grunting as they moved. Raven opened the back gate and helped Dupree sit down.

Nathan held in a breath when he saw the wounds. The lieutenant had taken a round to the side and another through his hand. It was remarkable he was still alive, but he'd lost a lot of blood.

"Lieutenant," Nathan said. "I know you're in a lot of pain, but I need to know about the men that shot you. I think they have my nephew."

Dupree winced and looked Nathan in the eye, lips quivering. "I'm sorry, Major," he choked and bent over, gripping his stomach. "We tried. I promise we tried."

"I'm sure you did," Nathan said. "I appreciate it more than you know. If there's anything you can tell me…"

The lieutenant coughed again, and dark blood seeped from between his fingers.

"Shit," said Raven.

Nathan waited for Dupree to regain his composure. The lieutenant licked his bloody lips, closed his eyes, and drew in a breath before opening his eyes again.

"The Sons of Liberty have Falcon," he said, his voice little more than a rasp.

"Who the hell are the Sons of Liberty?" Raven asked, looking from Dupree to Nathan. "And what's Falcon?"

Dupree reached up and gripped Nathan's hand. "Fenix," he said from between gritted teeth. "He called himself General Fenix. The Aryan bastards took Falcon to the Castle."

11

Colton was up early enough to watch the sun rise above the Rockies the day after the barbecue. Streaks of purple and yellow climbed above the highest jagged peak. To the south, smoke continued to fill the sky.

Mornings were his time, a peaceful hour to reflect on the day before and the day ahead. At least, they used to be. The cough of a diesel engine shattered the calm not long after Colton wandered outside. Lindsey Plymouth pulled into the driveway.

He held up a hand, motioning for her to wait, and then slipped back inside his house. Kelly and Risa were sitting down to eat a breakfast of bread and jam. Kelly pointed to a paper bag on the table.

"What's that?" he asked.

"Lunch," she said. "Don't forget to eat today."

Colton grinned, grabbed the bag, and kissed his wife and daughter goodbye. They followed him to the front door to watch him leave like they had virtually every morning before the attack.

"Mornin', Chief," Lindsey said. She waved at Kelly and Risa from the truck.

Despite the events of the day before, Lindsey didn't look too rattled. She smiled as he hopped into the passenger seat.

"Do you have good news or bad news for me this morning, Detective?"

Lindsey swiped her hair from her freckled forehead and looked in the rearview mirror as she backed out. "Little of both, Chief. I've already got a good list of people that qualify to be deputies. Got an Army Ranger and a guy that served two tours in Iraq as an MP."

Colton checked his bagged lunch. A tuna salad sandwich. Same thing he used to eat almost every day in Bond Park with Jake in the spring and summer, chatting about sports and fishing. It still hadn't quite hit Colton that he'd never have lunch with Jake again.

"What's the bad news?" he asked.

Lindsey started down the winding roads back into town. "Had another break-in. This time two men were spotted. I've already interviewed the clerk who thinks they're from the Harmony Foundation Treatment Center at the edge of the park."

"More addicts?" Colton said. "Jesus. I knew that place could end up being a liability. I want someone to head over there to see which residents have checked out or left."

"I'm already on it, sir."

"That it?" he asked hopefully.

"We're hearing reports of raiders over the new radio. Robberies, violence, and…a rape, sir."

Colton blinked. He had prepared himself for this, but hearing the word was a powerful reminder of how dangerous the world was becoming.

"You were right, Lindsey."

She tilted her head. "About what, sir?"

"Needing more deputies. I'm also going to run something by Mayor Andrews this morning. I've been thinking we should put spotters throughout the valley, now that we're going to have more bodies to help."

"Not a bad idea," Lindsey said. "Maybe we should assign someone to the Crow's Nest at Prospect Mountain at all times."

Colton nodded. "We're going to need more rifles. Might need to ask around if some of our residents are willing to donate some for our new officers."

"I'll put that on my list, sir." She paused, and then shot him a sideward glance. "Why do you have to run this stuff by Mayor Andrews? Woman doesn't know a damn thing about protecting Estes Park. She owns an art store, for God's sake."

"She's the mayor. She was elected. That still means something."

"Yeah, but—"

"You going to start questioning me like Don?" Colton asked.

Lindsey shook her head. "I've got your back one hundred and ten percent, sir." She parked the truck in front of town hall. Colton opened the door and went to get out but hesitated, remaining halfway inside the vehicle. Hearing about the rape and the increasing violence had him on edge.

"You watch your back out there today, kiddo," Colton said.

Lindsey's pale cheeks flared. "Kiddo?"

"Sorry. I meant to say Detective Plymouth."

"Uh-huh."

"Just be careful." He wished he had someone to send out there with her, but his officers were all busy protecting critical facilities or at road blocks that Don had assigned them.

"I'll report back in a few hours," Lindsey said. "Good luck with Mayor Andrews."

He patted the top of the truck and then walked into town hall. The mayor's office door was already propped open. He knocked anyways and stepped into the room. To his surprise, Don wasn't out checking on patrols—he was sitting in the chair in front of Gail's desk with his cowboy hat on his lap. He nodded at Colton, but didn't make an effort to stand.

"Good morning," Gail said.

Colton looked at Don. "What are you doing here?"

"Sergeant Aragon is here to discuss a few items," Gail said.

"Sergeant Aragon has work to do," Colton replied. "These daily briefings are supposed to be between just us two."

Gail took off her glasses and set them gently on the table. "Colton, please have a seat. Let's not make this meeting any more difficult than it needs to be."

She gestured for the chair next to Don.

"I'll stand," Colton said. He controlled his anger by counting to ten in his head. Starting a fight now wasn't going to do anyone any good.

"Suit yourself," Gail said. "Let's get right down to it. I want an update on what's going on outside this valley."

Colton gave her a rundown of the major law enforcement and recovery activities since the EMP attack, including the capture of the Todds, as well as his plans for elk hunting and water preservation. He finished with the task that he'd given Detective Plymouth to find new officers.

"How many officers?" Gail asked.

"As many as it takes," Don said before Colton could answer. "We can't let anyone in. We have to cut off the borders."

Colton narrowed his eyes at the sergeant. They'd butted heads before, but Don had never shown this kind of attitude. Maybe it was because Jake was gone, but Colton had the feeling Don had finally decided to make a power play.

"I'd like to be in charge of the deputizing," Don said. "Lindsey is a smart young lady, but she isn't trained in hiring."

"She's more than capable, and I've already put her in charge," Colton said.

Gail tapped her finger on the desk. "Back to the elk. How are we going to protect the herds? We need to be careful about how many we kill."

"I've already talked to Ranger Field, and he's going to help monitor the hunts and make sure the rules are enforced."

"When the food is gone, we're not getting more," Don said. "We need to consider evacuating all non-locals. There's no way we can feed everyone indefinitely."

"*Evacuating?*" Colton clenched his fist. "Is that what you'd call it?"

"Anyone who doesn't have a valuable skill set is a burden on our town," Don said. "You're the one who told our officers to not let anyone in who can't contribute."

"I also said anyone already in town the night of the attack would be safe here." Colton's fingers twitched as though they wanted nothing more than to curl into a fist and sock Don in the jaw. "I'm not going back on my word, Sergeant."

"All due respect, but you've made some poor decisions lately," Don said. "First with the handling of the murders, letting Raven and Nathan take our best vehicle, and then using medical supplies on a woman who probably won't live."

Colton shook his head. "Not this bullshit again."

"Stop it, both of you," Gail said.

Colton continued to glare at Don, who held his gaze.

"If you're both done," she said, looking between the two men, "there's something else I want to discuss. Our jail was never meant for holding prisoners long term. What do you suggest we do about Milo and Cindy Todd?"

"Hang them," Don said.

Colton couldn't believe his ears. He gawked at his patrol sergeant. Was this the world they were living in now—a world where justice was decided in an office instead of a courtroom?

"That's insane," Colton said. "We can't start executing criminals."

"I'll do it if you won't," Don said.

"Are you sure they helped kill Officer Nelson?" Gail asked.

"Not a doubt in my mind," Colton said. "They would have killed me, Lindsey, and Raven in the forest off Devils Gulch, too."

Gail bowed her head and massaged her wrinkled forehead. When she looked up, she gave an order Colton wasn't sure he could follow.

"Execute them, Chief. We have to be strong. We have to show everyone that Estes Park will not be broken by violence and fear."

"Damn straight," Don said, his black eyes gleaming.

If Colton didn't know better, he'd think the sergeant was excited about the notion.

What the hell was happening to the people of his town?

***

Sandra was exhausted, but she made herself put on a clean set of scrubs. It was her last pair, so she'd need to figure out the best way to wash her laundry soon.

Teddy was first on her rounds when she got to the hospital for another fourteen-hour shift. She stopped at her station and put on gown, gloves, facemask, and goggles, all necessary for extra protection while checking his wounds. Necrotizing fasciitis was a complex condition. It required constant monitoring and lots of antibiotics. If Teddy didn't heal soon, they would have to venture out of Estes Park to find him the meds, or else they'd have to cut off any newly infected tissue. Hyperbaric oxygen chambers and other high-tech treatments were not an option with the power off.

Teddy was sleeping on his back, blond hair matted to his head. She checked his vitals with care, trying not to wake him. His pulse, blood pressure, and respiration were normal, but she could tell he was running a slight fever by the sweat on his forehead. She checked it with an old-school thermometer and watched the mercury rise to one hundred and one degrees.

Teddy blinked several times when she dabbed his forehead with a cold cloth. When he finally focused on her, a smile dimpled his cheeks.

"Hi, sweetie," she said. "How are you feeling?"

"I'm kinda hot." He craned his neck to look around. "Is my mom here?"

"No, she's looking after my Allie right now."

Teddy raised his stump and examined the bandage. "It hurts this morning."

"I'm going to check it in a second, okay?"

He nodded and rested his head back on the pillow, his smile gone. Over the past few days, Sandra had seen his mood slipping. It was beginning to sink in that his arm was gone. He always looked away when she checked the dressing, as she was doing now. He'd been in the hospital for weeks now after being rushed here with gangrene-like symptoms. At that point he had already been suffering from the flesh-eating bacteria, and it had been too late to save his forearm.

She slowly rotated his arm in her gloved hands to examine the site of the amputation for inflammation. It all seemed to be healing nicely, until she saw the red, swollen patch of skin.

"Am I okay?" he asked.

Sandra hesitated, wondering if she should call Doctor Duffy over right away. She bandaged his arm back up and smiled. "Don't worry. I'll be back soon, okay?"

"Okay," Teddy said. He positioned himself on his side, hugging a stuffed bear against his chest.

Sandra walked back into the main area to look for Doctor Duffy. He was standing outside the isolation room where they were keeping Martha.

Duffy looked up from a clipboard as she approached. "Sandra, good morning. How's our youngest patient?"

"Teddy has some inflamed skin around his elbow."

"I'll go take a look," Duffy said. He cursed under his breath. "We're running low on antibiotics."

"I know," Sandra said.

"Martha's in pretty rough shape, too," Duffy said. "She still hasn't said a single word since Colton and Don dropped her off. Colton asked me to try and figure out what happened out there. I'd like to see if you can get her to talk when she wakes up."

Sandra looked through the glass panel into Martha's room. She was sleeping, her chest slowly moving up and down. Duffy arched his bushy brown eyebrows and held the door open for Sandra.

"Check her vitals," he said. "I'll go check on Teddy."

Sandra nodded.

Duffy stepped back into the other room and Sandra prepared to check Martha's vitals. Just as the door clicked shut, Martha's eyelids fluttered open.

"Doctor Duffy," Sandra cried out. "She's awake!"

Footsteps pounded the tile floor outside, and Duffy opened the door a second later. He joined Sandra at the bedside.

"Ma'am, can you hear me?" Duffy asked.

Martha struggled to raise her eyelids. Half open, her eyes flitted from Duffy to Sandra.

"I'm Doctor Duffy and this is Nurse Spears."

The woman looked at Sandra with frightened eyes. "The children," she mumbled through cracked lips. Her voice broke, and she brought a hand up and pointed to her mouth.

"Water," Sandra said. "She needs water."

Duffy returned with a bottle and helped position the straw at Martha's mouth.

She took several long gulps, then jerked her head away from the straw.

"The children," she said again. She was breathing faster, lungs wheezing. "You have to find the children."

Duffy looked at Sandra, then back at Martha.

"What children?" he asked.

"The soldiers...they took the children on the road. Have to find them." Martha gasped for air. You have to—" Her voice cracked again, and her eyes rolled up into her skull as she lost consciousness.

***

Raven put another blackened rock on top of the pile covering the fresh grave. Hundreds of years ago, his ancestors had buried their dead like this, but Raven never thought he would be doing the same thing on the side of a highway.

"He was a hero," Nathan said.

"There wasn't anything else you could do for him," Raven said.

They had spent the night trying to save Lieutenant Dupree's life while the fires raged around them. Four hours before sunrise, the Marine had succumbed to his wounds.

Raven stood beside the grave in the gray morning haze and looked out over the smoldering valley below, shaking his head. Dupree hadn't been able to tell them much before he died—and what he had said left Raven wondering if the lieutenant had gone crazy. He'd been ranting about castles and birds and Nazis.

"You follow any of what he was saying?" Raven asked.

Nathan nodded thoughtfully. "Ty's code word is 'falcon.' Not sure about the castle, but it sounds like some kind of Aryan Brotherhood, white supremacist types are behind the kidnapping."

"So you think we're looking for a bunch of skinheads?" Raven asked.

"Yeah, and I think we should get moving," Nathan

said. His boots sank into the mud as he walked back to the Jeep. The rains had finally suffocated the fires and turned the charcoaled terrain into a soggy mixture of mud and ash. Their CBRN suits were smeared with the black residue.

Nathan held the Geiger counter toward the sky. The chirp of the counter sounded, rising into a steady tick.

"I'll be damned," Nathan said. "The radiation readings have gone down. Makes sense, I guess. Last night's storm must have further precipitated the radiation."

"Precipitated?" Raven asked.

"Yes," Nathan said confidently. "We should be good to take our suits off."

Raven didn't hesitate in removing his helmet. He pulled it off and took in a breath of steamy air that carried the overwhelming scent of smoke.

"Come on," Nathan said. "I want to cover as much ground as possible today."

He glanced down at Dupree's grave one last time and then patted Raven on the shoulder.

"We're going to avenge him, and we're going to find Ty," Nathan said.

Raven pulled his ponytail behind his head and tied it in a knot on the way back to the Jeep. He wasn't overly optimistic, and he was beyond exhausted. He shook away the fog of war, something he hadn't experienced since North Korea.

Raven went to open the Jeep door but stopped when something strange caught his eye. He stared at the blackened carcass of an animal resting by a boulder on the side of the road. Bending down, he pulled out a quill from the dead porcupine. He held it in his fingers, a chill going through his fatigued body. He set the quill on the dashboard and grabbed a cloth from his backpack. He dabbed it in water and then wiped his forehead clean.

"Shit. This is the end of the world, Major. No doubt about that now," Raven said. "I thought maybe we could come back from this, but I think this is the end of the line for the human race."

Nathan swallowed a piece of granola and tilted his head to one side. "What?"

"I said the same thing to Colton the other night. The signs are all around us."

"Yeah," Nathan said. He dumped water onto a cloth to scrub his face. "North Korea did nuke us. I'm not sure if the country is going to bounce back for a while, but I don't exactly think this is the end of our species."

"It is," Raven said with confidence. For some reason, the revelation didn't bother him as much as he thought it would.

"Maybe not today, and maybe not tomorrow," he said, "but this is the end of civilization as we know it. The old Sioux woman has finally finished her quilt."

"Huh?" Nathan said.

Raven started the engine and began driving down the hill. "There's a Sioux story that tells of a place where the prairie meets the badlands—a place with a hidden cave."

"You're starting to sound a bit crazy, man."

"Just listen," Raven said. He paused and rolled his window down slightly. "Inside the cave lives a woman. She's been there for thousands of years working on a blanket strip of her buffalo robe. Beside her sits Shunka Sapa, a massive black dog. He watches her while she flattens the porcupine quills with her teeth for the quilt. A large fire burns in a pit. This fire has been going for thousands of years inside this cave, and over the fire burns a pot of Wojapi, or berry soup."

"Does this story have a point?" Nathan asked.

Raven steered around a vehicle and kept talking. "Every once in a while the woman gets up to stir the soup, and the big black dog pulls the quills from her blanket strip."

"So what?"

Raven shook his head as they approached the Humvee on the bridge. "This is where that ambush happened," he said.

White ash surrounded the deflated tires. Every window had broken, and the paint was burned away. An explosion had blown the top open like a turtle shell that had detonated from the inside.

"I have a feeling some of these skinhead bastards are also soldiers. Not just this General Fenix asshole that Dupree mentioned," Nathan said. "Who else could get a drop on Dupree's unit?"

Raven slowly drove over the bridge, a gray mist rising around the vehicle. He'd had the same suspicions about their chases. From here on out, Raven had to keep an eye on every bluff to ensure they didn't end up like the lieutenant and his team.

Nathan had the same idea. He gripped his carbine in both hands.

"You going to finish your story or what?"

"Yeah, sorry," Raven said. "The Sioux legend says that when the woman finishes her blanket strip, the world will come to an end."

Raven scooped the porcupine quill off the dashboard. "I found this on the side of the road back there."

"It's just a coincidence."

"No," Raven said. "It's not."

He eased off the gas when he saw bodies on the road ahead. He brought the Jeep to a stop. The nearest corpse was so badly disfigured from the flames that Raven couldn't see the features. He stepped out onto the street and bent down to read the nametag on what was left of the man's uniform. Raven put his sleeve over his nose to keep out the scent of burned flesh.

"Looks like this guy was with the Colorado National Guard," Raven said. "Last name was S-something. Shit, I can't make it out."

"Let me see," Nathan said. He hustled around the Jeep to take a look.

"Doesn't make any sense," Nathan said. "Why would the Marine team have been ambushed with a Colorado National Guard unit?"

"You think the guard unit were in on it?"

Nathan was already moving back to the truck. "No idea, man, but we don't have time to sit around and investigate."

"We're just going to leave these bodies out here?" Raven called out after him. "You don't even want to drag them off the road?"

Raven already knew what Nathan's answer would be. They didn't have time to bury these soldiers like they had Dupree. He jumped back in the vehicle, feeling like he was betraying the ghost of every Marine that had ever died by leaving Dupree's men and the guard unit on the road. He didn't like to admit he was sentimental, but leaving a man behind, even a dead one, threatened to bring him to tears.

I will come back, Raven promised. He eyed the quill on the dashboard again, hoping Nathan was right about the Sioux story only being a coincidence.

12

"I have a plan," Ty said quietly.

Micah sat up in the bed across the small room. Emma was next to him, sleeping.

"A plan for what?" Micah whispered.

"To get us out of here, but I need your help," Ty replied.

Using his hands, he picked up his legs and moved them over the side of his bed. He paused to listen for footsteps in the hallway outside. Hearing none, he reached over for the handles of his wheelchair and positioned it in front of his bed. He was skinny, but his lean arm muscles and lots of experience allowed him to move into the chair with ease.

"Where are we going to go?" Micah asked.

"Anywhere but here. These men want to use us for something bad," Ty said.

Emma stirred and rubbed her eyes. "I don't feel good." She scratched at a sore on her face.

Footfalls cut Micah off before he could reply. They rapped down the hall and stopped outside the door. There was a click, and then the metal door shrieked open.

Carson stepped into the room and pulled off his baseball cap to run a hand over his shiny scalp.

"Get up," he said, snickering. "Those of you that can."

Ty clenched his jaw. He really, really didn't like Carson.

"I need to go to the potty," Emma said shyly.

"Great, just my fucking luck," Carson muttered. Body odor drifted into the room with him as he walked over to her bedside.

"Watch your language around the kids," came a second voice.

Standing in the entrance was Dr. Rollins. Ty still didn't know how to feel about the doctor. Was he a good man? If so, why was he helping General Fenix? All Ty knew was that he had to get out of here before the General could use him.

"How are you feeling, Ty?" Dr. Rollins asked.

"I'm fine, but I have to go to the bathroom, too."

The doctor walked over to Ty's bed and crouched down in front of him. He reached into his vest pocket and pulled out a piece of licorice. "Go ahead," Dr. Rollins said, holding out his hand.

Ty narrowed his eyes at the candy. He was hungry, but he didn't want anything from these men. "Give it to Micah or Emma."

Emma licked her lips and held out her hand, but Dr. Rollins frowned, hesitating. He tossed the candy to the girl and turned back to Ty.

"General Fenix wants you healthy, and it's my job to make sure you stay that way," he said. "Come on, help me with them, Carson."

Dr. Rollins grabbed the handles of Ty's chair and wheeled him into the hallway.

"You stink, mister," Emma said.

Ty couldn't help but chuckle at her serious tone.

"Shut up," Carson replied.

Dr. Rollins pushed Ty around the corner into a hallway with crates of supplies. The other kids were being held in a room in this passage. He had already mentally mapped out where the rooms were in relation to the hospital, but he wasn't sure how to get back to the big storeroom where he'd first arrived. There had to be a way out from there, if only he could find it again.

Carson walked ahead and pushed open the door to the medical center. Inside, there were three beds, two of them occupied. Tommy, his arm in a sling, tried to sit up. He winced and then smiled when he saw Ty.

"How you doing, buddy?"

Ty waved but didn't say anything. He'd thought Tommy was nice, but now he wasn't even sure of that.

Dr. Rollins rolled the chair past the operating room. An elevated metal table was centered in the small room. Off to the side was a trashcan overflowing with bloody rags. They moved into a third room where there were open showers and several toilets partitioned off with wood walls. Carson and Dr. Rollins helped Ty out of his chair and onto the toilet seat. He hated needing their help, but he was also used to relying on other people to get around and do certain things.

When Ty had finished, Dr. Rollins pushed him into the main room near Tommy's bed.

"I'll be right back," the doctor said.

"Hey," Tommy said quietly. He ran a hand over his shaved head and looked to see if anyone was listening. "You want to get out of here?"

Ty perked up. "Can you help me? Won't you get in trouble?"

"Not if we don't get caught. Don't tell anybody, okay? Gotta keep this a secret."

"Let's go, you little shits," Carson called out from the door of the bathroom.

Tommy winked at Ty. "I'll come for you later. You just wait."

Dr. Rollins returned with more pills and a bottle of water for Ty. Once he'd taken the medicine, the doctor wheeled his chair out of the med ward. Ty lifted a hand to wave goodbye to Tommy, but the young man shook his head subtly.

Right, Ty thought. *It's a secret.*

Ty wasn't sure why Tommy wanted to help him, but maybe it was because of what Ty had suspected earlier— that Tommy was a good guy caught up with some bad people, just like his mom told him could happen if Ty wasn't careful.

Instead of taking a right, Dr. Rollins took a left into the hallway while Carson herded Micah and Emma to the right toward their room and the room where the other kids were being held.

"Where are we going?" Ty asked, twisting in his chair.

"Remember what I told you earlier," Dr. Rollins whispered. "Just do as they say."

Ty gripped the armrests and peered around the next corner. They came upon a wider passage with thin metal train tracks on the floor. The doctor kept to the right of the rails.

Wood supply crates marked *Danger: Explosive* were stacked along the rocky walls. At the next junction, Dr. Rollins took a right into an even wider hallway. More of the wood boxes were stacked to the ceiling. Orange rain barrels and metal crates were positioned along the tracks. Overhead, Ty saw a ventilation shaft with boards blocking the entrance. Ty tried to keep all of it straight in his head in case he needed to come back this way again.

A chain of lights hung from the ceiling, several of the

bulbs flickering. Ty couldn't see the other end. The ground sloped down as they made their way deeper into the shaft. Everything here was damp from the water running down the walls. They passed several small rooms with cots, some of them occupied by sleeping soldiers.

Finally, Dr. Rollins slowed and directed Ty's chair toward an open door. Four metal tables were set up inside, guns and beer cans littering their surfaces. Six men were studying the maps draped over the surface of the closest table. In the center of the group stood General Fenix. He looked up, a toothy grin spreading across his face.

"Little Mr. Montgomery," he said. "It's so great of you to join us."

Fenix nodded at Dr. Rollins and the doctor walked away, his footsteps echoing down the hallway. With him gone and Tommy in the medical ward, Ty was on his own. The other men took seats on a leather couch at the other end of the room. They turned away, seemingly uninterested in the meeting.

The General moved behind Ty and said, "Don't be scared, kid."

The wheelchair was moving a moment later. Fenix pushed Ty up to the nearest table and then walked over to a wooden cabinet that was stocked with beer, liquor bottles, and cans of pop. He grabbed a can of Sprite, popped the lid, and set it down in front of Ty.

"It's warm, but it's still good. Go ahead, take a drink. You know you want to."

Ty looked at the can. He was thirsty, but he shook his head.

"No?" Fenix said. He scooped the can up and slowly brought it to his lips, watching Ty. "Last chance."

Ty shook his head again. With a shrug, Fenix chugged the can down.

"Ahhhhh," he said, wiping off his mouth. "Refreshing. If you change your mind, I have more."

He tossed the can aside and then grabbed a laptop sitting on the table. He swiveled the screen to face Ty.

"Okay, let's get to it," Fenix said. He leaned over and hit one of the keys. Ty suddenly saw a face on screen— his own. He hardly recognized himself in the video feed. His dark hair was disheveled, and his green eyes were swollen from crying. He had lost some weight, too, and he'd already been skinny to begin with.

"I'd like you to do something very simple. I'd like you to say hi to your mom." Fenix sat at the table next to Ty.

Ty tore his gaze away from the video and looked at Fenix. "You're trying to trick me."

"Kid, I'm going to ask you this one more time before I'm apt to get cross. And I don't think you want to make me mad, do you?"

Ty remembered what Dr. Rollins had told him. "No, sir," he mumbled.

"Good," Fenix said, satisfied. He leaned across the table, pushed a key on the laptop, and moved out of the way.

Ty stared at the screen for a moment, shivering in his chair. "Mom...?"

Fenix nodded several times and gestured for him to continue.

"Mom, it's me. I miss you. Where are you? Why haven't you come for me? I'm not hurt, but these men are holding me captive in a place called the Castle and—"

Fenix swiveled the laptop so it was facing him. His smile was gone now, replaced by an icy stare. "Madame

Secretary," he said in his smooth, deep voice. "My name is General Dan Fenix, and I'm the leader of the Sons of Liberty. We've taken it upon ourselves to restore order in these parts. Our mission is to take back our country from those that would have us enslaved."

"That's right!" one of the men on the couch called out.

"We have your son, Secretary Montgomery, and for the right price, you can have him back. I'll need ten million in gold bars and a list of weapons to be delivered at a place of my choosing. This is not a negotiation. If you don't deliver the gold and weapons within twenty-four hours, you'll be getting your son back significantly more damaged than he is now. And if you fail to comply with my requests...well, let's just say you won't be getting him back at all."

Fenix shut the laptop with a loud, definite click.

***

Charlize Montgomery sat in the cockpit of her F-15 Strike Eagle. She knew she was dreaming, but like most of her dreams, she did not feel in control of her actions. She was just a spectator to an event that had occurred over a decade ago.

The fighter jet tore through the air, but the horizon remained unchanged, like she was hardly moving at all. The harder she fought to wake, the more powerful the grip of the dream became.

She curved west toward a highway snaking through the terrain. There wasn't a moving car in sight, but she could see a cluster of idle vehicles. At first she thought this was the highway in Florida clogged with the refugees fleeing Orlando, but the landscape was different. Instead of grass and wetlands, there was sand.

Smoke rose in the distance, thinning as it spread higher into the sky from the burning oil fields to the east. Charlize realized then she wasn't even in the United States. She was back in Iraq.

More plumes drifted away from a city. The sight wasn't unusual for the warzone. Often times the retreating army would set the fields ablaze to cover their escape or burn the resource to prevent it from falling into enemy hands.

The F-15 roared and dipped down to 3,200 feet AGL. She was low enough to see the charred vehicles on the road. The sight reminded her this wasn't a dream—it was a nightmare. The memory was from a reconnaissance mission that occurred over a decade ago in Iraq.

She dipped down to one thousand feet, just like she remembered it, close enough that she could see the cooked bodies in the vehicles, but also close enough that any enemy forces in the area would have a great opportunity to put her in the sand.

At least she wasn't alone. Five other F-15s were out there, combing the area for potential enemy combatants. Her mission now was to capture yet another human rights violation of the local population and pass it up the food chain to brass. The politicians and diplomats would cry about the war crimes, and she would return to drop bombs on the bastards responsible.

As she came in for another run, she saw more remains of the refugees in what was likely an attack by Al-Qaeda forces. The sight that day had invoked another memory of the images she had seen of the Highway of Death during the first Gulf War. Hundreds of Iraqi Regular

Forces and their fleet of vehicles were bombed by American forces during the night while fleeing Kuwait.

The people in the dream weren't soldiers though—they were civilians. Men, women, children, and even the body of a dog caught in the crosshairs littered the road. Some of them remained in their vehicles; others had tried to flee the artillery shelling and machine gun fire.

She relayed the information to her wingman, voice catching when she described the scene. On her third pass, she swooped down to five hundred AGL to take photos with the pod cameras. The jet ripped over the graveyard, snapping pictures of the massacre.

She pulled up, and the jet curved away for a fourth and final run. The engines screamed as she gave the bird some extra juice. Every warning sensor suddenly went off, chirping and flashing in the cockpit. A surface-to-air missile streaked toward her jet from one of the burned vehicles.

Even though she was dreaming the nerves in her body all tightened at once. Normally losing the missile would have been easy in the thirty-million-dollar aircraft, but she was so low to the ground that she only had a second to release flares and tear away from the projectile.

The g's lashed at her body as the F-15 jerked upward. The flares did their job, but the blast from the missile was so close it jolted the aircraft from behind, peppering the right wing with shrapnel. The nose of the jet continued tearing toward the clouds.

She was still in business.

Now she had some unfinished business of her own. Whoever had just taken the pot shot at her was about to get toasted.

Two dots raced across the skyline at two o' clock. The

cavalry was on the way, but she ignored their warnings to retreat. This son of a bitch was all hers. She just had to get him before he could fire another missile.

As she circled, she prepared to fire a missile of her own. The target clicked on her display when she lined the sights up on the old pickup truck, but she decided to use her M61 Vulcan six-barrel mini-gun instead. There would be less damage to the site, which they needed to preserve for evidence of the war crimes.

At the last second, she saw the man she was about to kill. She pulled the trigger after a slight hesitation, realizing the man wasn't a man at all. There were two boys, trying to operate the missile launcher together. They vanished in the 20mm round spray, and Charlize's heart caught in her throat at what she had just done.

Warning sensors chirped in her cockpit as her jet ripped through the sky. The blue sky faded to white, and she felt the tug of reality pulling on her. The chirping and beeping continued, but they weren't the warning sensors from her cockpit. These were the sounds of a hospital.

Muffled voices echoed in the distance.

"Madame Secretary, can you hear me?"

She moved her lips, but she couldn't seem to summon her voice.

Cracking an eyelid open, she saw two thin figures hovering under a light. The faces came into focus, an African American man and woman, both of them unfamiliar to her. The chirping of the machines faded to a steady beep.

"I'm Doctor Francis and this is Doctor Parish," the woman said. "Can you follow this pen for me?" She held up a pen and waved it in front of Charlize's face.

Charlize did as instructed and mumbled, "Where am I?"

"You're safe at Constellation, ma'am," replied Doctor Parish.

The bunker under the sea where President Diego had moved U.S. Northern Command, Charlize recalled, her brain slowly catching up with reality.

"How long have I been out?" she asked.

"A day, ma'am," Parish said.

"Have you heard anything about my son and brother?"

Francis and Parish exchanged a look.

"Ma'am, I think you should wait for—" Francis began to say.

"Tell me, and tell me right now," Charlize said firmly. Her head was pounding so hard it blinded her right eye. She reached up to grab her aching skull.

"Give me a second," Parish said. He stepped out of the room and into the hallway.

Doctor Francis remained at her side.

"Where's Albert?" Charlize asked. She tried to sit up, and Francis held up a hand.

"You need to relax, Secretary Montgomery. Albert is just outside."

Charlize rested her head back on the pillow.

A few minutes later the door opened and Parish stepped back into the room. Albert joined them and offered a brusque nod to Charlize.

"I'm sorry for not listening to you earlier, Big Al," she said.

His smile said he forgave her as he crossed over to stand by her bedside.

"General Thor is on his way," Parish said.

They waited another ten minutes for a knock on the door. General Thor walked inside with a man in a suit. Charlize sat up when she saw it was President Diego.

"Relax, Charlize," Diego said. "You're going to want to hear this sitting down."

"What? What's going on?" She pushed at the bed until she was sitting up straight with her back to the plastic headboard. Albert walked over to stand by her bedside.

"The USS *John Stennis* strike group was attacked by a North Korean submarine last night," Diego said. "The aircraft carrier was destroyed, and Captain Dietz and Lieutenant Marco perished in the blast."

"How?" Charlize asked. Her breath caught in her chest. "How did the submarine get through the ring of protection around the carrier?"

Thor shook his head. "They didn't precisely 'fire' on the USS *John Stennis*, ma'am."

Charlize exhaled the breath she was holding in. "Kamikazes?"

"Yes," Thor said with a nod. "The North Korean submarine snuck past the defenses and self-detonated before Captain Dietz could detect the diesel sub. The North Koreans must have thought President Diego was still on board to pull a move like that."

Charlize couldn't believe it.

"There's still one more submarine out there," Thor added. "We're working on finding it."

Diego fiddled with his red tie and said, "There's something else...we received a video of your son."

13

"Chief, the Stanley's on fire!" shouted Margaret.

Colton looked up from the map of Estes Park on the conference room table. He was in the middle of briefing everyone on the plan to place sentries at multiple places across the town. All around him, staff, officers, volunteers, and recruits turned toward the department's dispatcher. Margaret stood a head shorter than everyone in the room, but she had a hell of a commanding voice.

"Did you hear me?" she yelled. "I said the Stanley is burning!"

Colton moved for the hallway and bolted toward the front doors. Footfalls pounded the floor as he was followed outside. He pushed open the doors and stumbled into the cool afternoon. In the distance, plumes of smoke rose toward the clouds.

This couldn't be happening.

It took him ten precious seconds to snap out of his initial shock, and then he started barking orders.

"Officer Matthew, get the truck! Officer Hines, grab the gear. Margaret, get the word out to every officer and tell them to head to the Stanley!"

Colton pulled up his duty belt. It was looser around his waist. Had he already lost that much weight since the attack?

Two minutes later, the Chevy rattled up around the side of town hall. Colton took the passenger side, and

Hines jumped into the back carrying several packs of gear and heavy turncoats. Several other volunteers climbed in with him. At Colton's nod, Matthew peeled away from town hall.

The Chevy chugged up MacGregor Avenue, and Colton used the time to put on one of the heavy coats. Gray and brown hills rose in the distance, speckled with evergreens. The beauty was once again overshadowed by a disaster as he slipped on a pair of gloves.

Matthew pulled right onto Wonderview Avenue, and Colton cursed when the small gold cap on top of the Stanley came into view. Flames licked the left section of the white neo-colonial hotel. They hadn't spread to the central or the right wing, but it was only a matter of time.

"Can't this thing go any faster?" Matthew asked, looking at the gauges.

Colton would have told him not to push it too hard—Jake had rebuilt the truck from old parts on the weekends, and he wasn't a hundred percent confident in his friend's skills as a mechanic—but he was too busy staring in horror at the burning building. Flames flickered out the windows and over the roof. At the bottom of the structure, a line of people were passing buckets of water.

It wasn't going to do a damn bit of good.

Storm clouds rolled across the horizon, but they were heading east, away from the park. Rain wasn't going to save the Stanley. Neither were a few buckets of well water. Without pressurized fire hoses, it was like spitting on a bonfire.

The last seconds of the drive seemed like an eternity. If they lost the Stanley, the stranded tourists and townsfolk sheltered there would be homeless.

Hundreds of people had gathered on the terrace out

front. Smoke rolled across the scene, shifting in the afternoon wind and blowing into the white tents set up on the lawn behind the hedge maze, gardens and fountains. Colton had to get them away from the building.

"Get back!" he shouted out the window.

Jim Meyers, the manager of the hotel, was on his knees praying.

How about trying to put the fire out? Colton thought. He opened the door before Matthew brought the vehicle to a stop and jumped out.

Motion from the front entrance to the hotel caught his eye. An elderly couple staggered out of the front door, coughing. The man helped his wife across the front veranda, but fell as he reached the steps, barely catching himself on the railing. Four American flags hung over white pillars holding up the balcony above them. The symbols of freedom whipped in the smoky wind as the fires closed in.

"Hines, help those people!" Colton shouted. "Matthew, get the crowd back." He turned to look for Jim. He was standing now, running his hands through his thin hair.

"Jim, is anyone else inside?" Colton yelled.

"I… I don't know."

"Well, find out!" Colton looked back to the volunteers who'd joined him. A few were helping direct people away from the burning building, but too many were standing and staring, mouths agape.

"Somebody throw me a gas mask!" Colton shouted. Hines dug through a pack and tossed over a mask. Colton snatched it from the air and stuffed it into his pocket while running toward the left wing.

"Chief, you forgot your helmet!" Hines shouted.

Colton turned and caught the helmet like a football and then continued toward the building. There were at least twenty people in the bucket brigade, and at the front of the line stood Lindsey, the collar of her shirt pulled up over her nose. He approached with a hand shielding his face, the heat of the flames already tingling across his exposed skin.

A window shattered on the second floor, flames exploding outward.

"Watch out!" Colton shouted.

Dale Jackson was standing under the window wearing his volunteer firefighter turncoat, helmet, and gloves. The retired veteran had made good on his promise to change his ways after Colton had caught him waving a gun at Nathan and Sandra the night of the EMP attack, and since then he'd been one of the first to help out when anyone needed it. Dale jumped away, but the showering glass sliced through his coat and cut into his tattooed bicep.

"Ah, shit!" he shouted.

"Get back!" Colton yelled.

Colton worked his way up to Lindsey. Her face was filthy and flushed. The heat intensified as the fire spread over the building. It wouldn't be long before the blaze would force the group to retreat.

"We need more water!" she yelled. "Where's the fire department?"

"What fire department?" Colton shouted back.

Lindsey grabbed a bucket and threw the water on the building. She handed it back to Colton, and he passed it down the line.

"Where the hell is Don?" Colton asked.

Lindsey coughed from the smoke. "Don't know."

The fire had spread up to the third floor. Another window broke. Colton grabbed a bucket, tossed it on the side of the building, grabbed another, and kept going, hoping that maybe the rain clouds would change direction.

Over the commotion came a frantic shout. "Where's my husband? I can't find my husband!"

Colton looked over his shoulder at an older woman with gray hair struggling toward the building. Hines was trying to hold her back, but she pulled from his grip.

"Colton!" Hines shouted.

Wood splintered overhead with a deafening crack. The roof began to cave in on the left wing, flames belching out into the sky. The blaze stung his exposed skin, and sweat beaded beneath the heavy coat he wore.

"Everyone back!" Colton shouted. He pulled Lindsey away as she went to grab another bucket.

"No!" she snapped. "We have to—"

Colton dragged her back just as a piece of burning wood hit the grass where she'd been standing. Sparks landed on her jeans. She fell on her knees, beating out the embers, but he quickly pulled her back to her feet.

"Come on!" he shouted. The other people working to save the Stanley dropped their buckets and ran. The heat of the flames hit Colton's neck like a slap. They had moved just in the nick of time.

On the other side of the lawn, the tourists were huddled in a group; some of them crying, others looking upon their temporary home in a state of shock. A man with a WWII veteran hat bowed his head, gripping the armrests of his wheelchair with arthritic fingers. The woman who had lost her husband screamed, pulling on

Hines to let her go.

"Get back!" Matthew shouted. Hands out wide, he corralled the crowd back across the lawn.

"Damn it, Dale," Lindsey shouted. Colton turned to see Dale still standing in front of the flames, holding two buckets of water, veins bulging in his neck. He tossed both buckets and then scrambled for more. Colton started toward him, determined to drag the man away before he got himself killed, when a hand grabbed his sleeve.

"Chief," said the gray-haired woman. "Please, my husband is still in there!"

"All right, ma'am," Colton huffed. "Where did you last see him?"

She pointed to the second floor, just above the veranda. Flames danced behind the classic colonial windows.

"Shit," Colton muttered.

Lindsey joined them, wiping soot from her forehead and then coughing into her sleeve. Dale finally retreated from the fire and jogged over, blood drenching his arm.

"Someone still inside, Chief?" Dale asked. He coughed into his sleeve and then cupped his lacerated bicep with a glove.

"Her husband," Colton said.

Dale jerked his chin at the building. "I'll go find the old guy. I've been in worse than that back in Iraq. Once saved a kid—"

"No, it's too dangerous, and you need to get your arm looked at," Colton said. "I'll go."

"Like hell. Not without me." This time it was Lindsey talking. She looked like she could barely stand, but there was a determined set to her jaw.

Colton didn't have time to argue. He took off for the porch before they could protest. A figure wearing a cowboy hat came running through the smoke around the east wing. For a moment, Colton thought it was Jake's ghost, but then saw it wasn't his old friend—or a friend at all—it was Don.

"Where you going, Chief?" Don shouted.

Colton pointed at the balcony on the second floor. "Got a man trapped inside."

"The building is a total loss. I'm sorry, but I can't let you go in there, it's far too dangerous."

Don put his hand on Colton's shoulder, pushing him back from the hotel.

"Get your hand off me, Sergeant," Colton growled.

Someone rushed by Colton and Don. It was Dale, and before anyone could stop him, the veteran loped up the stairs and ran through the open doors into the lobby, spearing the smoke with his helmet.

Colton pulled out his gas mask and secured it over his face as he ran after Dale. The mask wouldn't do much to protect him from the heat or carbon monoxide, but at least it would block the smoke particles as long as there was at least twenty percent oxygen. He had to make this quick. Without much thermal protection or an oxygen tank, he wouldn't last long inside the building—and Dale didn't have a mask at all.

Keeping low, Colton moved through the smoke-choked porch and stepped into the lobby. Visibility was shit, but at least this part of the building wasn't on fire. He took in raspy breaths, struggling for air as he moved.

He hadn't been inside the Stanley for a long time, not since he'd taken Kelly to the historic bar and restaurant for an anniversary celebration years ago. If he remembered correctly, the stairs were straight ahead.

Colton walked as low and as quickly as possible, hands waving in front of him to stop from running into anything. The smoke was heavy here and he couldn't see the staircase, but he could make out the reception desk to his left, and the golden elevator on his right. He crouched down and moved forward until he saw the bottom of the carpeted stairs.

A cracking sounded like the earth splitting in two. Colton stood and then jumped back just as the ceiling gave way, dumping burning wood, plaster, and furniture onto the floor in front of the stairs.

He shielded his face from the fire with an arm and looked up through the gaping hole to the second floor. A chair tumbled out of the opening, shattering at his feet. Colton frantically brushed off the sparks that stuck to his clothing.

"Dale!" he shouted, his voice muffled by the mask. He couldn't see much of anything through the plastic, and he knew he didn't have long before it started to melt. Even worse, he could hardly breathe.

Unable to stand it anymore, Colton tore off the gas mask and pulled his collar up over his nose. He coughed into the material and desperately searched for a way around the spreading flames to the stairs. His vision burned and blurred from the smoke and intense heat, but he managed to see a gap around the fire. Maybe if he could get around it...

"Over here!" someone shouted. He whirled to look for the voice, but the curtain of smoke was too thick. Even with the sunlight coming through the front doors, he couldn't see much. The walkie-talkie crackled on his hip, but he was afraid of dropping it if he tried to answer now.

"Help me with him!" yelled the same strangled voice.

A large, misshapen figure emerged on the other side of the fire at the bottom of the staircase. Two men, Colton realized, one of them leaning on the other as a crutch.

Colton flattened his body and moved around the flames to help. Fire licked at his pant legs. He took a step back and then leapt over the burning floorboards.

"Help me carry him," Dale said. He coughed violently and hoisted the man up with Colton's help. The fire raged over the debris where the ceiling had caved in. Static crackled from the radio again, and then there was a voice that sounded like Margaret, but Colton couldn't make out the words.

"Let's make a run for it," Dale choked. They barreled around the section of burning floor. Moving as one, they carried the moaning elderly man through the lobby, out the front doors, across the porch, and down the stairs.

As soon as they were outside, they dropped to the ground. Lindsey, Hines, and Matthew ran over with buckets of water. They tossed them onto Colton, Dale, and the unconscious man, dousing the embers that smoldered on their clothes.

"You're a crazy son of a bitch, Dale," Colton said. He pushed himself up, shivering from the combination of the cold water and the wind.

"Found this guy on the stairs," Dale managed to say.

Lindsey was on her knees next to the unconscious man. Air wheezed from his lungs. His wife came running over and dropped down by his other side.

"Chief!" someone shouted.

Colton looked over his shoulder at Detective Tim

Ryburn. He bent down to put his hands on his knees, gut hanging over his duty belt.

"Chief," he said. "I... I ran here as fast as I could. Margaret's been trying to get you on the radio."

"I've been a little bit busy," Colton said.

The flames had reached the right wing of the Stanley now. Another section of roof collapsed into the heart of the building, burying over a hundred years' worth of memories, artwork, and history.

The walkie-talkie on Colton's belt buzzed again just as Ryburn finally caught his breath. "Chief, there's been a jailbreak."

Colton coughed and shook his head. "What are you talking about? Who broke out?"

"That thug, Theo," Ryburn said, wheezing. "A group of armed men took him from the jail. They showed up right after we got word the hotel was on fire."

Colton looked at his other officers. He had ordered his entire department away from their posts, including the jail, in an effort to save the Stanley. He looked back at the inferno. This wasn't some accident. This was arson—a distraction to get them away from their critical facilities. He felt the realization like a fist to the gut.

They'd been played.

He plucked the radio off his belt. "Margaret, do you copy?"

"I'm here, Chief," she replied.

"Are you okay?"

"Yes, but..." Margaret said. "Those men didn't just take Theo. They took all our supplies, too."

— 14 —

The rain had subdued the forest fires along the highway, but the flames had done plenty of damage to the terrain, burning all the way up to the treeline around the jagged mountains to the south.

Nathan held up the Geiger counter to check for radiation. The reading came back minimal again. The rain had not only stopped the fires—it had also cleared a lot of the radiation. No one would be able to plant crops around here anytime soon, but at least the ground wasn't completely toxic.

He pulled out the analog radio from his bag, hoping that he would finally be able to reach his sister. He turned to the channel and said, "Major Sardetti calling Lieutenant Marco or Secretary Montgomery. Does anyone copy? Over."

No one answered.

After a few attempts, Nathan put the radio back in his rucksack. "Haven't been able to raise anyone for over nine hours. I don't understand."

"You sure you're on the right channel?" Raven asked.

Nathan shifted his rifle from one hand to the other. His broken arm was killing him, but he didn't want Raven to see it. "Yeah, I'm sure."

"This feels a lot like the night of attack, when we were completely cut off," Nathan said. "I'm worried something else has happened."

Raven kept his gaze on the road, eyes shifting left to right. The man was on constant alert. Four hours of driving on Interstate 70 and searching the side roads hadn't turned up anything but corpses. Nathan had lost count of the bodies. Most had died from radiation poisoning, but they'd found a few clusters of people who'd been shot. The Sons of Liberty must have moved through here, but it was impossible to say how long ago or even which direction they'd been heading in.

"We need a new plan," Raven said. "Following the bodies isn't working."

"Maybe it's time to let *me* come up with a plan," Nathan said. "I say we set a trap and ambush these fuckers like they did the soldiers back on the bridge."

Raven wagged his finger back and forth. "I think I figured you out, Major. You want me to die, so you can have Lindsey. But she's mine, man. Feel free to date my sister when I'm gone, though. As long as you treat her right."

Nathan wasn't sure how to respond to that, so he forced a smile. He liked Sandra, but the last thing on his mind was dating.

"You break my sister's heart and I'll break your other arm," Raven said.

Nathan laughed this time. "I'm not interested in anything besides finding my nephew and getting back to my sister, don't worry."

"Yeah, yeah," he said, looking at the dash. "I better fill up the tank after this hill."

Raven pulled off to the side of the road along a slope that descended to a lake. Thousands of fingers of smoke rose from the cooling timber all around them. The one good thing about everything being black was it was easy to spot any potential hostiles.

Nathan stepped out and raised his AR-15 to scope the road. Three burned-out cars covered in ash remained where they had died six days earlier. He zoomed in on a single body that was nothing but charred flesh and bones.

He stretched his aching muscles after finishing the scan. There wasn't anyone out here. Not anyone alive, anyway. He returned to the Jeep, where Raven was preparing to funnel gas from a can into the fuel tank.

"Need some help?" Nathan asked.

"Nah, just watch our backs."

Nathan limped back to the other side of the Jeep to check the area Raven had already cleared. A patch of terrain to the north had survived the fires, leaving an island of green in an ocean of black. He pushed the scope to his eye and magnified on a red tent under a massive ponderosa pine.

"You see that tent?" Nathan asked.

"Yeah, but no people. I'm guessing whoever pitched that is dead inside."

He set the gas canister in the back of the truck, grabbed his rifle, and walked over to the edge of the road. Wind gusted across the two men, rustling their filthy clothing.

"Think we should have a look anyway?" Nathan said. "If someone's alive up there, maybe they saw something and can tell us—"

The rattle of an engine cut him off. The sound rose over the wind, faded, and came again. Nathan and Raven darted for cover behind the Jeep.

"Where's that sound coming from?" Nathan asked.

"South, I think."

Raven and Nathan shouldered their rifles and crept

around the Jeep. The cough of the engine grew louder, and a Humvee crested the road to the south, zooming over a hill and speeding down the open stretch.

"We have to hide," Raven said. "Everything else on the road is covered in ash."

Nathan followed Raven into the ditch. They scrambled down the rocky side and got down on their stomachs. From this vantage, Nathan couldn't see the road, but he could hear the diesel engine approaching. It didn't sound like it was slowing.

"Set a trap," Nathan whispered. "Let's see if my plan works."

"We don't know if these are the guys."

"Yeah, but—"

Raven held up a finger to his lips as the vehicle slowed on the road. The Humvee slowed to a halt just above them. Doors opened, and multiple pairs of boots hit the pavement.

"Keep your eyes open," said a man's voice.

"I'll check the back of the Jeep," answered another.

Nathan slowly pushed his muzzle up, but all he could see was the top of the Jeep and the hazy sky. All he needed was a single thread of evidence that these were the assholes who had taken Ty. Then he was going to move in.

The top of a shaved head and two bushy eyebrows emerged overhead. Another shaved head appeared. This one had a Swastika tattoo on the left side.

Skinhead bastards.

"I don't see anyone out here," one of the men in the truck said. He moved out of sight. The other man remained, the top of his head in Nathan's sights.

"There's a tent over here!" someone shouted from the

other side of the road. "We should check that shit out."

"Hold up, Jimmy," came a new voice. "You got to check out the supplies in this Jeep. We hit the jackpot! The General is going to be really happy."

The man moved away from Nathan's red dot sight, vanishing from view. He looked over at Raven. Despite their injuries, Nathan was confident they could take these Aryan assholes down right here.

But that wouldn't help find his nephew.

Unless he left one of them alive.

Nathan heard another new voice on the road, bringing the total contacts to five.

"Check out this crossbow," the man said. "That is freakin' sweet."

Raven's eyes widened.

Five men was a lot to take down, even with surprise on his side, but Nathan couldn't let them take their gear and the Jeep. Being stranded out here was as good as a death sentence.

"Engine is still hot, boss," someone said above.

Nathan flashed a hand signal to Raven, directing him to take the two guys on the right. That left Nathan with the three on the left. They had to move fast, and they had move now!

Nathan felt the pre-battle jitters as he mentally prepared to take their lives. It was different than flying his jet into combat. He would be able to see the men he killed, look them in the eyes, something a pilot didn't have to deal with when dropping bombs or launching missiles.

His heart had been beating calmly, but as soon as he jumped up with his rifle, it slammed against his ribcage. Two men in black fatigues were removing gear from the back of the Jeep. They looked in his direction, and the one on the right shouted the alarm.

Nathan fired two shots into the first man's side, sending him staggering away. He trained the barrel on the second man, who was fumbling for a holstered pistol, and dropped him with a shot to the temple.

Gunfire came from Nathan's right. Raven's shots punched through a soldier's neck, a geyser of blood spraying the windshield of the Jeep. He dropped to his knees and clutched the mortal wound.

A bearded soldier on the right scrambled for cover on the other side of the road and dove into the ditch. Nathan focused his gun on a thick man with an athletic build to his left who had taken off running. He aimed for a pair of wide, linebacker shoulders and fired a shot that tore through the back of his ribcage.

The muscular man crashed to the pavement with a thud, limp and dead. Nathan felt a tinge of satisfaction and roved his rifle to find the final target and finish the job. This time he was going to aim to maim and not kill.

"Eyes up!" Raven shouted.

In the turret of the Humvee, a sixth man emerged. He grabbed the M240 and aimed it at Nathan.

Raven dropped to a knee and fired two shots that pinged off the armor shield surrounding the big gun. It barked to life, sending 7.62 mm rounds in Raven's direction. He rolled out of the way and then jumped into the ditch they had been hiding in.

The gunner raked the machine gun back and forth, spraying rounds into the pavement. Then he moved the barrel toward Nathan, but Nathan already had his sights on the gunner's head.

"Eat this, you Nazi loving prick," Nathan muttered.

His voice didn't sound like it belonged to him as he squeezed off a shot that hit the man in the center of his black baseball cap, sending his shaved skull jolting backward with such force it broke his neck.

Bullets peppered the Jeep to Nathan's left. He ducked down for cover as more rounds slammed the metal. Where the hell was the shooter?

"No!" Raven shouted. At first Nathan thought he was screaming about his precious Jeep, but then a flash of steel whizzed past Nathan and crunched into someone standing behind him.

He whirled to see a seventh man collapse to the ground, screaming in pain and holding onto the handle of the hatchet Raven had buried into his breast. Nathan snapped into action, on high alert as he moved to the other side of the Jeep to search for the final soldier, the one that had lunged into the opposite ditch. The man was on the run, already halfway to the island of trees with the tent.

Raven aimed his rifle, but Nathan held up a hand. "We need him alive. Shoot him in the leg."

A crack sounded, and the thin, short man hit the dirt about one hundred yards from the road. Nathan turned back to the guy who had snuck up on him. He squirmed in pain on his back, feet slapping the concrete.

"Where the hell did you come from?" Nathan muttered. He slung his rifle over his back and kicked the man's gun away. Then he leaned down next to him, getting right to the point. "Where the fuck are the kids?"

"Don't kill me," the guy pleaded. He looked up, his bearded face contorted in agony. "I didn't hurt nobody. I swear it."

Nathan grabbed the handle of the hatchet. "I asked

you a question."

Lips trembling, the man still didn't answer. He closed his eyes and said something under his breath that Nathan couldn't make out. Might have been a curse or a prayer. It didn't matter. Nothing mattered but hunting down the bastards who had kidnapped his nephew and ambushed Lieutenant Dupree and his men.

"Suit yourself," Nathan said.

He twisted the blade a quarter of an inch. The man shrieked in agony. Nathan released his grip on the blade and waited for the skinhead to come back to reality, but his eyelids slowly drooped over his eyes as he slipped toward unconsciousness. A slap to his face pulled him back. He glared at Nathan, eyes burning with rage.

"Tell me where you took the kids," Nathan said.

"Fuck you," the man replied. He spat in Nathan's face and let out a hoarse laugh. Maybe he knew he was going to die, or maybe he was just that big of an asshole. Either way, Nathan could tell he wasn't getting any information from this one. He stood and considered leaving him there to die slowly in pain, but he didn't want the liability when he turned his back.

"Join your friends in hell," Nathan said. He plucked the hatchet from the man's chest. Blood gushed out of the cavity. He let out a scream as Nathan brought the blade down square in the middle of his forehead. The sickening crack echoed like a gunshot.

Nathan thought he would feel something like satisfaction, but all he felt was more pain. He wiggled the hatchet free and stood.

Raven waved from across the road. He was kneeling next to the injured man. Nathan stopped to check the bullet holes in the Jeep. There were two in the hood and several in the windshield. Almost every window had been shattered.

"Shit," he said. Nathan walked around the side of the Jeep when he saw his rucksack on the ground next to one of the corpses. The analog radio was right next to the pack. He bent down to examine the radio, cursing again at the sight of the shattered casing and protruding wires.

Nathan closed his eyes and snapped them back open again. Their one form of communication with the outside world was completely trashed. He stood and ran over to Raven.

"Radio and the Jeep are fucked," Nathan said when he got there. He handed the bloody hatchet to Raven, who gave him a cockeyed look, flared his nostrils, and then looked back down at the injured man wriggling on the ground.

"You fuckers shot my baby," he said in an incredulous high-pitched voice.

"I'm sorry," the man cried. "I was just—"

"We'll take their Humvee," Nathan said. He studied the man lying at his feet. He was covered in tattoos of hate symbols.

"Nathan, this racist piece of shit is named Joe," Raven said, patting the man's shoulder. Joe grimaced in pain. "Joe here has agreed to take us to meet his racist piece of shit friends at a place called the Castle. In exchange, I've promised not to cut his nuts off."

***

General Thor returned with another man Charlize didn't recognize. They set up laptops on a table in front of her bed.

"Madame Secretary, this is Colonel Mark Raymond. He will be leading the briefing about your son. I may have to duck out early to deal with the situation off the coast of Palm Beach. We're still running rescue missions to see if we can pull anyone from the water."

Charlize nodded. She understood Thor had other things to worry about with a war going on. A hostage situation was probably low on his priority list.

"Good afternoon, ma'am," Raymond said. He was a tall man with a bulbous nose and thick brown hair. "I've been unable to reach your brother on the channel you provided. We're still not sure if he reached out to Lieutenant Marco, either. The comms are a mess."

Charlize nodded again. She felt like a robot, but she didn't want to interrupt.

Raymond placed his laptop computer on a table in front of her bed. "Normally this briefing would be conducted by the FBI or perhaps the DOJ, but since the country is under martial law, the military is handling the case."

He typed a passcode into the computer and then angled it so she could see better. On screen, her sweet baby boy looked up with droopy eyes, his hair a mess. Her heart ached at the sight, but at least she had proof he was still alive. Raymond hit a button, and Ty's high voice came from the speakers.

"Mom, it's me. I miss you. Where are you? Why haven't you come for me? I'm not hurt, but these men are holding me captive in a place called the Castle and—"

The camera panned to a bearded man wearing fatigues. Blue eyes, cold as ice, stared back at her.

"My name is General Dan Fenix, and I'm the leader of the Sons of Liberty. We've taken it upon ourselves to restore order in these parts. Our mission is to take back our country from those that would have us enslaved."

Charlize ground her teeth as she watched the man fold his hands and smile at the camera.

"We have your son, Secretary Montgomery, and for the right price, you can have him back. I'll need ten million in gold bars and a list of weapons to be delivered at a place of my choosing. This is not a negotiation. If you don't deliver the gold and weapons within twenty-four hours, you'll be getting your son back significantly more damaged than he is now. And if you fail to comply with my requests…well, let's just say you won't be getting him back at all."

The feed shut off.

Charlize fought to keep her voice level as she asked, "Who the hell is General Dan Fenix?"

Raymond closed the laptop. "That's a good question. At first we weren't sure. I searched our databases to look up anyone by that rank and name but came up empty."

"The reason for that is simple," Thor said. "General Fenix was never a general. He was an Army captain who served two tours of duty in Iraq and one in Afghanistan. In 2005, he was dishonorably discharged after evidence surfaced he had ordered several civilians killed."

Raymond took over. "There were conflicting reports about those deaths. Some of his men seemed to have covered up what really happened in Iraq, and the others were too afraid to speak up. Fenix returned to Colorado and vanished off the map for several years. He resurfaced in Denver. The Feds were watching him—apparently he started a group affiliated with the Aryan Brotherhood called the Sons of Liberty. Although they seem to be a different sect with their own beliefs."

"The Sons of Liberty are basically white supremacists that hate the government and everyone who isn't white," Thor said. "Unlike the traditional skinhead, these guys are way more political. It's disgusting their name plays homage to the Founding Fathers."

"I was thinking the same thing," Raymond said. He massaged his jaw nervously. "We believe Fenix has been building his own personal army since he returned home from the war."

"The truth is that we don't know how many men he's been able to recruit or what kind of weaponry he's managed to amass," Thor said gravely.

"And now they have my son," Charlize said. "We have to find him."

"That's going to be difficult," Thor said. "We have no idea where he is, and we're strained for resources as it is."

Charlize breathed deeply through her nose, reminding herself that Thor had never been a father. He didn't understand how callous his remarks sounded.

"What about the area where Lieutenant Dupree was ambushed?" she asked.

"We don't know if it was Fenix and his men who killed Dupree," Raymond said.

"Of course. I'm sure it was a different highly skilled and well-armed paramilitary group in the middle of Colorado that took out those Marines," Charlize said. Frustration was bringing out her sarcastic streak—a tendency that Clint had always reminded her to curb. But her right-hand man was dead now, and she would be damned if she sat around talking to these men a moment longer while her son was in danger. Charlize swung her legs over the side of the bed.

Thor and Raymond stood simultaneously, while Albert

offered Charlize his hand.

"The doctor said you need your rest, Madame Secretary," Thor said.

"I rested. Now I'm getting up to speed on this Fenix son of a bitch." She smoothed out her loose-fitting sweat suit and swept her roughly chopped hair back from her forehead, trying to pretend that she still cut as commanding a figure as she once did on the Senate floor.

"We can't give him what he wants, ma'am, and you know that," Thor said. "Fenix is a terrorist, and the United States—"

"Does not negotiate with terrorists," Charlize said, finishing his sentence. "I know, and I agree."

Raymond looked at her quizzically. "Then what do you plan to do?"

She met his gaze steadily. "I'm going to hunt him down and kill him."

***

Sandra held her breath and pulled back the bandage covering Teddy's elbow. The flesh was mildly red, and there was no sign of a worsening infection, but that didn't mean he was out of the woods. The news of the Stanley and the loss of the medical supplies and food had everyone in the hospital on edge. They needed the antibiotics to keep Teddy alive, and aside from what they had on hand at the medical center, they were all out.

She slowly rewrapped his arm.

There was a knock on the door to the small isolation room they had moved Teddy into. Doctor Duffy opened the door and gestured for Allie to come inside. She fiddled with the white mask covering her face. Creek trotted up to the doorway wearing a plastic suit Sandra had found for him.

"Sit," Sandra instructed.

The dog obeyed and remained in the open doorway. He looked like an alien, but it was for Teddy's protection. Any germs could threaten his already weakened immune system.

"Teddy, I'd like you to meet my daughter Allie and my brother's dog, Creek," Sandra said.

Teddy shined at the sight of his new friends. "Hi, Allie, and hi Creek."

Creek sat on his hind legs in the doorway.

"He looks funny in that suit," Teddy said with a chuckle.

"I know," Sandra said. "Kind of like an alien doggy."

Creek stood and let out an affectionate whine.

"I wish I could give him a treat," Teddy said. He twisted to look at Sandra. "Can I later?"

"Uh, Nurse Spears, can I talk to you?" said Doctor Duffy. He stood behind Creek in the doorway and gestured for Sandra with a hand. She could tell by his tone and frown that he wasn't happy.

"Allie, you watch Creek, but make sure he stays sitting right there, okay? I'll be right back."

Her daughter dipped her head and up down. "Okay, mom."

Creek tried to follow, but Sandra snapped her fingers and the dog relaxed on the floor. He placed his head on his gloved paws as Allie kneeled next to him and stroked his plastic suit.

"Watch Teddy and Allie for me, boy," Sandra said. She knew it broke protocol, but she had taken every precaution possible, and Teddy needed this. Morale was in some ways even more important than the antibiotics keeping him alive.

Creek let out another low whine as she left the room. He was really missing Raven, and so was Sandra. Not hearing from her brother for almost twenty-four hours had torn at her insides. She knew he could take care of himself, but the roads were getting worse by the hour. Every time she heard a vehicle pull into the parking lot, she would peek out from the emergency room to see if it was Raven.

She followed Doctor Duffy down the hall, waiting for a lecture, but instead he stopped outside of Martha's room and bowed his head, sighing. "I need your help, Sandra. As you know, Colton wants to know what happened to Martha, and I can't get her to talk to me. Can you try?"

"Sure," Sandra said.

She went to open the door, but Duffy put a hand on her wrist. "Do you know what's happening out there? I mean, is it true? Was the fire at the Stanley intentional?"

The rumors had circled around the hospital, but Sandra didn't know what to believe. She had to focus on her job and leave the policing up to Chief Colton.

"I don't know," Sandra said. She opened the door and walked inside the dark room lit only by a solar lamp. She put it on the bedside table and sat down next to Martha.

"Hi, Dr. Kohler, it's Nurse Spears."

Martha blinked and slowly rolled her head to the side.

"How are you feeling? Are you thirsty?" Sandra asked.

Martha licked her dry lips and Sandra helped her take several sips from a straw. Then she used a cloth to wipe Martha's forehead dry.

"I'm here to talk to you about what you said earlier.

About the kids."

Martha swallowed the last of the water in her mouth and looked at the ceiling, closing her eyes, and then snapping them open.

"The soldiers..." Her voice cracked and she tried to speak again. "The soldiers took the kids."

"What soldiers?"

Martha bowed her head, then looked back up to meet Sandra's eyes. "They weren't American soldiers. One of them had a Swastika tattoo."

Sandra nearly dropped the cloth in her hand. She had walked into the room with a dozen questions running through her mind, but now she just had one. Could these be the same men who took the supplies and set fire to the Stanley, and the same people who took Nathan's nephew?

"I found two kids on the road. I was going to take them to Denver with me, but I failed them..." Martha said. "I failed—"

"No, you did not. You did what you could." Sandra dabbed Martha's forehead with the moist cloth. "You don't have to tell me anything that's too scary to remember. I'm just trying to figure out if these were the same men my brother and my friend Nathan went to look for. Nathan's nephew was taken from the Easterseals camp south of here."

Martha brushed the cloth away from her forehead. "I saw a boy in the back of that pickup in a wheelchair."

Sandra hesitated. "A wheelchair?"

"Yes," Martha said. She rested her head back on the pillow, but kept her eyes on Sandra.

"I hope your brother and this Nathan are skilled soldiers because the men that shot me won't hesitate to kill them or anyone who gets in their way. They had evil in their eyes, Nurse Spears."

— 15 —

Colton paced back and forth, trying to get a grip on the situation. Mayor Andrews, Tom Feagen, and a handful of other administrators were standing in the hallway outside the town offices. Everyone was arguing.

If Jake were here, he would have shouted in his booming voice, silencing them in a heartbeat. But Jake wasn't here, and Colton was on his own.

"Quiet!" shouted a woman. Lindsey was pushing through the crowd. "Let the Chief speak," she said.

The side conversations quieted down.

Colton nodded at Margaret. Despite her earlier insistence that she was fine, the dispatcher was shaking. He hated asking her to go through it again, but he wanted the mayor and her staff to hear it firsthand. She told them what she'd told Colton earlier—a dozen men in black ski masks had stormed the station, pointed a gun in her face, and demanded the keys to Theo's cell.

"Were these men soldiers?" Gail asked when Margaret had finished.

"No, I don't think so," Margaret said. "But they did have what looked like really old military trucks. The type I remember seeing transport soldiers in Vietnam. The backs of their trucks were filled with crates and canned food."

"So they hit our supply depots first," Don mused. "That would have taken planning and coordination."

"How did they get past our road blocks?" Feagen asked.

"We don't have the resources to guard every single road," Colton said.

"Did you see where they went?" Gail asked Margaret.

Detective Ryburn stepped forward. "I did. They were heading toward the park entrance."

Colton pivoted so he could look the detective in the eye. "Why the hell didn't you tell me that earlier?"

"The Stanley was burning," he said. "I'm sorry, Chief, but there wasn't anything I could do. Some of them even had automatic rifles."

Don held up a hand. "Wait, back up. You said they were heading into the park?"

Ryburn nodded, his chin jiggling.

"That's where we're storing the meat," Don said.

Colton drew in a long breath. "Jesus, these guys knew where we were hiding everything."

"How?" Gail asked.

"Good question," Tom Feagen said. "It was your job to make sure our facilities were protected, Colton. Now what are we going to do?"

"What will we do for food?" someone asked.

Gail scowled. "And medical supplies."

"And where are we supposed to house the tourists?" asked Officer Hines.

The questions came in a flurry around Colton. He took a step backward. It was all too much—the questions, the pressure. He had lost control of the town in a single afternoon.

"We'll find a way," Lindsey said. "Right, Chief?"

She looked at him with the hopeful gaze that he would expect from a rookie soldier looking to a commander for reassurance before a battle. Colton didn't have any to give.

"We have to get our supplies back." He pulled out his Colt .45, flipped open the loading gate, thumbed the hammer, and spun the empty cylinder to inspect the chambers.

"Grab the pickup, Lindsey," Colton said. "Don, you coordinate with our officers and volunteers to see if you can figure out what these guys took. Margaret, stay on the radio. I'm heading up Trail Ridge Road."

"No," came a firm voice.

Colton snapped his full cylinder closed and turned to Gail.

"I've talked it over with the others, and I'm putting Sergeant Aragon in charge of the police department and Estes Park militia," she said.

He could only stare at her for a moment. "What the hell are you saying?"

"You're not in charge anymore, Marcus," she said. "We still want you on the force, but it's time for a change in leadership."

Don put his cowboy hat on and stepped next to the mayor, but Lindsey walked over and stood by Colton.

"You can't do this, Mayor," she said. "This isn't Chief Colton's fault."

Officers Matthew and Officer Hines, along with Detective Ryburn, remained where they were standing— unwilling to take a side, or perhaps waiting to figure out which side to take.

"If Jake were here—" Colton started to say when Gail cut him off.

"He's not. I'm sorry, Marcus, but Jake is dead. And you haven't kept your promise to protect this town. It's time to let someone else try…before it's too late."

The words stung Colton deep, like a hot knife scraping his bones. A hundred things rushed through his mind, memories of better times and dreams for the future.

Hines and Matthew slowly moved over to Don's left side, but to his utter shock, Ryburn walked over to Colton. Lines had been drawn, three against three. But Don had the support of the town administration.

Colton balled his fists.

Don saw that and raised a brow as if to taunt him. Colton narrowed his eyes at the sergeant. God, he wanted to jack Don in the face and knock him on his ass, but that wasn't going to do anything but make Colton feel better. The true test of a man was doing the right thing even when clouded by anger. His father taught him that when he was just a boy. Too bad no one had taught Don what a real man was.

"Fine, Mayor," Colton said, relaxing his hands. Without Jake, Raven, and Nathan to stand by his side, he had no choice but to back down. In the end, the town came first. His family came first. He would not make things worse by resisting the decision of the majority.

Colton pulled off his chief of police badge and handed it to Gail.

"You can take mine, too," Lindsey said. She fumbled for her shield, but Colton put a hand on her arm.

"Don't," he said. "The force needs you."

She scowled, but stepped down. As Colton left, he heard Don giving the same damned orders he'd been delivering before Gail demoted him.

A few minutes later, Lindsey and Ryburn followed him outside.

"This is horseshit!" Lindsey said. She ran alongside,

her face redder than her hair. "You can't let Don take charge. He's a jackass."

"A real jerk," Ryburn agreed.

"It's not my call," Colton said.

Lindsey looked at the ground. "I hate to do this, Chief, but I'm gonna need the keys to the truck back. Don is sending me up to the park to check on the meat."

Colton pulled the key from his pocket and held it out, even though giving up Jake's truck felt like a betrayal. "Did he say you had to go alone?"

Lindsey grinned, looking more like her usual self. "Why don't you drive? I'll take shotgun."

"Let's go," Colton said, closing his fist around the key.

Lindsey took the passenger side, and Ryburn jumped in the back. The drive out of town was met with silence, Lindsey looking out the window and Colton focusing on the road. They all knew the men who had taken their supplies were long gone now, but the threat lingered and Lindsey loaded her AR-15.

"I'm sorry, Chief," she said.

"Better stop calling me that."

She shook her head and turned back to the window.

Twenty minutes later, they were winding up the long road into Rocky Mountain National Park. Snow framed the sides, a foot at first, then an entire wall the height of a man. A chilly breeze rushed into the open windows.

Colton had plenty of time to think about everything that had happened, but his primary concern right now was that meat. They had at least two weeks' worth, plus a week from the dozens of elk and other game they had killed to feed the town. That meant three weeks of survival without having any outside help. Without it, they were going to be scrambling to keep everyone fed, especially with their canned and dried food stolen.

At twelve thousand feet above sea level, the bitter breeze stung Colton's lungs. He rolled up his window and parked the truck outside the Ranger station.

"Where the hell is Ranger Field?" Colton asked. He was supposed to be guarding this place, but the old Indian motorcycle that Field had been driving was gone.

Colton got out of the truck and un-holstered his Colt .45. He thumbed back the hammer and stepped onto the snow. Breathtaking views of the Rocky Mountains surrounded him on all sides, but he was focused on the open doors to the metal sheds next to the ranger station.

He crunched over the snow, already knowing the frozen goods and the meat were all gone, but needing to see it for himself.

"Ryburn, go check the station for Field," Colton said, automatically taking command of the situation as he'd always done. "Lindsey, you check the other sheds."

Colton walked to the first building and stepped inside, breath coming out in an icy poof. Sunlight shone through the open door, illuminating a snow-covered floor still marked with the impressions of meat and the other goods they had stored here. In the center of the room, a single glass bottle of pickled herring protruded from the snow.

"The other sheds are all empty, sir," Lindsey said.

Colton pulled the bottle out of the snow and found a piece of paper tied onto the side. He retreated back outside and held it into the sun.

"What's that?" Lindsey asked. She wrinkled her nose. "Seriously? I hate pickled fish. Of all the things to leave…"

Colton untied the note and read the message.

You can blame Raven Spears for your missing loot. I wouldn't have even known about Estes Park if it weren't for him. Your first mistake was trusting that weasel, and your second mistake was putting my cousin Theo in jail. Estes Park is a nice place. I might have to come back for another visit soon.

Sincerely — Nile Redford

"What's it say?" Lindsey asked.

Colton almost laughed. He shook his head, handed it over to her, and then turned to look at the view. Behind the ranger station, arms of smoke from the smoldering ruins of the Stanley rose into the sky. Below, the Estes Park valley stretched out like a bowl. The Fall River wound through the flat meadows, and a herd of elk, little more than a constellation of brown dots from this distance, moved along the banks at the water's edge.

Ryburn rounded the station a moment later. "No sign of Fields in the station," he reported.

Colton cursed and lit a cigarette he had bummed off Officer Hines. The situation had gone from bad to worse with Ranger Field missing. He feared the man was buried in the snow somewhere out here.

After taking a drag, Colton took a final look out over the valley. The only thing the town had left was clean water and the wild game in the park—and the game wouldn't last forever. Two of his officers were dead, and he feared more would die in the violence that ensued from the starving citizens.

For a fleeting moment, he felt relieved that he was no longer in charge. The feeling passed in a heartbeat when he looked back at the place where he had married his high school sweetheart and raised a daughter. He wasn't in charge anymore, but he was going to be damned if he let anything happen to Estes Park.

***

The Humvee growled down the road. Raven had traded his Jeep in for the upgraded military vehicle, but he hated leaving his baby behind. He would be back for her soon. Just like he would be back for Creek. He was really missing his four-legged best friend. Nathan was a poor substitute.

He pushed down on the gas pedal and the Humvee rocketed up a hill. His eyes flitted over the canvas—a drab landscape, gray rocks, and grayer sky.

"Eyes up," Nathan said to Joe from the back seat. The racist little prick was groaning from the pain. Nathan slapped the kid every time he began to lose consciousness.

"You can't die yet," Nathan said. He continued the interrogation with a backhand to Joe's chin.

"How many of you are there?"

"I—I don't know," Joe said.

Nathan put his thumb into the bullet wound in Joe's leg, prompting a screech of agony.

"Please," he cried, whimpering like a child. "Please don't kill me."

Raven looked away from the rearview mirror. They were coming up on a canyon with high rock walls. Shadows crossed the road. Easing up on the gas, Raven ducked down to look at the outcroppings as they entered the gully. He was searching for a glint of metal or scrap of color that didn't belong in the gray rocks. The second he took his eyes off the road, the tires jolted over a rock.

He swerved just in time to miss a skirt of scree that

had spilled onto the pavement. The trail of loose rocks spread until the road was completely blocked. Raven slammed on the brakes just in time to avoid a collision.

"Looks like a rockslide," he said.

"Is there a way around?" Nathan asked.

Raven backed up to find an alternate path, moving into the shadows. A crackling noise came from the back seat.

"Hey, is that a radio?"

Nathan pulled up a backpack from the floor behind the passenger seat. He rummaged through the contents and found a handheld radio.

"I thought you checked this bag, Raven."

"I thought you checked it," Raven replied.

Nathan turned the radio on and a voice came over the channel.

"Liberty 1, this is Snake Nest. Do you copy? Over."

"Shit," Nathan said.

"Liberty 1, Liberty 1. Snake Nest, do you copy?" repeated the voice.

Raven gestured for the radio. "Gimme."

"What are you going to say?" Nathan asked.

"Just trust me."

He grabbed the radio from Nathan and brought it to his lips.

"Copy you. Snake Nest, this is Liberty 1."

"Where the hell have you been, Liberty 1? You missed your last check-in."

Raven couldn't help but grin, getting into the character. "We found some loot back on Interstate 70. We'll be back in a few hours."

There was a pause that felt like an eternity.

"Roger that, Liberty 1. The General looks forward to

seeing what you brought him. Over."

Raven turned off the handheld. "Who the fuck is the General?"

"Answer him," Nathan said, squeezing Joe's arm.

"General Fenix," Joe mumbled. "He's the leader of the Sons of Liberty."

"That's the guy Dupree was talking about, right?"

Nathan nodded and looked at Joe. "You're with the Aryan Nation or what? How many of you fuckers are there?"

Joe didn't answer. He shifted in the seat next to Nathan and brushed up against the door, moaning in pain.

"How many soldiers are there in your group?" Raven asked.

Nathan grabbed Joe and pulled him away from the door. His eyes had rolled into his head and his lips pursed. The wrap covering Joe's leg was saturated with blood. It looked like he'd lost a lot—maybe too much. Raven didn't feel so much as a flicker of remorse. Skinhead bastards got what was coming to them.

"I don't think we're getting much more out of our friend," Raven said. "We have to stick to the original plan."

Raven pulled around the debris pile, the tires jolting over the loose rocks. After powering through the last stretch, he continued through the windy ravine at fifty miles an hour. Gray clouds rolled overhead, only a sliver of sun peeking through their belly. Raindrops pelted the windshield, seeping through a bullet hole and onto the dashboard.

"The first turn-off is about a mile ahead," Nathan said.

"I know," Raven replied. He had memorized the map

Joe had sketched out for them. He claimed it was the back way to the Castle. Totally unguarded. Raven and Nathan were both skeptical, but they had no other choice than to check out the road. They would find a place to ditch the Humvee and move the rest of the way in on foot.

"Hand me that radio," Nathan said. "I'm going to try and see if I can get ahold of my sister or someone who can reach her."

Raven handed it back to Nathan.

"You ever hear of this General Fenix?" Nathan asked while he was fiddling with the channels.

"Nope," Raven said. "But I know the type. If he's part of the Aryan Nation, then he sure as hell isn't going to like me."

Nathan caught his gaze in the rearview mirror. "You're sure you're up for this?"

Raven took a moment to think before he answered. Running the gauntlet was one thing, but heading into a lion's den to face the kind of men who would skin him alive was another. Sandra, Allie, Creek, and Colton needed Raven. But so did Nathan, and so did his nephew and the other kids being held hostage.

"I'm up for it, Major, but I need you to make me a promise. If something happens to me, I want you to look after my family. You have connections through your sister. Make sure that Estes Park gets supplies and help."

"You have my word, Raven. I promised Colton the same thing."

Raven held up a hand. "One more thing. If I die, you better tell Lindsey that I went down in a blaze of glory—especially if I didn't."

Nathan scanned through the channels, reaching out to

anyone who might be listening. Raven sped through the ravine while they waited for a response that never came.

They drove in tense silence. Up ahead, Raven saw something hanging from a tree that made his blood run cold.

"I think we're about to enter enemy territory," Raven said, pointing. He pulled off onto the shoulder of the road and backed into the shadows of a bluff.

"Is that a..." Nathan's voice trailed off.

Raven pulled the binoculars from his vest and narrowed in on the figure of a man stretched out in a T-shape, lashed to the branches of an oak. A vulture pecked a ribbon of flesh away from his neck.

"They crucified the poor son of a bitch," Nathan said.

Joe groaned. "Liam didn't see eye to eye with the General, so the General took his eyes." He coughed and rested his head against the seat.

"Damn," Raven breathed. These bastards were even worse than he'd imagined.

"Took his eyes," Joe mumbled to himself. "He'll take yours too, and do worse to the injun."

Raven shook his head, thinking of the Sioux story about the end of the world.

It tells of a place where the prairie meets the badlands—a place with a hidden cave.

Well, there was a nice rolling meadow ahead, and behind them was a stretch of rocky, arid terrain and a network of caves in the mountains—if Joe was to be believed. All they needed was a black dog, and yet another of Raven's childhood stories would come to life.

Nathan tightened the rope around Joe's hands and then tied it to the door. He finished securing the prisoner with tape over his mouth. Nathan grabbed one of the six

M4s they had taken from the dead Sons of Liberty, and climbed into the passenger seat.

"Keep moving," he said.

Inside the cave lives a woman, Raven thought, repeating the story in his mind as he drove. *She's been there for thousands of years working on a blanket strip of her buffalo robe. Beside her sits Shunka Sapa, a massive black dog.*

"I think I figured out who Shunka Sapa is," Raven finally said.

"What?" Nathan looked over. "Oh, from the Cherokee story?"

"The Sioux story. Big difference, Major."

Nathan plucked the map off the dashboard. "General Fenix is our Shunka Sapa, right?"

Raven nodded. "Yeah, I think so."

"According to Joe, we're almost there. Let's put that black dog down."

"Recon first, Major," Raven said. "I don't trust a thing this punk says."

Nathan agreed with a nod. "I'm going to try the radio one more time." He ran through the channels while Raven checked his gear.

Crossbow and hatchet? Check. Glock? Check. MK11? Check. Hand grenades? Check. They had plenty of ammunition and weapons for the hunt. He caught himself. This wasn't a hunt—this was a battle.

Nathan cursed and tossed the radio aside. "Still nothing. I've got a bad feeling about this."

Raven didn't know what to say, so he merely put the Humvee in gear and rolled on. They were coming up on the man on the tree. His shaved head was bowed, his chin tucked against his naked chest. His hands and feet were nailed into the bark. It was hard to tell how long he had been strung up, but his flesh was already decomposing.

He gunned the engine and sped down the road that cut through the meadow. A fence of foothills lined with pine trees provided a natural barrier at the end of the valley. The road twisted up into the mountains beyond.

"You see the turn-off?" Raven asked.

Nathan was already scoping the jagged cliffs that towered over the road. There were plenty of perches for a sniper, but they hoped the Humvee and the radio would allow them to sneak behind enemy lines.

Still, Raven didn't like it. This was starting to bring back memories of the raid in North Korea eighteen months ago. Even for a trained soldier, heading into enemy territory never got any easier. Without intel, and with only a two-man team who were both injured and exhausted, it was going to be almost impossible.

Letting out a discreet sigh, Raven focused on the plan. Recon and scouting came first. They would also try one last time to reach Nathan's sister or someone else who could call in support. If that failed again, they would do a risk assessment.

On the right side of the road was a lake with a mirrored surface, and to the left, a lush forest of pines. Raven slowed on the approach, looking for the entrance to the frontage road that would take them to the so-called Castle. Instead of the path, he saw another body strung up on the base of a ponderosa pine on the left side of the road.

"Christ," Nathan said. "More of them?"

He was looking to the right side of the road. Raven turned to see another corpse crucified to a tree there. He stopped the Humvee in the middle of the shadowed road, engine humming.

These bodies weren't Sons of Liberty soldiers. The dead people—a man on the left side and a woman on the right—appeared to be in their mid-twenties and were dressed in civilian clothing. They looked like campers.

Nathan pointed at a National Park Service sign about a quarter mile down the road. "That's the turn-off."

"And this is a warning," Raven said, nodding at the dead.

It reminded him of what the Apaches did to their prisoners—and the stories of what the American Army did to the American Indians. Both sides had butchered each other, scalping, slaughtering, and stringing up the dead.

But this wasn't the fucking Oregon Trail. This was the twenty-first century. This type of brutality wasn't supposed to exist in the American West anymore. The Aryan Brotherhood displayed a level of brutality Raven had never seen in his lifetime.

"Stay frosty," he said to himself.

Nathan kept his rifle shouldered, looking for targets as Raven pulled down the frontage road and entered a tunnel of trees. The canopy overhead nearly blocked out the mountain peaks in the distance. Darkness shrouded them as they drove slowly down the road. There wasn't a single sound of nature inside the forest. No chirping birds or bugs—no sign of deer or rabbits.

"This place gives me the creeps," Nathan said.

"I hear that, brother," Raven agreed.

The dirt road snaked through the forest and began to rise over another hill. As they neared the top, Nathan suddenly lowered his rifle and said, "Back, back, back!"

Raven saw the stone lookout tower at the same time. He could only see the top of the structure, but it was enough to send him peeling back in reverse.

"Joe wasn't kidding. They've got a castle," Nathan said. "Pull off behind those trees."

Raven steered the Humvee off the road and parked beneath the trees. It wasn't full cover, but they would camouflage the truck. They both got out, and Raven hefted the MK11 they had found in the vehicle over his shoulder. He had trained to use the semi-automatic sniper rifle back in the Marines. It was equipped with a swivel-based bipod, sound suppressor, mil-dot riflescope, and back-up iron sights. He could pin a tail on a donkey with the gun at fifteen hundred yards.

"Joe's unconscious," Nathan said.

"I say we leave him here. Come on, help me cover the Humvee."

After covering up the truck with fallen branches, they set off into the forest. Five minutes into the hike, Raven spotted the brown, rocky embankments framing the edge of the woods. A fence of Douglas firs grew out of the steep inclines. The slope descended a hundred feet to the pasture below and was covered in mossy boulders; plenty of places to hide.

They ducked behind one of the rocks and scoped the valley below. Raven checked the road and then moved the crosshairs back to the tower. It was more of a silo, made of stone with a lookout at the top. He put it at about twelve hundred yards out. Two men stood in the lookout at the top with their rifles angled out over the valley. A camp consisting of four buildings stood to the east.

"Two contacts," Raven reported. "But we're clear up here. This is the perfect vantage."

Nathan held up a pair of binoculars. He did a

thorough scan of the valley while Raven checked their six.

"Looks like some sort of camp," he whispered. "That's got to be where they're keeping the kids. I see a couple of contacts patrolling, but that's it."

Raven took another look. A stone building and several log cabins were nestled under the ridgeline to the east. It was the same type of architecture Raven had seen in other national parks, built during the New Deal when President Roosevelt created the Civilian Conservation Corps to put America back to work after the Great Depression. Several men patrolled the camp with automatic rifles. Raven counted three of them and only one clunker pickup truck.

"My guess is these fuckers hightailed it up here to seek refuge after the attack last week," he said. "They don't appear to be that organized."

"We can't underestimate them," Nathan said.

Raven nodded grimly. He had underestimated Brown Feather, and he wouldn't make that mistake again.

"Try and get ahold of your sister again," Raven said. "If you can't, then we attack at dark."

16

Rows of torches burned in Bond Park. Tonight, Cindy and Milo Todd were to be executed for killing Officer Rick Nelson.

Colton stood next to Lindsey, stoically watching the scene. He'd told Kelly and Risa to stay home—he couldn't stand the thought of them witnessing this. All Colton could think of was a Ku Klux Klan lynching.

"This feels wrong," Lindsey said.

"People need to know the law still exists," said a voice.

Don approached, carrying a shotgun in one hand. A new gold star was pinned on his breast. "When the men who burned down the Stanley and took our supplies hear about this, they'll think twice about coming back to Estes Park."

"I don't think Mr. Redford's crew will be worried," Colton said.

"Justice will be served to those that break the law, including this Mr. Redford," Don said. He spat a wad of tobacco onto the ground when Colton didn't reply.

"Don, don't you have anything better to do right now?" Lindsey asked.

"Look, I'm sorry about how things went down in the Mayor's office today, but you don't have what it takes to get us out of this mess, and I think you know it," Don said, never taking his eyes off Colton.

Colton balled his right hand into a fist and pivoted like

he was about to throw a punch. Don flinched and took a step back.

"Congratulations on the new job, Chief Aragon," Colton said. "I hope to God you're as tough as you think you are."

He walked away, leaving Don to prepare the nooses and contemplate what came next.

Lindsey followed Colton toward the knot of curious residents that had formed in the parking lot beside the park. Several folks stood along the railing on the deck outside Claire's Restaurant, and there were more standing on the balcony of La Cabana Mexican Grill.

In the flicker of torchlight, he recognized most of the faces. Many of them he had known his entire life. His job—his duty———his duty had been to keep them safe, and he had let them all down.

"Are they really going to hang those people?" someone asked.

"Sure are," another person said. "They deserve it."

"I'd shoot them myself," said another man. "Rick was my neighbor. He was a good man."

June Roberts, a retired woman who worked at the Safeway part-time bagging groceries, interjected. Her voice was soft but firm. "We can't just kill them. That makes us no better than they are."

Colton bowed his head, trying to hold off the anger by counting in his head. Every time he tried, he kept coming back to the pointlessness of each death that had occurred over the past week. He scanned the crowd for his wife, just to make sure she hadn't come. He was glad he didn't see Sandra or Allie in the crowd, either, but he did spot Rex and Lilly Stone. Both of them watched Colton, their faces blank.

One person he couldn't find who should have been here was Mayor Gail Andrews.

A commotion came from the back of the crowd. Colton followed its source to see Milo and Cindy being led from the station by Officer Matthew and Officer Hines. The prisoners shuffled, hands cuffed and feet shackled together by a connecting chain.

"Where's Gail?" he asked Lindsey.

She shrugged. "No idea."

She better be here.

Father Frank Nolte emerged from the crowd. He was dressed in a black shirt with a white collar. Colton had known Frank for thirty years. He'd married Colton and Kelly, baptized Risa, and most recently presided over Melissa Stone's private funeral. Before the attack, he'd been gearing down to retire, but Colton had a feeling he was about to become a very busy man.

Frank loosened his clerical collar and said, "You're sure there's no other way, Marcus?"

"Not my call, Father," Colton said. "Don's in charge now."

A woman shouted over the din of the crowd. "You can't hang us!"

It was Cindy, and she was pulling on her chains, yanking her brother away from the gazebo. The crowd, now several hundred strong, would be unstoppable if they decided to protest.

"You can't do this!" Cindy shouted. "Please, please!"

"It was Eric! Eric killed that cop!" Milo yelled.

Don pumped his shotgun and angled it at them. "Both of you, be quiet. You will have your time to speak in a few minutes."

"I wish they'd get on with it," someone said behind him. Colton turned and saw Gail, her eyes fixed on the makeshift gallows.

Apparently the mayor had decided to show up after all.

"We're really going to do this?" Colton asked.

"We've already discussed this, Marcus. We *have* to do this."

Colton faced her. "You're wrong."

"I wish I was," she sighed. "This isn't going to be the last time we have to do something like this."

"No! Please!" Cindy shouted again.

Hines pulled Milo and Cindy toward a long wooden footstool that had been set up under the nooses. Don pointed the shotgun at them. "Up," he ordered.

"Please, please don't do this!" Milo begged. "It was Eric. He's the one that hit that cop in the head with the rock!"

"Yeah, it was Eric!" Cindy shouted. "You already killed him. This ain't right!"

Don angled the gun at Cindy, and she finally stood on the stool. Once she and Milo were both under the nooses, Father Frank performed the sign of the cross.

There were a few shouts from the crowd, but most citizens simply waited in silence. Colton suspected a good portion of them didn't expect them to follow through with the execution.

"Stop!" Cindy shouted. "I'm sorry, I'm sorry! I swear to God, this wasn't my fault."

She locked eyes with Colton. There was something in her gaze besides anger, but it wasn't regret. It was fear. He guessed Cindy would say anything right now to save her own skin.

Don cleared his throat and then announced, "Cindy and Milo Todd, you have been found guilty by a jury of your peers in the murder of Officer Rick Nelson, the kidnapping of Detective Lindsey Plymouth, and the attempted murder of several police officers. Estes Park, Colorado, and the United States of America is under martial law, and the punishment for your crimes is death."

"We never even had a trial!" Milo shouted.

Cindy lowered her head, sobbing uncontrollably, snot flowing freely from her nose.

"The Estes Park administration reviewed the case and found you guilty of the crimes I just stated," Don said. "That's the law now."

"Do it!" someone shouted. Colton turned to see Kyle, the thirteen-year-old son of their neighbors, punching the air with his fist. "Hang them!"

Don raised a hand, and the crowd quieted.

"We all know the country is at war," he said, his voice booming over the park. "A war that we will only survive if we deal swiftly and violently with our enemies. There will be many tough decisions from here on out. Some of them won't be popular. Others will be questioned. But Cindy and Milo made their decision, and they will receive their justice."

"Please," Cindy begged.

"Father Nolte will now say a prayer," Don said.

Colton saw Frank's lips moving, but he only heard bits and pieces of the prayer. The crowd continued to watch in silence. A mother in the front covered her son's eyes, and several people walked away.

Cindy continued to beg for her life, but Milo just stared ahead, his gaze vacant and withdrawn. Sweat dripped down his forehead, and a wet spot had blossomed around his crotch.

In Afghanistan, Colton had once towered over a Taliban soldier that was on his back, leg busted and torso full of bullet holes. The man was going to die, and he had known it. The body did some awful things when that happened.

Frank finished his prayer and looked to Don.

"Do you have any final words?" Don asked.

"I'm sorry," Cindy cried. "I'm sorry."

Milo sneered, suddenly snapping out of his stupor. "You're all going to burn in hell for this."

Don looked at Gail, and she nodded. "Proceed, Officer Hines," he said.

Colton couldn't believe it—Don didn't even have the guts to do this himself. He had asked the younger officer to do it instead.

Officer Hines climbed the ladder behind the makeshift gallows and slipped bags over their heads. Frank made the sign of a cross again, held up his Bible, and recited the Lord's Prayer in a trembling voice.

Hines looked back at Don, who nodded. After a moment of hesitation, Hines kicked the stools away one at a time. Cindy and Milo dropped, the ropes tightening around their necks. Legs still shackled, they squirmed and jerked like frogs.

Somewhere in the crowd, a baby starting crying. Colton turned to see Rick Nelson's wife in the front row. She was holding her crying daughter in her arms, staring at the two hanging bodies with complete hatred.

Colton forced his gaze away and left before the Todds stopped kicking.

***

Charlize and Albert approached the double doors to U.S. Northern Command side by side. It was just after nine o'clock at night, but she felt wide-awake.

According to the doctors, she had been taken down by a combination of things: an infection, low blood sugar, and fatigue. She'd needed a few days of rest—and her body had made the call to shut down. The new antibiotics were helping, and despite the constant headache, she was starting to feel better already. Once he'd been convinced that Charlize was going to be okay, Albert had given her another frank chat about not listening to him when he'd tried to take her to the medical ward.

Two Marines came to attention as Charlize approached the double doors. The man on the left pushed them open to the two-level room beyond, which was currently buzzing with activity. It was the same basic setup she had seen in the PEOC and on the *USS John Stennis*. Monitors fed images of hotspots around the United States. On the right wall was the feed from a video camera inside a Humvee rolling down a highway.

Two more monitors displayed aerial footage from helicopters, and a third showed checkered farmland somewhere in the Midwest, all of it burning. There were a dozen other monitors showing views of highways clogged with vehicles, refugees, and destruction.

So this is what's been happening while I was asleep.

President Diego stood at the central table next to General Thor. He drank coffee from a mug with the presidential seal on it while Thor briefed him.

Colonel Raymond, Thor's second in command, jogged up the steps while Charlize observed the room. He stopped at the top of the stairs. "Please follow me, Secretary Montgomery."

"Colonel, have you gotten any closer to finding out where Fenix is holding Ty?" she asked.

"No, ma'am, but it's a large area and we only have one bird in the area right now. Most everything that was at Buckley AFB was killed in the EMP blast, but we're moving some working aircraft there." He paused on the step below her and looked up. "From one parent to another, we will find your son. I've got my best team working on this."

"Thank you, Colonel," she said.

The reassurance was exactly what she needed to prepare for her first briefing since leaving the USS *John Stennis*. President Diego held up a hand when he saw her, but he didn't smile. He stepped away from the table and met her at the bottom of the ramp.

"Good to see you back on your feet, Charlize. A lot has happened since you were out," Diego said. "Follow me."

"I'll be right here, ma'am," Albert said. He smiled. "Always."

Charlize smiled back at him. He had done so much for her over the past week, especially after losing Clint. She owed him her life. When the time was right, she was going to get him to open up—and maybe even get him to start calling her by her first name—but not until he was ready.

Thor walked with them to a conference room tucked back in a corner of the room. Inside, a long table furnished the narrow room. A dozen military officers and civilians glanced up from the folders in front of them. Charlize only recognized a few of the faces.

"I'd like to introduce you all to the Secretary of Defense, Charlize Montgomery," Diego said.

"Hello," Charlize said, raising a burned hand. She took a seat next to Diego and he passed her a folder marked *Confidential*. She cracked the seal as Thor began speaking.

"Good evening, everyone. We have a lot of ground to cover. I'll start with an update on the North Korean threat. As you all know, the USS *John Stennis* was attacked and destroyed. We lost some good men and women, but the enemy sub was also destroyed. The bad news is we think there is another one out there. Colonel Raymond will explain what we're dealing with in a few minutes but first, let's talk about the recovery efforts here in the United States."

Thor turned to a wall-mounted monitor and waited for it to come on. A map of North America appeared on screen.

"This is the EMP blast umbrella. As you can see, it extends to the borders with Canada and Mexico, in locations marked in red."

Charlize had seen a similar map four or five days ago, but she was shocked to see that the red EMP umbrella extended well into both neighboring countries.

Thor switched to another map, this time of just the United States. "This is the radiation zone," he continued. "We predicted twenty-five percent of the population would perish in the first two weeks. Those numbers were low. Reports coming from the Midwest are higher than originally projected. Add to that the chaos in our major cities, and we're looking at thirty percent. We've also had difficulty setting up the Survivor Centers for logistical reasons."

"Recovery is my main focus," Diego cut in. "We're

receiving lots of support from our allies across the pond, but we can't count on much assistance from Mexico or Canada, due to their own situations. I've readjusted our military assets to protect the convoys moving the generators to the radiation-free zones in the States. Our goal is to protect those populations and get the power back on in places we can still save." He glanced at Charlize. "Now that you're back on your feet, I'd like you to help with this effort."

"Sir, all due respect, but our main focus should be destroying the North Korean submarines and any forces they may still have lurking out there," Charlize said. "That's why I gave the order to deploy HSM squadrons before I left the USS *John Stennis*. Can someone tell me what we have deployed right now as counter measures on top of my request?"

"Yes, ma'am," Raymond said.

Several people shot what might have been judgmental glares at her. She didn't exactly blame them. An entire team of Marines and a valuable helicopter had been sent to find her son, and here she was talking about re-prioritizing the main focus of the government.

"My point is that we can't afford to be attacked again," Charlize clarified. "The recovery efforts depend on our ability to prevent another attack."

Raymond finished thumbing through a folder and pulled out a sheet of paper. "We've added four P-8 Poseidons and three squadrons of F-18 Super Hornets to the hunt. We're casting a wide net and will find the remaining sub eventually."

"Eventually?" President Diego said, frustration rising in his voice. "Charlize is right. We can't afford to be attacked again. I don't understand how some archaic old junker submarines are slipping through our net of detection."

"It makes me wonder if they are having help," Charlize added. "The sub will have to surface to refuel and charge their batteries."

"Yes, ma'am, that's true, but it's possible they refueled without detection, or that they refueled before getting close to U.S. waters. Our best chance will be catching it with radar on the surface, or seeing its snorkel," Thor replied.

Charlize felt like a hypocrite for her next order, but it was the only way to protect the United States. "Mr. President, I would highly encourage you to consider reallocating some of our remaining aircraft, specifically F-18s, just like you are readjusting military assets to protect the convoys. We need as many aircraft involved in the hunt for this final sub as possible. There's no telling what the North Koreans still plan to do after the kamikaze stunt they pulled with the USS *John Stennis.*"

Diego thought for a moment. She half-expected him to ask her if ending the air search for her son was part of that order, but he simply nodded and said, "Make it happen, Charlize. If there is anything else you need, just say the word."

"Thank you, sir," she replied.

"What's next?" Diego asked.

Thor gestured toward a thin man in a white lab coat with a red goatee and short-cropped hair to match. "This is Doctor Peter Lundy. He's our leading scientist, with a PhD in electrical engineering and a second PhD in physics. Secretary Montgomery, you will be working with him closely."

"Hi, everyone, and welcome, Secretary Montgomery,"

Lundy said. "As many of you know, I'm the manager of this facility. Constellation was designed to protect the United States from a catastrophic event. Using new technologies, we're laying out an ambitious plan to get the grid back up in the following locations over the next twelve months."

The radiation zones on the main screen vanished, and circular areas marked with SCs bloomed across the screen.

"We're focusing on two Survival Centers in each state while we work on getting the grid up nationwide," Lundy continued. "Each SC will be designed to support populations of one hundred thousand people. That's—"

"Two hundred thousand people per state?" Charlize interrupted. "What about everyone else?"

"You've missed a lot while you've been out," Diego said again. "The situation out there is dire. This should put it in perspective for you. Go ahead, General."

Thor typed at the laptop in front of him and then pivoted his chair to face the main screen. On the screen, a team of soldiers was running down a highway clogged with vehicles under a bright sun.

"This is a team of Navy SEALs at a checkpoint on Highway 75 outside of Miami," Thor said.

The feed wobbled and then leveled out as the SEAL with the mounted cam stopped and climbed onto the hood of a sedan. Standing there, he roved his helmet from left to right, providing a wide view of the road. Humvees with soldiers in turrets were pointing their guns at the thousands of refugees slogging toward the barricade.

A gunshot rang out, and the SEAL jumped back to the pavement, sending the feed swooping toward the sky and then back to the Humvees. When he was back on his feet, he flashed a hand signal to his team, and Charlize caught a glimpse of their fatigued faces. She recognized them as the same team that had escorted her to Constellation.

Charlize tilted her head. "I thought these men were holding the line south of Orlando?"

"They were, ma'am. That line has fallen. They're trying to keep refugees from overwhelming Miami now. This video was taken a few hours ago by Senior Chief Petty Officer Fernandez's helmet cam."

He fast-forwarded the feed. Fernandez ran along the shoulder of the road with his team. He shot a glance over his shoulder at the convoy of Humvees blocking off the highway. The soldiers in the turrets had fired into the crowd, knocking men and women down like bowling pins. A group of civilians poured around the vehicles anyway, and the Humvees reversed, the gunners still firing.

Fernandez suddenly dropped to the ground, and one of his teammates reached down and grabbed him under the arm. The chief was gripping his chest with one hand, blood already seeping between his fingers.

The Humvees reversed, and one of them stopped next to Fernandez and his men. The team helped their leader into the truck, and the feed shut off.

"All across the country, similar scenes of chaos and violence are erupting," Thor said. "Gangs and hate groups are terrorizing cities and roadways. Even ordinary citizens like those you just saw have done terrible things in their panic and desperation."

"Simply put," Diego said, looking at each member of his Cabinet in turn, "I'm afraid the America we knew is a thing of the past. When I said my main focus is on recovery, I meant we should focus on salvaging what we can from the ashes and preventing the total destruction of our country."

***

Ty grabbed onto a stone ledge inside the observation tower. They were somewhere in the mountains, but he didn't recognize any landmarks. He breathed in the fresh air, which carried a pine scent like the candles his mom would burn in the winter. After being cooped up inside the Castle, he wasn't complaining about being brought up here, even though it was General Fenix who had accompanied him up the dark elevator shaft.

The wooden box they had ridden to the top of the tower creaked and groaned behind them. Carson stood at the open metal gate and manually lowered the elevator back down using a rope and pulley system.

"Send that back up with our friend!" he shouted.

Fenix placed his elbows on the ledge next to Ty and folded his hands together. He took in a long breath, exhaled, and said, "It's nice up here, isn't it, kid?"

Ty didn't say anything, and kept his eyes on the view. Rays of ghostly moonlight spilled from the guts of clouds drifting across the sky. The light cast a carpet of white over the sea of trees. A waterfall slid down the rocks to the right of the tower, dumping into a stream that wound through the valley below.

"You don't talk much, do you?" Fenix said. "I don't blame you. I'm sure you're scared and probably want to go home, but I'm going to tell you a secret. The world as you knew it is over. That means no more Happy Meals or trips to the toy store."

"I don't eat fast food," Ty said. He kept his gaze on the rocky ledge under the waterfall. Something was out there, moving around in the shadows.

"Whatever, kid. Point is, you're not going home even if your mom pays up. There's nothing left out there. You're going to have to toughen up," Fenix said. "I'm here to help you with that."

Carson walked over and raised an archaic looking hand-held video camera. "Don't mind me," he said. "I just like home movies."

Fenix snapped his fingers to get Ty's attention. "You do know what happened the other night, right, kiddo?"

"My name is Ty, not *kiddo*, and my mom is going to make you wish you were dead."

Fenix laughed, but it wasn't a nice laugh. "You're a snippy little bastard, aren't you? Well, let me tell you something, *Ty*. Your mom is late, so I think we're going to have to send her another video."

The cart in the shaft creaked, and Fenix walked over to the gate. Tommy, his arm in a sling, stepped out. He smiled when he saw Ty.

"Hi, General, the doc said you wanted me to come up here," Tommy said.

"Yup, I have a mission for you, young man," Fenix said. "It has to do with our friend here, Ty."

Tommy hesitated before walking out onto the platform. Carson set the video camera down on the ledge.

"Little Mr. Montgomery doesn't like to talk, and I thought someone younger might have better luck," Fenix said.

Tommy's gaze flitted to Ty and then back to the General. "Sure, sir," Tommy said. "Whatever you say."

Fenix turned toward Ty. "Would you be willing to talk

to Tommy?"

"Um, okay," Ty said uncertainly.

"What do you want me to talk to him about?" Tommy asked.

"Well, I thought you might explain to Ty about your plan to escape," Fenix said.

Tommy tried to raise his injured arm to protect himself, but Carson was too fast. He shoved Tommy over the ledge with ease. Tommy let out a cry that echoed through the valley. Three beats later, he hit the rocks below, his scream silenced by the shattering of bones.

"You're next, kid," Carson said.

Fenix dragged him out of the chair. Since he couldn't kick, Ty couldn't do much but squirm his upper body. He hit Fenix around the head and shoulders, anyplace he could reach, but the man didn't even flinch.

"You're going to make this worse," Fenix said with a grunt. "Grab his legs, Carson."

Carson set the camera on the ledge so it faced them. Fenix and Carson swung Ty over the side, and the world turned topsy-turvy. He was now dangling over the edge of the tower, staring straight down at Tommy's ruined body in the shape of a pretzel on the rocks below.

"No!" Ty screamed. "Please, put me down!"

A light shone on the side of his face. He craned his neck to see Carson directing a flashlight and the video camera. Fenix held Ty by his feet and ankles, smiling down at him. The men were recording this entire thing. Once again Ty was a spectacle, and the only man who could help him was dead below.

Ty clamped his jaws shut. He didn't want his mom to hear him screaming.

"Charlize Montgomery, this is General Fenix again. I

don't think you took my last message very seriously."

Fenix let him drop a few inches. Ty couldn't help screaming this time. He flailed, fingernails scraping the smooth stone surface of the tower. There wasn't anything to grab onto.

Carson moved the camera over the ledge to look at Ty's face and then directed it at Tommy.

"If you don't meet my demands, your son will end up like his friend down there. That's what happens to people who defy me."

Ty looked away from Tommy's broken body to the waterfall to the right of the tower. Motion flickered across the ledge. A mountain goat strode out onto the rocks, hooves clicking on the rocks. It watched Ty in the moonlight.

"You have forty-eight hours or your son dies," Fenix said.

An instant later, the ground fell away as Fenix and Carson pulled Ty to safety. He kept his gaze on the goat, which remained frozen as if it thought they couldn't see it as long as it didn't move.

"Sorry, kid," Fenix said with a wide, toothy grin as they set him back in the wheelchair. "This is just business."

He looked over at Carson. "Get that video uploaded and fired off via satellite, asap. Hopefully Ty's mother takes the Sons of Liberty a bit more seriously now."

"Will do, sir," Carson replied. "You sure were smart to build a faraday cage and stockpile all this old technology."

"I told you it would come in handy." Fenix took in another long breath of air and looked over the ledge, shaking his head. "Man, I really liked Tommy. Shame he was such an idiot."

"He wasn't much good to us with his injured arm anyway," Carson said. He grabbed onto the back of Ty's chair and pushed him back to the elevator shaft. The radio on his hip crackled as he pushed him to the gate, a message relaying from the speakers.

"Snake Nest, this is Liberty 1, we're on our way back with some goods. I think you're really going to like what we found on the highway."

17

Nathan tucked the radio back on his hip. "They bought it. Time to move to the next stage."

"You're sure about this?" Raven asked.

"I hope that's a rhetorical question. We have to do this. There's no one else to help."

"Yeah, but there's only two of us." Raven swiped a strand of hair that had stuck to the camouflage paint on his face. "I faced worse odds in North Korea, but there were more of us to face them together."

"I thought that's why you decided to pull our plan from the textbook on guerilla warfare. Make it look like there are more of us than there are, right?"

"Yeah," Raven said again. His tone lacked confidence.

Nathan looked down at the map of the camp they had drawn with a stick in the dirt after their recon. He shone his flashlight on each crudely sketched structure as he recapped the plan. "We've got two hostiles in the tower, two more guarding the building here, and two more here. A patrol of three more men are covering this area."

He pointed at one of the buildings. "I believe this is where they are holding the kids." He traced a finger over the dirt. "This path heads into the mountains to the north. You said you didn't see anything back there, right?"

"You saw the map Joe had on him. The only thing back there are some abandoned mines that are probably all caved in. I scoped the area before dark and didn't see anyone coming or going, which leads me to believe these guys are it."

Nathan unwrapped his last granola bar and bit off a chunk. He swallowed and then pointed at the entrance to the camp.

"I'll drive the Humvee here and wait for you to open fire. As soon as you start shooting, I'll bail and find the kids. Your job is to draw these guys away from the buildings…and to avoid hitting me."

Raven wrapped his ponytail and tucked the end into the collar of his camouflaged fatigues. They'd been lucky to get clothes, weapons, and nutrition, courtesy of the dead skinheads. Both men had dressed for war tonight.

Raven wiped another streak of paint across his forehead and let out a long sigh. "What if things go south?"

"Then you hightail it out of here. I don't want you trying to rescue me, okay? Go back to Estes Park and get help. One of us has to make it back."

After a moment of hesitation, Raven nodded again. "Don't worry, I got your back, Major."

"I know," Nathan said. He knew how crazy the plan sounded. He had a broken arm, a sprained ankle, and his entire body hurt. Raven was in better shape, but not by much.

But they had the element of surprise, automatic weapons, a Humvee, and something the skinheads didn't have—heart.

Nathan reached out with his bandaged fist, and Raven bumped it back.

"Shit, that kind of hurt," Raven said when he pulled his hand back, chuckling. "I guess that's not a good sign."

"You're a tough son of a bitch, brother. You'll be fine."

Raven shrugged a shoulder. He turned away, but Nathan tapped his sleeve.

"Thank you, Raven," Nathan said. "I'm grateful to have you with me."

"You saved my sister and niece. Least I can do is get myself shot up for your nephew."

Raven flipped the night vision goggles over his camouflaged features.

"Happy hunting," Nathan said.

They parted ways, both of them knowing that the odds were good that they wouldn't make it out of the Castle alive. Raven slipped out of the forest and down the slope of the hill to the outcroppings of rocks. He carried his MK11, but he had access to plenty of extra firepower. They had placed five M4s in strategic nooks along the bluff under the cover of darkness. As soon as Nathan drove into position, Raven would run from nest to nest and open fire to make it look like there was a small army up here. Then he would pick off each target with the MK11. Or maybe he would start with the MK11. Either way, Nathan trusted Raven to get it done.

On the way back to the Humvee, Nathan managed his thoughts just like he always did before climbing into the cockpit of his F-16. He couldn't let the desire for revenge get the best of him now. They had come too far for that. He had to be smart about this.

Nathan checked on Joe when he returned to the truck. The plan was to keep him tied up, but that plan changed when he saw Joe wasn't breathing. Nathan placed two fingers to his neck, checking for a pulse that wasn't there.

It was hard as hell to feel anything for these men. They

had made their decision to join with the wrong side, and they would pay with their lives.

Working quickly, he untied Joe and pulled him from the truck. Then he moved the body to the passenger seat, propping him up in what he hoped looked like a natural pose. He turned on the truck, headlights splashing across the road. The high beams cut through a light curtain of fog drifting across the road below. He rolled the window down to let in fresh air. This was it.

Unlike the forest they had passed through to get here, the night was alive with sounds. Bugs chirped, and a bird cawed in the distance, the calming music of nature filling the truck. In a way, it felt almost like this was just a leisurely drive through a park. But then the headlights captured the tower and the two soldiers outside—including their shaved heads and high-powered rifles.

Nathan gritted his teeth and continued down the road at thirty miles an hour. He could see the roofs of the cabins now, and the three men patrolling outside. Another soldier stood warming his hands next to the fire pit in the courtyard.

Taking one hand off the steering wheel, Nathan grabbed his M9 and kept it near the door. The two men stepped away from the guard tower and strode to the road in a relaxed manner. One of them held up a gloved hand.

Nathan hadn't planned for that and eased off the gas. He'd thought he would be able to drive right into the camp. Instead, he came to a stop about two hundred yards from the entrance, hoping these men couldn't see his face in the moonlight—or the fact that Joe was dead.

The guard on the left walked toward the Humvee, while the one on the right remained in the road. Nathan aimed his M9 at the driver's door as the man approached.

"Come on, Raven," Nathan whispered. The only reply was the pounding of his heart. He could hear it beating like a riveter in his chest. He raised his foot, prepared to stomp the gas, when a streak of red whizzed by the truck like a meteorite.

Nathan didn't hear the gunshot, but he saw the bullet hit the dirt. Raven's first shot had missed. The skinhead stumbled backward and Nathan pointed his M9 out the open window.

Pop, pop!

Nathan dropped the guy with shots to the eye and nose. The second guard took a 7.62 mm round to the chest, blood gushing from the wound and coating the ground. Raven had come through. From over a thousand yards out, it was a hell of a shot.

There was a fleeting moment of silence in the valley as the other guards realized what was happening. Then the real gunfire started. Muzzle fire from one of Raven's nooks illuminated the rocky bluff behind the Humvee. Return fire flashed across the camp from every direction.

Nathan punched the pedal and sped toward the entrance. The skinheads outside the buildings ran for cover, leaving their posts just like Nathan had hoped. A heavyset man lumbered into the road with a rifle aimed at Raven's position. Nathan pointed his M9 out the window and got off two shots that sent the man diving for cover.

The radio Nathan had forgotten about suddenly barked to life.

"Snake Nest, this is Tower 1. We're under attack, I repeat—" The voice was silenced, and a body plummeted from the top of the tower in the rearview mirror as Nathan raced toward the camp.

Four down. Not bad, Raven.

Nathan swerved off the road and saw the fat skinhead running away from the gunfire. The headlights captured his thick, tattooed arms and the back of his shaved skull. He glanced over his shoulder, his face a mask of terror as Nathan plowed into him.

The crack of metal on bone drowned out the gunfire as the man was knocked down and crushed under the weight of the Humvee. He put the vehicle into reverse and ran the guy over again for good measure. There was a muffled screech and then silence as Nathan steered back toward the camp. As soon as he turned back onto the road, gunfire lanced into the windshield. He ducked down as rounds bit into the seats. Two of the bullets tore through Joe's corpse.

"Shit," Nathan muttered. He slammed on the brakes, put the vehicle in park, and grabbed his M4. Another flurry of shots hit the front of the vehicle, punching through metal. He bailed out, losing the radio in the process. Keeping low, he bolted for the cover of the nearest tree. His ankle screamed at him, but adrenaline kept him moving.

Rounds speared the Humvee, shattering windows and pinging off the armored turret. Safely behind the tree, he counted the sound of the rifles. There were at least three or four, maybe more.

Nathan risked a glance around the right side of the tree. A skinhead half-hidden behind a barrel outside the first cabin saw him and squeezed off a burst. The bullets hit the tree, peppering Nathan with bark.

Holding in a breath, Nathan moved around the left side of the tree and fired a three-round burst that hit the barrel. Return fire cut into the tree before he could raise the red dot sight.

He placed his back against the trunk and waited.

There was a brief lull in the gunfire. Exhaling, Nathan bolted from around the tree and took up position behind a boulder. He popped up and fired a shot that hit the guy behind the barrel in the neck.

Nathan was up and moving before the body hit the dirt.

Two more muzzle flashes came from the camp, but neither of them were focused on him. He centered his rifle on the last flash and then pulled the trigger. A shout, then silence.

Nathan stopped behind another tree to catch his breath and change his magazine. A stick crunched somewhere to his right, and he glanced over to see a tall man with an athletic build looking down the iron sights of his rifle.

"Got you, you piece of shit," the man snarled.

The top of his shaved skull suddenly flew up like a white toupee caught in a fierce wind. Nathan didn't stick around to check if he was dead. He moved fast with his rifle roving for targets, his broken arm throbbing with pain. He raked the muzzle back and forth.

Nothing moved across his field of vision.

Had they done it? Were all the skinheads down?

"I'm coming, Ty," Nathan whispered. He ran to the nearest building and grabbed the handle, but it clicked, locked. He took a step back and kicked the door open with his good foot to reveal a room filled with crates.

Nathan cursed and ran for the second cabin. He opened the unlocked door, but found only more supplies.

Where the hell were the kids?

A bullet hit the dirt when he moved back outside. He

looked up at the cliff. Was that a warning?

Hold the fuck on, Raven.

Nathan got to the third cabin when he heard the rattle and cough of engines.

He froze.

Not just a few engines. Dozens of them. Some of them sounded like the whine and splutter of old motorcycles and dirt bikes. Others were the deep roar of diesel engines, possibly military vehicles. The enemy's cavalry was en route. He had to get moving.

Nathan ran for the third and final cabin.

"Come on Ty, please be here," he said.

He opened the door. A man hiding inside raised a pistol and fired. The shot hit the frame of the door just above Nathan's head. He answered with a three-round burst into the man's chest and then stumbled back outside.

The kids weren't here.

Ty wasn't here.

This wasn't the Castle. It was just the forward operating base.

Nathan's mind raced. Either Joe had lied, or maybe he hadn't known as much as he pretended. Either way, Nathan was fucked if he didn't get moving.

He ran for the Humvee, his ankle hurting so badly it felt like he was ripping the muscle. If he could reach the truck, maybe he could get back to Raven and find a way out of here. They'd have to regroup, scout the area again. Joe had mentioned tunnels in the mountains, but searching those would require more time.

Headlights swept over him. Nathan jumped into the Humvee just as the bikes came into view. Behind them, pickup trucks full of soldiers and two Humvees drove down the road feeding into the back of the camp.

Heart kicking, Nathan slammed the door. The engine was still on, but it was making a rattling sound. When he shifted into reverse, the truck jolted and then stalled. He tried it again, but got only another grinding noise.

"Come on! Come on!" he shouted, trying again.

Nathan decided to abandon the truck. He grabbed his rifle and moved back outside just as one of the motorcycles zipped down the road. Several more circled around him, cutting off his escape.

"Drop your rifle!" someone shouted.

"Hands on your head, asshole!" yelled another voice.

Nathan hesitated, calculating the odds. He finally lowered the gun and dropped it to the dirt. He raised his hands above his head and slowly got to his knees.

Nathan looked up at the hill, silently sending a message over and over again.

Run, Raven.

Nathan had failed, but Raven was still out there. He knew in his heart that Raven would come through on his promise to save Ty, just as he would have watched over Sandra and Allie if their positions were reversed.

Over the angry shouts and curses came a surprisingly polite voice. "Well hello," the voice said. "We weren't expecting company."

Nathan looked up at a man with thick hair and a well-groomed beard shot through with gray. He raised a fist with brass knuckles, arched both brows, and said, "Welcome to the Castle. I really don't think you're going to enjoy your stay."

***

Sandra opened the front door for Allie. Colton had given them a lift to Raven's house, and now he was lingering on the porch, looking like a man with something on his mind.

He let out a sigh. "I really wish you would stay in town, Sandra. I told Raven I would look after you while he's gone. The man who took our supplies and broke Theo out of jail is the same man your brother owes a lot of money to. Name of Nile Redford."

"Mr. Redford... That snake." Sandra remembered that name all too well. She looked at the shotgun propped next to the front door and then sat on the porch swing.

"You sure you won't come stay with us?" Colton asked.

"Yes, I'm sure. I've got this gun and Creek to look after us. I feel safer up here, anyways."

"You know you're welcome at my house. Kelly loves company, and I bet the girls would like a sleepover."

"Don't worry about me, Chief. I can look after myself."

Colton sighed a second time. "I'm not the chief anymore, Sandra."

"What?" Sandra planted her feet on the porch, stopping the porch swing. "Why the hell not?"

"Long story. I still haven't told my wife yet."

"Who's in charge?" Sandra asked.

"Don Aragon."

Sandra sniffed. "That guy is a piece of work."

"It was his idea to execute the Todds," Colton said. "Well, him and Mayor Gail."

"That's one thing we agree on, then. Now people will know what happens when you mess with Estes Park."

"You sound just like them," Colton said with a shake

of his head. He put one hand on his duty belt and the other on the grip of his pistol, and turned to look at the sky.

"I'm sorry, but I'm sick of people like the Todds, Mr. Redford, and Brown Feather thinking they can just take whatever they want."

Colton nodded like he understood.

"We'll be fine," she continued. "Go home and spend some time with your family."

"I'll stop by the medical center tomorrow and check on everything there," Colton said. "Goodnight."

"Goodnight," Sandra replied. Using her toes, she pushed the swing. It rocked back and forth. Creek watched Colton from the dirt at the bottom of the porch, ears perked. Allie came back outside and sat down beside Sandra. She chewed on a half of a peanut butter sandwich.

"When is Uncle Raven going to come home?" Allie asked.

"Soon, baby. Soon." Sandra stroked her daughter's hair and studied the dazzling stars in the black bowl overhead. She loved it out here. Estes Park had been a haven from her past, a place where she could start over and raise Allie among good people.

At least, it had been a haven. Things were different now. The violence and fear had stripped away her peace of mind.

Her eyes flitted from the stars to the shotgun propped up against the siding. She doubted Mr. Redford would come back, but she was prepared if he did. She wasn't scared of him, especially after being kidnapped by Brown Feather. Nothing could be worse than that.

A falling star caught her eye. It streaked over the

jagged teeth of the mountains to the east.

"Wow, did you see that?" Allie asked, sitting up.

Another meteorite broke through the atmosphere and tore through the sky, leaving behind a trail of fire.

"Is that the Raven Mocker, Mama?" Allie asked.

Sandra pulled her hand from around her daughter's back. "What? Who told you about the Raven Mocker?"

"Um… Uncle Raven did?"

"Of course he did," Sandra said with a frown.

Allie looked at the sky with curious eyes. "Does that mean someone is dying out there?"

Sandra shook her head. "It's just a story. It's not real."

"Will you tell it to me?"

"No, it's too scary."

Sandra relaxed against the cushion. She used her feet to push off again, the swing creaking back and forth.

"I promise I won't get scared," Allie said.

Creek lifted his head to look at them as though he wanted to hear the story too.

"Please?" Allie begged.

"Fine," Sandra said. She pulled Allie close, using her arm as a wing.

"The Raven Mocker is a witch from an old Cherokee tale. It was used to explain meteorites and falling stars, which is what we're seeing now."

"A witch? Like in *The Wizard of Oz*?"

"This is a male witch—a man who takes the form of fire when he sails through the sky, leaving behind sparks and making a sound like a high wind."

"I don't hear any wind," Allie said.

"That's because those are just shooting stars and not the Raven Mocker. The story says he appears at night when someone is dying."

"Do you think Uncle Raven is dying?"

Sandra reared back at the question. "Allie, no! Why would you say that?"

Creek let out another low whine and moved up the steps to sit next to the swing.

"It's okay, boy," Sandra said. She reached down to pat his head. "I know you miss Raven. I miss him, too."

Sandra looked back to the sky just as another falling star streaked over the mountains. This time she heard the rushing of the wind.

18

Raven zoomed in on the Humvees and the pickup trucks that surrounded Nathan on all sides. Soldiers fanned out across the camp with their weapons at the ready, some of them yelling orders. For skinhead pricks, these guys seemed way more organized than Raven had expected. Where the hell had they gotten all of these old vehicles and bikes? It was like they were prepared for the EMP attack...

Or hoping for the attack, Raven mused.

He centered the crosshairs of the MK11 on the man closest to Nathan. The pilot was sprawled on the ground, having been hit several times with brass knuckles. There wasn't anything Raven could do from here but watch. If he opened fire now, he was liable to hit Nathan.

Rounds suddenly lanced away from the camp, kicking up dirt and pinging off the boulders all around Raven. He lunged for cover and flattened his body just as another volley of bullets slammed into the other side of the rock.

He was really in trouble now. He cursed as he wiggled across the ground like a damn worm. If he did somehow manage to make it out of this one, he was going to reconsider his choice of career. Tracking had not been working out lately—all he ever seemed to find these days was trouble.

Rounds whizzed overhead. Dirt and chunks of rock rained down on his body. He pulled himself behind another boulder and looked up. He wasn't far from the ledge he'd shimmied down earlier. He could climb up and make a run for it through the woods, but where the hell was he going to go after that?

Headlights streaked across the road below. Now motorcycles and dirt bikes were heading his way. He counted four of them and then ducked back down as a bullet speared the air six inches above his head.

Rounds cut into the hillside. The bark of an M240 joined the chorus of war. They really wanted him dead if they were wasting that much ammo. He mastered his breathing and prepared to move.

You got this, Raven. You got this. Because if you don't got this, you're dead.

He scrabbled up the dirt slope. Then he jumped onto the ledge and rolled to relative safety. Rounds hit the hillside he had just abandoned, and cut through the trees overhead.

He changed the magazine in the MK11 while he was on his stomach and then pushed himself up to run through the dense forest. The chug of old motorcycles filled the air as they made their way up the road and through the valley. An idea seeded in his mind, and instead of running away from the road, he ran toward it.

Raven's crossbow and backpack were right where he'd left them next to a tree. If he was going to make his plan work, he was going to have to do this fast. He pulled a rope from his pack, unspooled it, and tied one end around the base of a ponderosa pine.

The gunfire continued on the other side of the hill to his right, and several rounds splintered through the trees. Headlights hit the top of the road ahead. He was running out of time.

Raven darted across with the rope in hand. When he reached the other side, he wrapped it around the thickest tree he could find.

The first dirt bike zoomed over the hill.

Raven waited for the next two bikes to appear. They were both motorcycles, a Harley and a Honda. He raised the rope and pulled it taut, careful not to get his hand caught. The drivers hit the rope at full speed, and they went flying head first over the handlebars. The fourth driver pulled over the hill and laid his bike down to avoid the wreckage. His body skidded over the pavement, but he kept his head up like a trained biker would have done.

Dropping the rope, Raven grabbed his crossbow and walked out onto the road. The first biker slowed and turned in a circle, tires skidding across the pavement, to look at his fallen comrades. His helmet homed in on Raven just as he let a bolt fly. The arrow crunched through his visor.

Raven tossed the crossbow on the ground, unsheathed his hatchet, and uppercut the fourth biker as he was trying to stand. The blade cracked through his jaw and shattered his bottom teeth. He let out a guttural screech that sounded more animalistic than human.

He left the blade in the man's chin, pulled his Glock, and finished him off with two shots to the back. Then he aimed at the drivers of bikes two and three. Both men were squirming across the ground, moaning and dragging broken legs.

Raven put a bullet into each of their skulls and then decided to double tap the trigger just to make sure they were dead since they were wearing helmets. The gunshots echoed away and silence fell over the road. He holstered the pistol and retrieved his hatchet. It took a good yank to pluck it from the man's chin. Several more teeth popped out in the process, splattering his pants with blood. He grabbed his backpack and MK11 from the shoulder of the road and paused to listen for more bikes.

The gunfire from the camp had ceased, and he couldn't hear any engines.

The crackle of a single radio broke the silence. He followed the noise to the fourth bike, a Harley with saddlebags. Inside one was a walkie-talkie. Raven tucked it into his vest. Then he hoisted the bike up, jumped on, and drove to the top of the hill. He unslung his MK11 and zoomed in on the camp.

It took him a moment to find Nathan. He was lying in the back of a truck, and he wasn't moving. Three other trucks pulled away, while a small army of foot soldiers fanned out across the meadows and road below. Raven lowered his gun and threw the strap over his backpack.

"Don't worry, brother. I'll be back with help," he whispered. He pulled a grenade from his pack, plucked off the pin, and tossed it over his shoulder at the other wrecked bikes. Gunning the engine of the Harley, tires screaming, he peeled away.

***

"How are we coming on the hunt for the other sub?" Charlize asked.

"We've got four HSM squadrons checking several potential zones as we speak," Thor said. "It's just a matter of time before we find the other sub."

"Good. It's time to go on the offensive, General. I don't care if we cross into sovereign waters. Our goal right now is to wipe the final North Korean threats off the map so we can focus on saving what's left of our country."

She looked back down at her laptop. Her eyes were grainy as she tried to focus them on yet another briefing. She had been sitting in this cold conference room with General Thor, Dr. Lundy, and Colonel Raymond for hours while she waited for news about her family. In the meantime, they had brought her up to speed on everything from military assets to the aid packages coming from abroad. America's allies were coming through with food, medical supplies, and other necessities, but distributing them was a problem. Their closest neighbors were also having problems with American refugees spilling across the Mexican and Canadian borders.

She finished reading a report about the status of the highway system in the Southeast and shut her laptop to look at her team. "Listen up, everyone. Aside from taking out the North Korean threats, we have to focus on clearing the roads and stopping the gangs and raiders from taking over. The Aryan group that has my son are not the only domestic terrorists out there that were waiting for something like this to happen."

"Agreed," Thor said. "But how do we clear thousands of miles with the resources we currently have?"

"Put together a special task force," Charlize replied. "Equip our semis and convoys with bulldozer blades, and send out troops to guard each shipment. We did that in Afghanistan, and we can do it here."

Raymond drew in a weary breath. "The problem with that is the fleeing refugees. You've seen the video. It's easy clearing a road full of vehicles, but people are a different story."

"We risk civilian casualties by expediting the movement of supplies," Thor said, direct and unsympathetic as always. "One way or the other, we lose American lives."

Charlize paused to think. Commanding troops was more difficult than flying a fighter jet solo. The last thing she wanted was to put more civilians in harm's way, but it was starting to feel like there were no good solutions.

"May I offer a more subtle approach?" Lundy asked, speaking up for the first time.

"Certainly," Charlize said.

He took off his glasses, polished them on a small cloth, and put them back on again. He was methodical about everything, and he spoke in a precise, clipped tone. "We could place radiation warnings in areas we're trying to clear. There's nothing like a biohazard symbol to keep people out."

"That's not a bad idea," Thor said before Charlize could reply. His eyes flitted to her for approval.

"I like it," she said. "Now let's—"

A rap on the door interrupted her. Albert stepped into the room without waiting for a response. Typically he kept a straight face, but now he was frowning, his eyes huge and worried.

"What's wrong?" she choked out.

"I've been told we have another video from General Fenix." Albert walked over and stood next to her. "The video should be on your computer, ma'am."

Charlize had thrown up after the last video. The image of Ty dangling over the side of that tower wouldn't leave her mind. Thor and Raymond stood and walked over as she typed in her credentials. The email was waiting in her new inbox. Swallowing, she moved the cursor over and clicked on the message.

The video was not of Ty. It showed a battered man on the concrete floor of a small prison cell. He was curled up in a fetal position, broken arm in a cast covering his face.

The camera panned up to a smiling General Fenix. "I thought I was very clear about what I wanted. At first I thought the assholes that attacked us were just two idiots, but then I realized one of those idiots was your brother."

The feed moved back to the man on the floor. He tilted his head up to reveal a bruised face she hardly recognized. Raising a hand, the man shielded his swollen eyes from the light.

"Nathan," she whispered.

Fenix moved back into the frame and kicked Nathan in the gut, lifting his body slightly off the ground. Her brother spat blood onto the concrete and then looked back up at the camera.

"Don't give 'em anything, Sis," he said, his voice thick.

"The clock is ticking, and things are not looking good for the Montgomery family," Fenix said. He raised his boot again. The video cut out just before it connected with Nathan's jaw.

***

Ty sat on his bed, listening to the screams coming from the hallway outside the room. The sound was scary, but maybe it was a good thing. If so many people were hurt all at once, it must mean there was fighting nearby. And if the Castle was under attack, then maybe someone had come to rescue him. Maybe his mom had finally found them!

A voice shouted over the screaming.

"They caught one of them," the voice said.

Footfalls approached the door to the cell. Ty put a finger to his lips, and Micah cupped his hand over Emma's mouth.

"Come on, we need to round up every available man just in case they come back," called a frantic voice.

"I heard we lost six of our boys," said another man.

"They brought a fucking army, man. Got snipers all along the ridge. We have to find them before they can report our location."

A high-pitched screech of agony sounded. "Stop, no, stop, stoppppp!"

Ty put his hands over his ears and watched the other kids do the same. By the time he pulled them away, the voices and the footfalls were gone, leaving only the sporadic wailing from the hospital down the hallway.

The minutes ticked away as Ty watched the door and waited for his mom to come rescue him. An hour passed, maybe more. The screaming stopped, and then the only sound was the plop of water in the bucket by the metal door. The shock of everything that had happened slowly wore off, and fatigue wrapped Ty up like a blanket. His eyelids felt heavy and droopy, but he forced them to stay open so he could watch the door.

She's coming. She'll be here any minute.

Ty looked down at his shaking hands and laced his fingers together. He wasn't sure what time it was exactly, but it felt like early morning. How long had he been awake? He couldn't remember the last time he'd slept.

You have to stay awake. You have to be ready to go.

Micah and Emma had fallen asleep in the bed across from him. They were curled up next to one another. Seeing them made Ty even more tired.

Maybe he could close his eyes for just a second.

As soon as he did, sleep took him.

Ty wasn't sure how long he slept. A voice woke him up, and he groggily blinked and looked around.

"Ty, wake up. Someone's coming," Micah said from the other side of the room. "Is it the good guys?"

The rap of military boots sounded in the hallway.

"Which room is it?" someone asked.

This voice didn't sound familiar to Ty. He used his hands to move his legs closer to the edge of the bed. His wheelchair was out of reach, but he wanted to be ready.

Another sound like something being dragged across the ground joined the rap of boots outside. The footfalls stopped just outside the door.

The hatch unlocked, and General Fenix stood in the shadowed entry, partially blocking the view of a battered man on the ground in the hallway. Ty moved slightly for a better view, but couldn't see past Fenix or the soldier that had the injured guy by the boots.

"I brought you a visitor, little Mr. Montgomery." Fenix helped the other soldier drag the bleeding man inside the room.

"Go ahead, have a look," Fenix said. "He came a long way to see you."

It took Ty a second to recognize his uncle, due to all of the cuts and bruises on his face.

"Uncle Nathan!" Ty yelled.

Nathan looked up at Ty, one eye so swollen he probably couldn't even see. He tried to talk, but all that came out was a groan. Fenix kicked him in the ribs.

"No!" Ty shouted. "Don't touch him, you bastard!"

Uncle Nathan looked up again, determined.

"I love you, Ty, and so does your mom." He coughed

and spat something dark onto the floor. "Everything is going to be okay."

***

A pounding woke Colton at one in the morning. He fumbled for the Colt .45 resting on the bed stand.

"Who is that?" Kelly mumbled. Risa's head popped up on her other side, eyes wide and frightened.

"Daddy, I'm scared," she said.

"Shhh, baby," Colton whispered. He walked over to the window and peeled back the curtain to see a man standing on the front step. He was draped in shadow, but a familiar old Chevy pickup was parked in the driveway. Colton had been sleeping so hard he hadn't heard the clunker drive up.

The person on the step knocked again and yelled, "Colton!"

Not a man, after all. The voice belonged to Lindsey.

He stepped away from the window and lowered his gun.

"Everything's okay," Colton reassured them. "It's just Detective Plymouth."

"At this time? It's the middle of the night," Kelly said.

"Stay here," Colton said. He knew whatever Lindsey had to say wasn't going to be good. He rushed down the stairs, bracing himself for the bad news, and opened the door before she could start pounding on it again.

Her face was waxy in the moonlight, her freckles standing out against her pale skin like flecks of blood.

"What's wrong?"

"Too much to tell," she said. "Come hear for yourself."

He followed her to the pickup truck. Instead of getting behind the wheel, Lindsey pulled out the digital radio that Leroy Travis had donated. Colton grabbed it and brought it to his lips. "This is Colton. Go ahead, over."

Raven's frantic voice sounded over the channel.

"Chief, shit, Chief. I screwed up bad." A chopping noise roared in the background, so loud he could hardly hear Raven. Was that a helicopter?

"Need men...guns," Raven said, his voice breaking up. "A fucking tank if you got one."

"Slow down, Raven," Colton said. "I can't hear you. What the hell was that noise?"

The background noise abruptly cut off.

"Sorry," Raven said. "That better?"

"Are you on a chopper?"

Raven laughed, a manic edge to his voice. "In a manner of speaking. That was a Harley."

"Start at the beginning, Raven."

There was a long pause followed by another rustling sound. A minute later, Raven came back online.

"Sorry, Chief, thought I heard bikes." There was another pause. "Nathan and I ambushed a gang of skinheads on the road, led by a guy named General Dan Fenix. Bunch of jumped-up Aryan assholes calling themselves the Sons of Liberty. We tracked them to a location called the Castle last night and went in to find Ty."

"What? Why the hell didn't you wait for backup?" Colton asked.

"Because our radio was shot. This is one of theirs," Raven said. "I know. I fucked up. We thought we found the kids, but they weren't at the skinheads' camp. Fenix has an army, and they captured Nathan. We have to get them out before they kill him and the kids, Chief. We need men. Lots of men and lots of guns."

Colton shook his head. He didn't even know where to start, so he simply said, "Where are you?"

"South of Estes Park. I don't know...pretty far. Maybe forty miles. I've been driving for a while. There are still fires out here, and I need help. I can't do this on my own."

Colton could hardly believe he'd just heard those words from Raven Spears. A voice came from the porch before he could answer.

"Is everything okay, Marcus?"

Kelly was standing in the doorway. Risa came down the stairs and sat on the bottom step, gripping her stuffed animal in her arms. They both looked scared. He knew in that moment he couldn't leave them. Not even to save Nathan and his nephew, or bail Raven out of whatever scrape he'd gotten into. At some point, he had to put the safety of his family before everything else. He had already failed his town—he wouldn't fail Kelly and Risa.

"It's okay," Colton told his wife. "Take Risa and go back to bed. I'll be up in a minute."

The radio crackled. "Chief, you there?"

Colton held the receiver up. His next words hadn't gotten any easier to say. "I'm not chief anymore."

"What the hell are you talking about?"

"I'm not in charge. Don is running the show now. We lost everything, Raven. Your old buddy Mr. Redford came to Estes Park while you were away. He took everything. Our meat, our supplies, our medicine. He burned the Stanley to the ground. Do you understand what I'm saying? Even if I was still chief, nobody else here would be willing to help you after what happened."

There was silence on the other line for several hard moments.

"Is my family okay?"

"They're fine, I checked on them last night. Sandra and Allie are staying at your place," Colton said. He turned to look at Kelly again. She was sitting on the step next to Risa, her long, rope-like braid falling over one shoulder. She met his eyes, and there was a question there: *Them or us?*

Colton raised the receiver again. "Where did these men take Nathan?"

"The Castle. It's an old camp a few miles north of Interstate 70. About sixty miles from Estes Park, or so. I'm not exactly sure. There are mines in the mountain behind the camp though. I figure that's where they're hiding out. They have a fucking army, Colton."

"Which is why you need to get your ass back here and make sure you aren't followed. There's only one thing we can do for Nathan now. We have to get a message to his sister and let the military handle this."

"No," Raven replied. "By the time they arrive, he *will* be dead. I made him a promise. He helped save my family, now I have to help save his." There was a pause, and then Raven spoke again, his voice rough. "So tell my sister and niece I love them, okay? And tell Creek he's a good boy. And…and hell, Marcus. Just don't let anything happen to them because of what I did, okay? Don't let my mistakes ruin their lives too. I'm sorry as I can be about Redford. But if I make it back, I'll take care of that asshole."

"I will look after your family," Colton said heavily. Static broke over the channel, the connection severed.

Colton turned to Lindsey. "Detective, I need you to

do me a favor."

She nodded. "Anything. Name it."

"I need you to get a message through to Secretary Montgomery before Raven gets himself killed."

— 19 —

Raven couldn't tell if the blood covering his fatigues was from the men he killed or if it was his own. It was probably a mixture of both.

An hour earlier, not long after he had spoken with Colton and learned of Mr. Redford robbing Estes Park blind, Raven had ditched the Harley and covered it with fallen limbs. Then he had slipped into the woods along the frontage road leading to the Castle. Since then, he'd been making his way through the forest, being slapped in the face with branches while the underbrush tore at his legs.

He was using the radio to monitor the movement of the skinheads in the area, staying just out of reach. Through the gaps in the trees, he noted a clearing that opened into a meadow. His trained eye caught motion in the knee-high grass. A baseball cap, and then a shiny bald skull bobbing up and down in the glow of the moonlight.

Gotcha.

Raven ran at a hunch, eyes flitting over the two-dimensional canvas for any surprises. Clusters of chokecherries scraped against his arms, but he ignored them. He barely felt the pain, and his fatigue had been replaced with the rush of adrenaline. He should have been going insane with worry, but instead he felt in tune with his surroundings. There would be time to deal with Mr. Redford later. As long as Sandra and Allie were safe,

Raven could zone everything else out.

He listened to the whistle of the breeze and the cry of a raccoon somewhere in the hills. Chirping bugs, crickets, and the croak of a bullfrog joined the din. Over all the sounds of nature came the faint voice of a man he was about to kill.

He reached the clearing and took up a position behind a ponderosa pine with a trunk wide enough to cover his body. This hill overlooked an open space with patches of late-summer wildflowers that seemed to glow in the moonlight.

Moving through the sea of knee-high grass, about halfway across the clearing, were the three men. They were headed for the base of a mountain on the other side of the field. The bluffs towered thousands of feet overhead, peaks tipped with snow.

Raven pushed the night vision goggles up and centered the scope of his rifle on the patrol. Two were carrying M16s, while the third had a shotgun.

He planned to take them down and then move in for the close-up work. Raven picked his first target, but just as he was about to pull the trigger, the silhouettes of more soldiers moved out of the forest below.

The three newcomers quickly overtook the patrol. They lifted a downed tree at the edge of the woods and moved it to the side, revealing a narrow dirt path that led up into the mountain. Raven could take three of them with his rifle from here, but six? That was too many to take alone, and he didn't want to draw reinforcements. He needed to wait until the two patrols separated.

While he sat there, he looked to the sky. The cloud cover had dissipated, leaving only fragments floating across the stars. He easily located the two pointer stars of the Big Dipper, Dubhe and Merak. Using those, he visualized an imaginary clock. Using basic math—the only kind he was good at, as Sandra would point out—he made calendric calculations to determine it was almost four in the morning. He had just under three hours of darkness before dawn.

At last, the first patrol headed west toward a stream. The other three stood guard at the open entrance to the dirt path. They were around fifteen hundred yards out by Raven's estimates. Killing all three would be near impossible, even with the Leupold Mark 6 riflescope.

He had to get closer, and he preferred to deal with the patrol heading back out first so he didn't get boxed in later when he went to infiltrate the Castle.

Raven melted back into the forest and stalked the three soldiers from a distance. Hugging the trunks of the trees around him, he watched them like a prowling wolverine. The vicious animals were known for ambushing larger prey at close range. That's exactly what he was going to do.

As he neared the patrol, he slung the rifle over his back and took off running. The trio was about to cross the creek at the western edge of the clearing. They moved in a straight line, more of a march than a patrol, which allowed him to move faster without fear of being sighted.

He darted through the woods and slid down a slope where a ravine divided the forest. At the bottom, he stopped at the muddy crossing. He stepped a few paces back, then ran and hopped over the three-foot-wide rift. Using the momentum from his leap, he climbed up the hill and back into the forest.

This time he moved more cautiously, careful not to slip on the beds of pine needles. He had lost sight of the men in the green hue of the night vision goggles, but he could hear them moving through the woods.

A Douglas fir provided a temporary refuge. Raven crouched next to its base and caught his breath. When his breathing had slowed, he pulled out his hatchet and knife, then peered around the tree. The three men were trudging through the forest with their rifles lowered. They didn't speak, but they moved without care, snapping twigs and crunching leaves like mindless beasts. Raven was going to enjoy gutting them.

Focus, Sam. Focus. Let go of your fear and anger.

He bent down to pick up a rock in the same hand that he held his knife. Listening to the footfalls, he could tell the man approaching to his left was the heaviest. Raven would deal with him last.

When the crunch of their boots sounded about ten feet away, Raven tossed the rock at a tree to his left. The crunch of footsteps abruptly ceased.

"Did you hear that?" one of the men said.

Without a moment of hesitation, Raven flung his hatchet at a muscular soldier holding an M16, burying the blade into his skull with a crack that scared two birds from a nest in the canopy overhead.

Raven darted behind another tree and raised his knife. Two seconds had passed since he'd thrown his hatchet. It took two more seconds to move around the side of the tree and flank the other two men. He came up behind a soldier carrying an M16.

He traced the blade across the man's thick neck from ear to ear. The blade cut clean and deep, blood shot out like a fountain. He relieved the dying man of his rifle as he fell and laid him down gently on the grass.

"Guys?" the heavyset soldier said. "Guys, where the

hell did you go? This shit ain't funny!" He pumped his shotgun and turned in the darkness, looking for his dead friends.

Raven prowled quietly in the shadows, enjoying the fear from his final chase. Ten seconds after he had flung his hatchet, he snuck up behind the overweight man and whistled from three feet behind his head.

The guy turned with his shotgun muzzle lowered to the ground.

Amateur wannabe soldier, Raven thought.

He lunged with his blade before the man could fire a shot. The tip sliced through a layer of fat under his ribcage and Raven twisted it deep, watching the white eyes of his enemy widen in the moonlight.

The man let out a guttural cry and dropped his shotgun. Raven withdrew the blade and stuck his prey in the side of the neck with a meaty thump. Blood gushed out, and the skinhead reached up in a futile effort to stop the flow. He grabbed Raven with his other hand.

Raven yanked from his grip, darted around to stab the kidneys with a series of short jabs that made the man screech like a pig being slaughtered, and then watched with grim satisfaction as the soldier clawed at the blood-soaked ground.

He retrieved his hatchet from the first kill, plucking it from the skull, and kicked the body of the second skinhead just to make sure he was dead. Then he checked on the third man. Somehow, he was still squirming. His legs kicked the dirt slowly, like a cricket with a cracked shell.

Raven got down next to him so he could meet his gaze. He snapped his fingers to draw the man's attention, but the spark of life was already draining from his eyes.

He didn't feel bad about killing this man. If anything, he was proud. His niece would grow up in a world with three less white supremacist assholes in it.

"Help," the skinhead wheezed.

"What's the magic word?"

The man managed to croak out, "Please...please..."

Raven laughed in his face.

The caw of a bird sounded, mimicking his laughter, and a flash of light speared through the sky. A meteorite, he realized.

The Raven Mocker.

Tonight, it was Raven's turn to bring a Cherokee legend to life.

***

If Charlize had to read one more report about bandits in Iowa or roadblocks in South Carolina, she was going to scream. She'd been trying to keep herself busy with work ever since the call had come from Estes Park. A detective from the police force there had relayed enough information to put together an operation to rescue her family. Teams from Buckley AFB were preparing to move on the Castle. There was nothing for her to do now but work—and wait.

Albert opened the door to the conference room holding two cups of coffee. She smiled when he set one of the cups in front of her and took a seat.

"Ma'am, do you have a moment to talk?" he asked.

Charlize closed her laptop. "Of course, Al, what's on your mind?"

He slowly sat down and massaged the outside of the coffee cup with his index finger, looking at it like he wasn't sure if he wanted to take a drink.

Charlize summoned the soothing voice that she used on Ty when he was upset. "It's okay, Big Al, you can talk to me."

"It's about my family," he finally said. "I know Jane and my girls are probably…" He paused and swallowed, choking a bit. "I know they are gone, ma'am, but I have a sister in Charlotte."

"Why didn't you say so before?"

He looked down at the table, then met her gaze. "You've been so sick, and so focused on your own family. I don't blame you for that. I'm just—"

"I totally understand. I've been selfish, and I apologize. I can't begin to know how badly you're hurting inside. I will do what I can to find your sister, I promise."

"Thank you, ma'am."

"What's her name?"

"Jacqueline," Albert said. "She's my twin sister."

Charlize raised a scorched eyebrow. "You never told me you have a twin."

"Sorry," Albert said, shrugging a large shoulder. "We're not identical, if you were wonderin'."

Charlize smiled. "I also didn't know you had a sense of humor."

He smiled back at her and then turned as the door opened, letting in a flurry of voices. Colonel Raymond stood outside. "An HSM team picked up a possible hit on the radar, ma'am."

"Show me," Charlize replied. She tugged on the sleeves of her new uniform, which included a white button-down shirt that almost covered her burns. Then she grabbed the Air Force baseball cap and put it over her cropped hair.

They moved into the circular command room, where General Thor stood rubbing his forehead. On the wall-mounted monitor, three MH-60R Seahawks armed with anti-submarine torpedoes and hellfire missiles glided through the skies.

A dozen other staffers were staring into the glow of laptops set up on the long table in the center of the room. The clock overhead showed 0600 hours. Charlize hadn't slept—her mind was racing too much to shut off. Everyone around her looked exhausted. This was the reality of war. Sleep, showers, and food were a luxury.

She crossed the room and stood next to General Thor and Colonel Raymond.

"Morning, Secretary Montgomery," Thor said. "We've had a radar hit about twenty-five miles east of New York City. There's a fleet of ten aid ships coming from Great Britain. The anomaly appears to be moving with the convoy."

Charlize cursed. "Those slick bastards are using the cover of the ships as disguise."

Raymond agreed with a nod. "I had the same thought."

"Did the Royal Navy send any protection for those aid ships?" Charlize asked.

"Yes, we have already contacted them," Raymond said.

"Good," Charlize replied. "How far out is our HSM squadron?"

"Five minutes," Thor said. "We have a strike group one hundred miles south of this location, but I've re-rerouted the USS *Michigan* and the USS *Georgia* to intercept. If this is the other North Korean submarine, they won't escape our tentacles."

Charlize took a seat at the table next to Raymond. She wanted to stand, to appear strong, but she needed to conserve her energy. Albert handed her the coffee she had left in the conference room.

"You're a saint, Big Al," she said, looking up at him. "Why don't you go get some rest?"

Albert opened his mouth, closed it again, and then said so quietly that only she could hear him, "I need to stay busy. Besides, I'd like to stay here with you until they find your brother and son."

"Have a seat, then," she said, tapping the chair to her left.

Charlize blew on the coffee and then took a sip. The minutes slowly ticked by as the choppers on screen tore over the waves in the early morning sun. If this really was the final North Korean submarine and they managed to sink it, then Charlize could focus entirely on the recovery efforts without fear of another attack.

And on the raid of the Castle, she thought. Charlize was trying her best to focus on her duties as Secretary of Defense, but worries about Ty and Nathan kept interrupting her concentration.

A crowd formed as the Seahawks closed in on the location. Several of the Royal Navy aircraft also moved into position.

President Diego and several other members of his Cabinet filed into the room. On screen, the container ships appeared. Charlize and Albert left the table and walked over for a better view.

There were six of the ships moving in a single-file line through the water. Thousands of metal shipping containers were stacked on the decks. Their contents would save countless lives—but only if the supplies made it ashore.

"They're about twenty-three miles from port," Thor reported. He remained standing with one hand cupping his jaw.

"That's close to New York," Raymond said. "What if they're planning another attack?"

Charlize nearly dropped her coffee on her lap when the middle ship of the small fleet exploded on the monitor. Shipping containers shot into the air like firecrackers and then plummeted back to the sea.

"Someone get me a SITREP!" Thor shouted.

"It's definitely a North Korean sub," Raymond said. "Just got a report from Eagle 1. He saw the torpedo trail. They're moving in for the kill."

"They better hurry before that sub dives," Charlize said.

The choppers on screen passed over the other container ships, providing a view of the decks and the supplies there. Then the view rolled east, away from the ships and after the sub.

"Eagle 1 and 2 are preparing to fire," Raymond said. "Stand by."

The lead Seahawk swooped lower, so close that Charlize could see through the clear water. The rotor drafts rippled the water in all directions like a boulder had been tossed into a pond. Several MK-54 torpedoes streaked away from the chopper and slammed into the waves, spearing down and down, the trails bubbling. A geyser of water shot up into the sky a moment later.

The other Seahawks moved into position and unloaded their payloads into the ocean. More geysers burst into the sky. There was a pause just long enough for

Charlize to think that they'd somehow missed. And then a massive red explosion blossomed out of the ocean like a flower on fire.

"Stand by," Raymond said again.

Charlize clenched her burned hands until they ached, waiting in anticipation for the report.

"Eagle 1 just reported in. Target destroyed," Raymond said with a relieved smile as the room erupted into cheers and applause.

A hand gripped Charlize's shoulder. She turned, thinking it was Albert, but this time it was President Diego.

"Congratulations, Madame Secretary," he said. "Now let's go see what we can do about rescuing your son and brother. Those strike teams from Buckley are in the air."

Raven stopped when he heard a distant chopping noise. He flipped his night vision goggles into place and scanned the terrain, wishing he had Creek's hearing. Seeing nothing, he fell into a run with his rifle at the ready. As he hopped over a fallen log, it became clear the sound wasn't from a motorcycle. It wasn't even coming from the road—it was coming from the sky.

Black Hawks.

Now that he'd recognized it, the sound was unmistakable. It was the sweetest song he'd ever heard.

At the edge of the forest, he crouched and dropped to his stomach. From there, he scoped the sky, still not seeing the birds. He lowered the sights to the back entrance to the Castle. The three men who'd been guarding the road were moving frantically. They carried a log away from the dirt path and dumped it into the grass. He zoomed in on dust rising through the trees. The rattle and clutter of engines sounded.

Raven was about to have company. He chambered a round and looked up just as the Black Hawks zoomed into view. Four of the birds buzzed in from the south, moving in combat intervals over the valley. Colton had gotten the call for help through to Charlize after all, but the cavalry was on the wrong side of the damn mountain!

The Sons of Liberty were escaping out the back door. Across the meadow, several trucks raced out of the forest. Raven scrambled for a better sniping position. He had to stop them before they got away.

He pulled out extra magazines from his vest and lined them up in the dirt. Then he set up the rifle and secured the bipod.

The first of the pickup trucks tore out of the clearing, kicking up a curtain of dust. The driver jerked east onto a road Raven hadn't seen from his vantage earlier. A Humvee followed the lead vehicle. Three more pickups and a second Humvee sped out of the woods.

Dirt bikes and several motorcycles raced alongside, tearing up the grassy shoulder of the road. There was no way he could stop them all, especially when they were moving in the opposite direction, but he could slow their escape and provide the military time to catch up to them.

Raven aimed for the lead biker. He pulled the trigger with the sights lined up on the wheel. The round hit the tire, sending the bike to the ground and the driver cartwheeling into a tree at the side of the road. The other bikes fanned out, but the trucks halted, bottlenecked on the road behind the crashed bike. Two men got out to move the bike.

A squeeze of the trigger dropped the first man, but the second dove for cover.

Answering gunfire cracked in the next valley, followed by an explosion that echoed through the night.

The battle had started.

Raven focused his fire on the first Humvee before the gunner in the turret could find him. The first two shots pinged off the armor, but the third hit the man in the cheek. He slumped back into the vehicle without firing a single shot from the M240.

All at once the doors opened and men jumped out

into the road, opening up with automatic rifles on his position. He ducked down, rounds whistling over his head. Then he rolled to the side behind the largest boulder and waited.

He couldn't wait forever. He could hear the rest of the convoy moving again.

The fleeing Sons of Liberty continued the assault, pinning Raven down with rounds that licked the dirt to either side, cracked off the rocks protecting his back, and slammed into the trees towering overhead.

When this was over, Raven promised himself to get a job where nobody would ever shoot at him again. Maybe Gail Andrews would hire him to work in her art gallery.

He exhaled and then dared to look through a gap between the boulders. The lead truck was moving again. In the back of the pickup behind the Humvee, he spotted a knot of small figures. The children were all piled into the bed, holding onto each other.

He had to stop that truck.

Raven ran for the woods. Rounds splintered the bark around him, sprinkling him with shrapnel. A jagged piece stuck him in the neck, stinging like a massive wasp. He ducked behind a tree and pulled the splinter from his flesh.

"Goddamn," he grumbled.

The shots peppered the trees to his left and he darted to the right where he took a knee behind a gangly juniper tree. The entire convoy was moving again and the sky was still void of choppers.

He had to get closer.

This is not a good idea…

Raven slid down the slope and took off in a sprint across the meadow, keeping as low as he could in the high grass. He tried to keep to the shadows, but the moon was bright tonight. Even with the camouflage paint on his exposed skin and his military fatigues, it was only a matter of time before he was spotted.

He checked the convoy. There was a thousand feet between him and the nearest vehicle, but they were moving at a fast clip. He was never going to make it across in time.

Raven opened his mouth to gulp the air as he ran, his lungs greedily accepting the oxygen as he pushed himself to the limits. He ran like a madman, focused on the bobbing heads of the children in the bed of the pickup. He spotted another prisoner, much taller than the others, slumped with his back against the cab.

Nathan was still alive!

Gunfire zipped by Raven. He had finally been spotted. Instead of diving for cover, he took a knee and aimed at the tires of the pickup carrying the hostages. A round whizzed by his face as he fired a burst at the truck. One of his shots punched into the bumper, but the second and third shredded the rear tire. The truck swerved off the road, nearly tipping over into the meadow.

The bark of the M240 pushed Raven to the dirt. He rolled on his side to escape the high caliber rounds that pummeled the ground where he had been a moment earlier. There wasn't a much more viscerally terrifying sound than the big gun. Raven greatly preferred being the guy firing the gun instead of the guy crawling away on his belly and praying not to get shot.

Not quite five hundred yards away, men were piling out of the second Humvee, which had reversed to help the disabled pickup. Three of the men ran to the truck, while the other three strode in his direction, weapons shouldered but holding their fire. These were trained soldiers, unlike the grunts Raven had taken down in the forest. He hoped Fenix was one of them so he could send the evil son of a bitch back to his Maker.

Your time is up, Shunka Sapa.

Rounds whizzed all around Raven as he dug his elbows into the ground. A bullet stung his trap muscle, taking off a layer of skin and forcing him lower. It was just a flesh wound, but that didn't mean it was painless.

He had trained for this exact thing, moving his body like a snake under barbwire while rounds cut the air above his helmet. Only this time he didn't have a helmet. And he was alone, facing an army of zealots who'd just as soon spit on his brown-skinned corpse.

Raven pushed his face against the dirt, tasting the cold earth. He was in battle mode, his senses on full alert, aware of every noise and movement. The gunfire moved to his left, giving him a window to fire off suppressed shots.

He reached forward and snapped the bipod into place. Then he pushed the butt of the rifle in the pocket of his shoulder. A bullet hit the dirt in front of him as he searched for someone to kill.

He centered the sights where he'd seen the flash from a muzzle. In the fading glow, Raven spotted the gunman and squeezed a round into his gut. Then he roved the muzzle to the left, where he shot another soldier making a run for the Humvee. The others all crouched for cover.

Two dirt bikes buzzed down the road, returning to provide covering fire, but Raven kept his attention on the turret of the Humvee, where the gunner was roaming back and forth for a target. He held a breath in his chest and fired a shot that took off the man's baseball cap. The surprised gunner had just reached up to touch his shaved head when Raven planted a bullet between his eyes.

The soldiers who had run to the pickup were unloading the children now. One of them had a child flung over his shoulders. Raven put a bullet in the man's kneecap, blowing bone and gristle onto the road. The soldier dropped the kid on the ground as he screamed in agony, clutching his mangled leg.

Both dirt bikes jolted onto the field in his direction. Raven took the first driver out with a shot to the arm, knocking him off the bike. The second biker lowered his helmet and raced for Raven as if he were going to plow him over.

Big mistake, bucko.

Raven fired two shots that both missed, but the driver had to put the bike down to avoid the third. Raven shot the man as he skidded through the grass.

Two minutes had passed since Raven had blown the tire on the pickup. It was amazing how much damage and chaos he had already inflicted. Screams, gunfire, and confused voices rang out from the road where the two vehicles remained. In the chaos, Raven spotted two men dragging Nathan toward the Humvee.

As much as he wanted to take them down, Raven couldn't get a clear shot and searched for another target. The final two men who had fired on him earlier were moving back to the truck. One of them turned and unloaded a burst in his direction.

Rolling to his right, Raven crawled to find a new position. He had to keep moving or he was going to lose Nathan, Ty, and the other kids.

Over the gunfire came the chop of helicopters—a sound that made his heart fire like one of the automatic rifles trying to kill him.

He popped back up to look for the birds but instead saw a man standing in front of him, tattooed right arm covered in blood where Raven had shot him. The biker bared his teeth and raised a knife the size of a machete.

One of the children screamed for help, and Raven's blood boiled over.

I don't have time for this shit.

Raven smacked the biker in the face with the butt of his MK11. He landed on his back, and Raven finished him off with a blow that caved his nose into his skull.

A big black bird suddenly emerged over the mountain and then swooped down over the forest. The door gunner in the troop hold fired on the escaping convoy with green tracer rounds.

"Hell yes!" Raven shouted. He kept low and advanced across the final section of the meadow. The Black Hawk drew the fire of the soldiers on the road, giving Raven an opening.

He fired a shot into the back of a soldier who was aiming at the helicopter. The next shot never came, the twenty-round box magazine empty. Raven pulled his side arm and sprinted through the grass. Warm blood ran down his chest from the flesh wound. He ignored it and focused on the road.

The second half of the convoy had escaped, but one of the pickups had returned to help load up the hostages. Raven counted four more of the men still trying to move the kids into the Humvee. Some of the children were fighting back, kicking, screaming, and biting. Nathan lay in the dirt, reaching out for one of the children who was dragging limp legs across the dirt.

For a split-second, Raven thought the kid had been

shot. Then he realized who it must be.

"Hold on, Nathan. I'm coming!" Raven shouted. He raised his handgun and bolted toward the little boy whose life he had promised to save.

***

Nathan extended his broken arm. He could only see Ty out of his right eye, but what he could see made him damn proud. Ty was determinedly dragging his paralyzed legs toward Nathan, keeping his head low during the gun battle as the world erupted into chaos around them.

He had Sardetti blood in him—that was for certain.

"Stay where you are!" Nathan shouted. "I'm coming for you."

All around them, gunfire cracked and bullets flew, some of them at the sky, others at the meadow. The Black Hawk circled overhead, the door gunner picking targets carefully. It wasn't the 7.62 mm rounds that had Nathan worried, though. Most of the SOL soldiers—if you could call them that—were lousy shots.

He caught a glimpse of return fire from the meadow and finally saw the figure that had ambushed the convoy. A slender man wearing camouflage paint ran across the field at a breakneck pace, a ponytail bouncing up and down.

"Raven, you crazy son of a bitch," Nathan mumbled. He felt a smile form across his broken jaw. Grinning hurt like hell, but he couldn't hold it back.

"Uncle Nathan!" Ty shouted.

"It's okay, buddy, just stay down!"

Shouts rang out from all directions. Digging his elbows into the ground, Nathan moved toward Ty. The

Sons of Liberty were falling apart, shouting and firing wildly.

Fenix's voice rose above the din. "Take down that fucking chopper!"

Boots squelched into the mud near Nathan's head. "Going somewhere, Major?"

Rolling to his side, Nathan looked up at the General. His features were stone, and his eyes were cold and calculating. Nathan had no doubt Fenix was going to kill him now.

"I love you, Ty," Nathan said, his voice coming out in a croak. "Don't look, buddy. Okay? Just look away."

A flash of motion came from his peripheral vision. Raven was firing madly with his pistol. He took down a soldier to Nathan's right. The body hit the dirt between Nathan and Ty. It was the smallest possible mercy, blocking the boy's view of whatever happened next.

Fenix was raising his M4 at Raven. Using every ounce of strength he had left, Nathan kicked Fenix in the back of the knee, throwing off his aim. The rounds whistled through the air less than a foot from Raven's side.

The General let out a grunt and stumbled. He collapsed to one knee in the dirt but quickly pushed himself up and grabbed his rifle. Raven used the stolen moment to grab Ty and pull him behind a truck. Two skinheads grabbed Fenix, trying to haul him back to the Humvee.

"We have to go!" one of them shouted.

The Black Hawk whined overhead, smoke hissing from the engine where a shot had penetrated the armor. Fenix laughed and yanked out of their grips.

"Get off me, you cowards." He fired his rifle at the disabled chopper. The rounds lanced into the bird and the pilots pulled away.

"I guess if I can't sell you Montgomerys, I got to kill ya instead," Fenix said. He redirected his rifle at Nathan's head.

"You can try and escape, but my sister will hunt you down and finish this. She will kill you," Nathan sputtered with confidence. He looked up at the smoking muzzle, trying his best to be strong in the last seconds of his life.

"No!" shouted a voice.

Nathan flinched at a crack. There was only a second of pain as the round splintered through his head and buried into his brain. Somehow, he was still aware—aware that the crack wasn't the gunshot, but rather his shattering skull—aware that this wasn't something he could survive. The fear rose to an apex when he thought of his sister and nephew, but then vanished with the sweet release of darkness that flooded over his mind. Charlize was safe. Raven would rescue Ty. There was nothing left for Nathan to do now but let go.

***

Charlize had chewed one of her fingernails bloody. Surrounded by President Diego, General Thor, Colonel Raymond, and Albert, she had watched the choppy feed of a mounted cam on one of the Black Hawks from Buckley AFB. The men stared in silence, all of them with arms folded across their chests. All except Albert, who was praying under his breath as he paced back and forth.

The hastily planned mission had gone smoothly at first. The four fire-teams of Army Rangers easily eliminated the defenses in the camp the Sons of Liberty used as their forward operating base. From there, the teams infiltrated the actual Castle through mineshafts, killing dozens of the escaping SOL soldiers. Unfortunately, Fenix had taken a different route with the main force of his personal army. He blew those shafts in his retreat, killing four Army Rangers in the blast.

The Black Hawk that had gone to search for the escaping soldiers had found half a convoy instead. The chopper had taken fire, and the video feed was cutting in and out. She watched in horror as the majority of the vehicles sped down a dirt road that led through a dense forest. The remaining vehicles were scattering. A Humvee tore through the meadow, and a pickup truck followed close behind.

"The pilots are putting down, Madame Secretary," said Colonel Raymond. "But they assure me that the enemy left the hostages behind on the road. Apparently a sniper ambushed the convoy before they could all escape."

Charlize looked around sharply. "One of ours?"

"No, ma'am. Frankly, we have no idea who he is or where he came from."

President Diego flung an uneasy glance at Charlize, but she focused on the screen. There was a sickening lurch in the video as the Black Hawk landed in the field, disgorging Army Rangers into the grass. The feed transferred to the helmet-mounted display from the leader of the fire-team. He motioned his men toward the pickup and dirt bikes still on the road. A figure near the truck was waving at them, both hands raised.

"Don't shoot, don't shoot! You got a friendly here," he shouted.

"That must be the sniper," Raymond said.

Charlize stepped closer to the screen, studying the pixels for any sign of Ty and Nathan. If they weren't there, or if the worst had happened and they were both dead, she wasn't sure she would be able to keep it together in front of these men.

At this point she really didn't care. If she lost her family, nothing else would matter.

"The other choppers are back in the air and pursuing the convoy, ma'am," Raymond announced. "We'll get those bastards, don't worry."

As the Rangers closed in on the road, a large hand closed over hers.

"It's going to be okay, Charlize," Albert said.

It was the first time she could remember him calling her by her name for a while. She realized then that Albert was her family, too. Maybe the only family either of them had left now. A sob tried to climb out of her throat, but she shoved it back down and straightened her back.

Onscreen, the Rangers strode out on the road, weapons flitting over the terrain. Bodies were sprawled in all directions. The sniper had killed at least a dozen of the enemy combatants. It was hard to believe one man had done that much damage.

A shot cracked as one of the Rangers finished off the SOL soldier trying to escape into the forest. The team-lead then trained his rifle on the man standing in front of the pickup truck.

"Hands on your head!" he shouted.

It was obvious this man wasn't one of the Aryan soldiers. For one thing, he had shoulder-length black hair. He put his hands on his head and got to his knees, still shouting that he was a friendly. Several kids sat in the dirt behind him, crying and holding onto each other.

Charlize searched their faces, but she didn't see Ty.

The lead Ranger lowered his gun and walked over to

the kids while two of the other Rangers spoke to the long-haired man. Charlize couldn't hear what any of them were saying. She gripped Albert's hand until her bones creaked and her burned skin threatened to split open over the knuckles.

"They have your son," Raymond announced. He cupped his earpiece again, and his smile slowly vanished.

"What is it?" she asked, barely recognizing the shrill voice as her own. "What's wrong?"

Raymond met her gaze. "They've also located your brother, ma'am," he said.

Charlize wanted to scream. If Albert hadn't been holding her steady, she might have run at the colonel and snatched the earpiece to listen for herself. "Is he alive? What's happening?"

"I'm so very sorry, Madame Secretary, but it seems that your brother has been killed."

— 21 —

Three days after Raven had returned from rescuing Ty Montgomery, Estes Park finally found the time to honor the dead properly. Rays of light from the setting sun speared through the clouds, illuminating the mounds of fresh dirt covering those lost in the aftermath of the North Korean attack.

Captain Jake Englewood. Officer Rick Nelson. Melissa Stone and the other victims of the Water Cannibals. There were almost a dozen graves in total. Major Nathan Sardetti wouldn't be buried here, but Colton said a prayer for him anyway.

An hour earlier, he'd given his condolences to both Jake's family and Rick's family without tearing up, but the tears had welled around his eyes after leaving the cemetery. He gripped the hands of his wife and daughter, holding on as if they were the only things keeping him anchored.

His heart was heavy, and his mind was filled with worry.

There'd be a lot more fresh graves soon. He'd done the math. Without food and medicine, they would lose seventy-five percent of the residents over the winter, maybe more.

He looked at Raven as they walked away from the cemetery. Creek, Sandra and Allie strolled next to him. The dog's tail had been wagging ever since Raven returned from the Castle, but most of the other townsfolk weren't happy about Raven's return after finding out about his connection to Nile Redford. Colton had no doubt Don had spread the information, but there was nothing to be done about it now.

Colton studied Raven from afar. Something had happened to him out there—something that had changed Raven. His jokes and smiles were absent, and he hadn't said a word about what he had done and seen.

Colton wasn't asking questions. Raven would talk when he was ready.

The Spears family joined them on the path back to town, the girls shyly waving at each other while Kelly and Sandra hugged. All of them had been through hell in the past week, but they were alive and Colton was going to do everything he could to keep it that way. He didn't need to ask if Raven felt the same way.

Lindsey jogged over to them through the departing crowd of citizens. She jerked her chin at Colton. "Need a word," she said. "You too, Spears."

The three of them walked a few paces away to the side of the dirt road.

"What's going on, Detective?" Raven asked. If Colton needed any more proof that Raven was troubled, it was that he didn't bother to look at Lindsey's figure or make even a half-hearted attempt at flirting. Sam Spears had grown up sometime in the last week, and Colton wasn't sure anymore if that was a good thing.

Lindsey spoke in a low voice. "Don is rounding up the new militia this afternoon. Just got wind of it. He plans on kicking out anyone who wasn't a citizen of Estes Park before the day of the attack."

"Son of a bitch," Colton said. "I hope to God some of

these new deputies don't follow the orders."

"I wouldn't bet on that," Lindsey said. "We got enough elk and salvaged supplies to last a few weeks if we purge the town of tourists. I doubt those men will say no if it means saving their families."

Raven looked down at the ground. "This is my fault, isn't it? If Mr. Redford hadn't taken the supplies, then we wouldn't need to kick anyone out."

"Don wanted this long before Mr. Redford showed up," Colton said. "Trust me, Raven, this isn't your fault."

Raven lowered his voice. "I'm going out there to look for Mr. Redford. I'll bring back everything he stole." He looked down at his dog, petting the Akita's soft fur. "Don't worry, boy. I'll bring you with me this time."

Creek wagged his tail and barked. Sandra glared at Raven and stalked over. Kelly did the same thing. Both women wore the same disapproving looks.

"I know that look, Sam Spears," Sandra said. "You're planning something, aren't you?"

"Come on, you might as well hear it," Colton said, waving them over. They deserved to know what was going on after all they had been through. He explained, as briefly as possible, what had happened and Don's plans to run the tourists out of town.

"I have an idea," he said after he had finished. "Hopefully, it'll prevent Don from starting civil war in town."

"Let's hear it," Kelly said.

"I'm all ears," Lindsey said.

"I'll make Don an offer he can't refuse," Colton said. "Thing is, even if we kick the tourists out, we're only buying ourselves a few weeks of survival. By the time those supplies run out, we'll be too weak to fight. We need to go after Redford while we still can, using our militia."

Lindsey smiled. "I agree, sir."

Raven nodded his approval. "That sounds like a great plan. I was just gonna shoot him."

"My patients aren't going to survive without antibiotics. We need medicine," Sandra said. "I'll do anything I can to help."

Kelly hesitated at first, but then nodded. "I'm not sure what use I'll be, but if this is what you think is right, I'll support you, Marcus."

"All right, it's settled then," Colton said. "I'll bring it up at—"

The distant rumble of a jet cut him off. Every face on the road turned to the western mountains just as a squadron of F-22 Raptors tore through the clouds. As the roar of the engines faded, Colton heard the shouts and cheers of the townsfolk. Over the cacophony came another sound Colton hadn't heard since the floods of 2013.

"Choppers, too," Lindsey said, pointing.

A long black silhouette emerged in the western sky. The Chinook was flanked by four smaller birds, all Black Hawks. Hanging from ropes attached to the belly of the Chinook was a blue shipping container.

The birds flew across the purple sky toward the heart of Estes Park. Everyone around Colton took off running to meet them. He remained frozen in place, still not believing his eyes.

"Come on, Marcus," Kelly said, taking his hand. With a wide smile, he ran with his wife and daughter toward Bond Park.

By the time they reached town hall, the Black Hawks

had already touched down in the parking lot and street. Soldiers were unloading boxes and stacking them in the grass.

Colton led his family to the front of town hall, where Mayor Gail stood with Don.

"I'll be damned," Don said, taking off his cowboy hat to mop his forehead.

The Chinook circled overhead and finally set the blue crate down in the middle of Bond Park before rising back into the sky.

"Nathan came through on his promise about helping Estes Park!" Raven shouted. He clapped his hands together and grinned, his first real display of emotion since he had returned. Creek barked and stood on his hind legs as Raven jerked his arms and legs. It took Colton a moment to realize that Raven was trying to dance The Robot.

"Boom! What do you think of them apples, Chief Aragon?" Raven said, chuckling. "I guess my mission to rescue Ty Montgomery paid off after all. I got friends in high places, man."

Don shrugged, clearly not amused. "You don't know this is because of you."

"Raven, you are the worst dancer I've ever seen in my life," Lindsey said with a laugh.

Colton chuckled, but not for long. He grew serious and approached Don.

"Well, *Chief*," Colton said. "Thanks to Raven, it looks like we got the help we need to get us through the winter, so I guess you won't be needing to kick anyone out of town after all."

Don looked at Gail. She took a moment to think on it, and then nodded. "Marcus is right. We have a lot to be thankful for today. You can tell the militia to stand down, Don. The tourists can stay for now."

"You got to be kidding me, Mayor," Don protested.

Creek bared his teeth at Don, who took a step back. Raven had stopped dancing and stood next to Colton.

"The mayor told you to call off the militia," Lindsey said.

Don hesitated another moment, glared at Colton, and then turned to his motley force of mercenaries and volunteer deputies, who had been standing around watching the real soldiers do all the work.

"Help them unload the supplies," Don ordered.

A detail of Marines and a large African-American man wearing the filthiest Air Jordan sneakers Colton had ever seen approached across the green space. They walked in formation around a woman wearing an Air Force baseball hat.

"Who's in charge here?" she asked.

Gail started to raise her hand, but then looked at Colton. After a pause, she turned toward the entourage of military officials with a politician's smile.

"I'm Mayor Andrews," Gail said.

Colton held out his hand as the woman in the Air Force hat approached. When she reached out to shake it, he noticed she had sharp green eyes that matched Nathan's.

"I'm Marcus Colton, ma'am, and I have a feeling you're Secretary Charlize Montgomery."

"You'd be right," Charlize said.

"I knew your brother only for a short while, but he was a great man," Colton said. "He did a lot to help our town."

"One of the best men I've ever met," Raven said,

stepping up to join them. "I was privileged to fight by his side."

A moment of realization passed over Charlize's stern features. She lifted a brow and said, "You're Raven Spears, aren't you?"

"Yes, ma'am, I am," Raven said with a ghost of his usual cocky grin.

"You're the reason I came here," she said, loud enough that the people milling around could hear her. "I wanted to meet the man who saved my son. Ty wanted to be here to thank you personally, but he's still recovering."

"I hope he's doing okay," Raven said.

"He's been through a lot. But thanks to you, I have him home."

Charlize continued down the line, nodding at Kelly and smiling at Risa. She shook several more hands as her security detail stood guard behind her. Colton wouldn't want to tangle with her bodyguard, who looked like he could bench press an elk.

"My brother made a promise to get your town help before he died," Charlize announced when she had finished shaking hands. "I'm honoring that promise today. He sure thought a lot of Estes Park."

She paused to look around with her hands on her hips. "My brother was right. You have a beautiful home up here. I hope these supplies will help get you through the winter. President Diego's goal is to try and have part of the nation's grid back up and running by this time next year. Until then, stay safe and know your government is still working for you. We *will* get through this, and we *will* rebuild."

"Thank you, Madame Secretary," Gail said, clapping. A few people in the crowd joined in.

Secretary Montgomery nodded. "I wish I could stay longer, but I have a lot of work to do."

"What about Fenix?" Raven asked. "Have you caught that bastard yet?"

"I've got ten gold bars for any man or woman who finds him," she said without a flicker of emotion. "Dead or alive."

Colton watched the security detail close in around Charlize like a Roman phalanx as they crossed the park and loaded into one of the Black Hawks.

The choppers rose into the sky, the whoosh of the rotors slamming into the citizens below. Colton followed them across the sky, gripping Kelly's hand and holding Risa close. He hoped there wasn't anyone out there watching the birds, but he had a feeling they had attracted plenty of attention. Men like Mr. Redford, General Fenix, and other enemies would be watching and waiting for a chance to strike. Estes Park was still at risk—even more so now that they had something worth stealing again.

It would take everyone in Estes Park—locals and tourists—working together to fight off the coming storm.

—End of Book 2—

Continue the adventure with

Trackers 3: The Storm

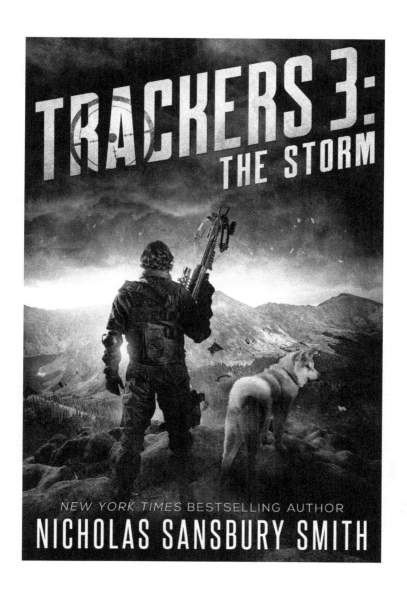

TRACKERS 3:
THE STORM

NEW YORK TIMES BESTSELLING AUTHOR
NICHOLAS SANSBURY SMITH

About the Author

 Nicholas Sansbury Smith is the New York Times and USA Today bestselling author of the Hell Divers series, the Orbs series, the Trackers series, the Extinction Cycle series, and the new Sons of War series. He worked for Iowa Homeland Security and Emergency Management in disaster mitigation before switching careers to focus on storytelling. When he isn't writing or daydreaming about the apocalypse, he enjoys running, biking, spending time with his family, and traveling the world. He is an Ironman triathlete and lives in Iowa with his wife, their dogs, and a house full of books.

CPSIA information can be obtained
at www.ICGtesting.com
Printed in the USA
BVHW041706130121
597765BV00007B/67